SAVE
YOU

BERKLEY TITLES BY MONA KASTEN

Save Me

Save You

SAVE YOU

MONA KASTEN

TRANSLATED BY RACHEL WARD

Berkley Romance
NEW YORK

BERKLEY ROMANCE
Published by Berkley
An imprint of Penguin Random House LLC
1745 Broadway, New York, NY 10019
penguinrandomhouse.com

Book design by Daniel Brount

Amazon, Prime Video, and all related logos are trademarks of
Amazon.com, Inc., or its affiliates.

Library of Congress Cataloging-in-Publication Data

Names: Kasten, Mona, 1992- author | Ward, Rachel, 1978- translator
Title: Save you / Mona Kasten; translated by Rachel Ward.
Other titles: Save you. English
Description: First edition. | New York: Berkley Romance, [2025] | Series: Maxton Hall
Identifiers: LCCN 2025006981 (print) | LCCN 2025006982 (ebook) |
ISBN 9780593954225 trade paperback | ISBN 9780593954232 ebook
Subjects: LCGFT: Romance fiction | Novels
Classification: LCC PT2711.A785 S3913 2025 (print) |
LCC PT2711.A785 (ebook) | DDC 833/.92—dc23/eng/20250513
LC record available at https://lccn.loc.gov/2025006981
LC ebook record available at https://lccn.loc.gov/2025006982

Originally published in German by Bastei Lübbe AG, Köln, 2018

First Berkley Romance Edition: September 2025

Printed in the United States of America
2nd Printing

The authorized representative in the EU for product safety and compliance is
Penguin Random House Ireland, Morrison Chambers, 32 Nassau Street,
Dublin D02 YH68, Ireland. https://eu-contact.penguin.ie.

For Kim

PLAYLIST

"Delicate" by Damien Rice

"You and Me" by Niall Horan

"Lonely" (feat. Lil Wayne) by Demi Lovato

"Dress" by Taylor Swift

"You Are" by GOT7

"Never Be the Same" by Camila Cabello

"Sticky Leaves" by Linying

"Lights On" by Shawn Mendes

"If I Be Wrong" by Wolf Larsen

"No Promises" (feat. Demi Lovato) [acoustic] by Cheat Codes

Lydia

James is drunk. Or coked-up. Or both.

It's been three days since anyone could really talk to him. He's just been on one long bender in our sitting room, draining bottle after bottle and acting like nothing's happened. I don't understand how he can be like this. Apparently, he's not even interested in the fact that our family is now in ruins.

"I think it's his way of grieving."

I give Cyril a sideways glance. He's the only other person who knows what's happened. I told him at his party, the night that James got off his face and snogged Elaine in front of Ruby's very eyes. Somebody had to help me get James home without either Percy or Dad spotting the state he was in. Our families are close friends, so Cy and I have known each other since we were kids. And even though Dad made me promise not to tell anyone about Mum before the official press release goes out, I know I can trust him and that he'll keep the secret—even from Wren, Keshav, and Alistair.

I couldn't have got through the last few days without his help.

He convinced Dad to leave James alone for a bit and told the lads not to ask questions for the time being. They're sticking to that, although I get the impression that with every passing day, they're finding it harder and harder to watch James destroying himself.

While my brother is doing his very best to shut off his brain, all I can do is wonder how I'm meant to cope. My mum is dead. Graham's mum died seven years ago. The baby growing inside me isn't going to have a granny.

Seriously. That's the thought running through my head on a perpetual ticker. Instead of grieving, I'm wrestling with the fact that my child will never know the embrace of a loving grandmother. What the hell is wrong with me?

But I can't help it. The thoughts in my head have taken on a life of their own—they escalate until I'm wallowing in catastrophic scenarios and I'm so scared of the future that I can't think about anything else. It's like I've been in a state of shock for three days. I guess something inside me—and James—broke horribly when Dad told us what had happened.

"I don't know how to help him," I whisper, watching James tip back his head and drain yet another glass. It hurts to see him suffering. He can't keep on like this forever. Sooner or later, he's going to have to face reality. And in my view, there's only one person in the world who can help him with that.

I pull out my phone for the squillionth time and call Ruby's number, but she doesn't pick up. I wish I could be angry with her, but I can't. If I'd caught Graham with someone else, I wouldn't want anything to do with him, or anyone associated with him, ever again either.

"Are you calling her again?" Cy asks, glancing skeptically at my phone. I nod, and he frowns disapprovingly. I'm not surprised by his reaction. He thinks Ruby's only interested in James for his money. I know that's not true, but once Cyril's made up his mind about a person, it's very hard to convince him to change it. And I might find it frustrating, but I can't resent him for it. It's his way of taking care of his friends.

"He won't listen to any of us. I think she might be able to get through to him before he has a total breakdown." My voice sounds weird in my own ears. So cold and flat—but inwardly, I'm the total opposite.

The pain makes it almost impossible even to stand up straight. It's like I've been tied up and spent days trying to undo the knots. Like my thoughts are whirling on a never-ending carousel that I can't jump down from. Everything seems pointless, and the harder I struggle against the helplessness rising up within me, the more completely it grips me.

I've lost one of the most important people in my life. I don't know how I can get through this alone. I *need* my twin brother. But all James will do is get shitfaced and smash everything that gets in his way. I haven't seen my dad since Wednesday. He's away, meeting with lawyers and accountants, settling the future of the Beaufort companies. He doesn't even have a second to spare on Mum's funeral—he's hired a woman called Julia to organize it, and she's been strolling in and out of our house for days like she's part of the family now.

The thought of Mum's funeral makes my throat clench. I can't breathe; my eyes start to sting. Hastily, I turn away, but Cyril notices.

"Lydia . . ." he whispers, gently reaching for my hand.

I pull away from him and leave the room without a word. I don't want the boys to see me cry. Sooner or later, they're going to start asking questions, whatever Cyril says; we can't stall them forever. They're not idiots. Even for James, this is out of character. OK, so he gets a bit out of hand sometimes, but he normally knows his limits. And the boys have clocked that right now, he doesn't. Keshav has started hiding bottles of the hard stuff from the bar, and Alistair "accidentally" flushed James's last few grams of cocaine down the loo—and that tells you everything you need to know.

I can't wait to put an end to all this secrecy. It won't be long now. The press release is going out at three on the dot, and then all the boys will know—and it won't be just them, either. The whole world will learn that Mum died. I can already see the headlines and the reporters doorstepping us and hanging around outside the school. I feel sick and stumble down the hall toward the library.

The lamps are on, casting faint light on the rows of shelves full of antique leather-bound books. I lean on the bookcases as I cross the room, my knees shaking. Right at the back, by the window, there's an armchair upholstered in dark red velvet. It's been my favorite spot in this house ever since I was little. This is where I came to hide away when I wanted some peace—from the boys, from Dad, from the expectations that go with the name Beaufort.

At the sight of this little reading nook, my tears flow all the faster. I curl up in the chair, wrapping my arms around my legs. Then I bury my face in my knees and cry quietly.

Everything around me feels so surreal. Like this is a bad dream that I could wake up from if I just tried hard enough. I wish myself back to the summer, eighteen months ago, when Mum was still alive and Graham could give me a hug when I was having a bad day.

I wipe my eyes with one hand and pull my phone from my jeans pocket with the other. As I unlock the screen, I notice streaks of mascara all over the backs of my hands.

I open my contacts. I haven't spoken to Graham for months, but he's still saved in my favorites, along with James's number. He doesn't even know about our baby, let alone that my mum died. I've honored his wish and haven't called him. It's been the hardest thing I've ever done in my whole life. We were in touch pretty much every day for more than two years, and then it suddenly stopped, practically overnight. It felt like going cold turkey.

And now . . . I'm having a relapse. I can't help it. I call his number and hold my breath as I listen to it ring. The ringing stops after a moment. I shut my eyes and listen intently, trying to hear whether or not he's picked up. At this moment, it's like I could actually drown in the lonely helplessness I've been feeling for days.

"Don't call me. We agreed," he says quietly. The sound of his soft, scratchy voice tips me over the edge. My body is shaken by a violent sob. I press my free hand to my mouth so that Graham won't hear.

But it's too late.

"Lydia?"

I notice the panic in his voice, but I can't speak, only shake my head. My breath is out of control, far too fast.

Graham doesn't hang up. He stays on the line, making quiet, soothing sounds. On the one hand, hearing him is churning me up more than ever, but on the other, it feels so safe and familiar that I press my phone even harder to my ear. I think his voice was one of the reasons I fell in love with him—long before I ever saw him in person. I remember the hours we spent on the phone, my ear sore and burning, remember waking up with Graham still on the line. His voice, gentle and quiet, deep, and just as piercing as his golden-brown eyes.

I've always felt safe with Graham. For ages, he was my rock. It's only thanks to him that I was able to move on from the thing with Gregg and start to look ahead again.

And even though I'm devastated, this feeling of security starts trying to fight its way back to the top. Just hearing his voice is helping me calm down ever so slightly. I don't know how long I sit here like this but, gradually, my tears stop.

"What's wrong?" he whispers in the end.

I can't answer. All I can do is utter a helpless sound.

For a minute, he stays quiet. I hear him breathe in a few times like he's going to say something, but at the last moment, he always holds back. When he finally speaks, his voice is hushed and full of pain: "There's nothing I'd rather do than drive over to see you, to be there for you."

I shut my eyes and imagine him sitting in his flat, at the old wooden table that looks about ready to collapse. Graham likes to claim it's an antique, but he actually pulled it out of a skip and revarnished it.

"I know," I whisper.

"But you know that I can't, don't you?"

Something in the sitting room just smashed. I hear breaking glass, then someone yelling. I can't tell whether they're hurt or having fun, but I straighten up all the same. I can't let James add a physical injury to the list.

"Sorry for phoning," I whisper, my voice broken, and I end the call.

I feel a stab in the heart as I get up and leave my little safe haven to go and check on my brother.

Ember

My sister is ill.

I wouldn't normally find that surprising—after all, it's December, it's freezing, and everywhere you look, people are coughing and sneezing. It's only a matter of when, not if, you're going to catch a cold.

But my sister never gets ill. Seriously, never.

When Ruby came home three nights ago and went to bed without a word, I didn't think anything of it. After all, she'd just come through the marathon of applying to Oxford, and it must have been mentally and physically exhausting. But the next day, she said she had a cold and couldn't go to school. That made me dubious because anyone who knows Ruby knows that she'd drag herself in, even with a temperature, out of fear of missing something important.

Today is Saturday, and I'm starting to feel really worried. Ruby's barely left her room. She's lying in bed, reading one book after another, and pretending that her eyes are red because she's ill. But she can't fool me. Something bad has happened, and she won't tell me what, which is driving me crazy.

Right now, I'm squinting through the crack around her door, watching her stir her soup without eating any of it. I can't remember ever seeing her like this. Her face is pale, and there are bluish circles under her eyes, getting darker with every day. Her hair is greasy and limp, hanging uncombed around her face, and she's wearing the same baggy clothes as yesterday and the day before. Normally, Ruby is the epitome of togetherness. It's not just her planner or her schoolwork—she takes pride in her appearance too. I didn't know she even had any slobby clothes.

"Stop lurking outside my room," she says suddenly, and I jump, caught. I act like I was coming in anyway, and push the door open.

Ruby raises her eyebrows at me. Then she puts the bowl of soup down on her bedside table, on the tray I brought it up on. I suppress a sigh.

"If you don't want it, I'll eat it," I threaten, nodding toward the soup. Not that it has the desired effect. Ruby gestures vaguely.

"Knock yourself out."

I groan with frustration as I lower myself onto the edge of her bed. "It's been hard, but I've left you alone for the last couple of days because I can see you're not exactly in the mood to talk, but . . . I'm genuinely worried about you."

Ruby pulls her duvet up to her chin, so that only her head is peeking out. Her eyes are dull and sad, like whatever happened to her has just this minute hit her with full force. But then she blinks, and she's back—or she's acting like she is. There's been a funny look in her eyes since last Wednesday. It's been like only her body was here, and her mind has been somewhere else entirely.

"It's just a cold. I'll be better soon," she says flatly, sounding like one of those lifeless computerized voices when you're on hold, like she's been replaced by a robot.

Ruby turns her face to the wall and disappears under the duvet again—a clear sign that as far as she's concerned, the conversation is over. I sigh, and I'm about to stand up when her phone lights up on the bedside table, catching my attention. I lean over slightly so that I can see the screen.

"Lin's calling you," I mumble.

All I hear is a muffled "don't care."

I frown and watch as the call ends and, a moment later, the number of missed calls pops up on the screen. It's in the double digits. "She's called you more than ten times, Ruby. Whatever's happened, you won't be able to hide forever."

My sister just growls.

Mum says I should give her time, but every day, it's getting harder to watch Ruby suffer. It doesn't take a genius to come to the conclusion that James Beaufort and his arsehole friends have something to do with this.

But I thought Ruby had got over Beaufort. So, what's happened? And when?

I've tried to analyze the situation the way Ruby would, and I've made a mental list:

1. Ruby was in Oxford for her interviews.
2. When she got back, everything was fine.
3. That evening, Lydia Beaufort turned up on our doorstep, and Ruby went off with her.
4. After that, everything changed. Ruby hid away and has barely spoken since.

Why???

OK. So, Ruby's list would probably be way more structured that that, but I've put things in a logical order, and clearly, whatever happened, it happened on Wednesday evening.

But where did she and Lydia go?

My eyes wander from Ruby, or rather the top of her head, which is all I can see poking out of her duvet, to her phone and back again. She won't miss it, I'm pretty sure of that.

"If you need anything, I'm next door," I say, even though I know she won't take me up on the offer. Then I give an extra loud sigh as I stand up and make a lightning-fast grab for her phone. I shove it up one sleeve of my baggy, loose-knit sweater and tiptoe back into my own room.

Once I've shut the door behind me, I exhale with relief—and instantly feel guilty. My gaze is drawn to the wall, as if Ruby can see me from her bed. She'll probably never speak to me again when she finds out that I've invaded her privacy like this. But as her sister, it's my duty to find out how to help. Right?

I walk to my desk and sit down on the creaky chair. Then I pull her phone from my sleeve. My sister makes a massive secret of everything that goes on at Maxton Hall, but obviously I know the kind of people she's at school with: rich kids whose parents are actual aristocrats, actors, politicians, or entrepreneurs. People with power and influence in this country, who quite often hit the headlines. I've been following some of Ruby's year on Insta for a while, so I know the gossip. Just the thought of what some of them might have done to Ruby turns my stomach.

I only hesitate for a tiny moment, then I unlock Ruby's phone and bring up her calls list. Lin isn't the only person who's been ringing. A number she doesn't have saved has called her loads of times too. I make up my mind and find Lin's details—after all, she's the only person from Ruby's horrible school I've ever met in person. Hesitantly, I hold the handset to my ear. She picks up after just one ring.

"Ruby," I hear Lin say breathlessly. "Thank God. How are you?"

"Lin—it's me, Ember," I interrupt her.

"Ember? What . . . ?"

"Ruby's not doing very well."

Lin goes quiet for a moment. Then, slowly, she says: "That's hardly surprising, considering what's happened."

"What *has* happened?" I burst out. "What the hell has happened, Lin? Ruby won't talk to me, and I'm so worried. Did Beaufort hurt her? If he did, the dickhead, I'll—"

"Ember." Now it's her cutting me off. "What are you talking about?"

I frown. "What are *you* talking about?"

"I'm talking about the fact that Ruby messaged me on Wednesday to say she'd made up with James Beaufort, and now today, I hear that his mum died last Monday."

Ruby

Ember's knocking on my door again.

I wish I had the energy to make her piss off. I get that she's worried, but I just don't feel able to psych myself up for anything, or to speak to anyone. Even my sister.

"Ruby, Lin's on the phone."

Frowning, I pull my head out from under my duvet and turn around. Ember's standing by my bed, holding out a phone. I squint at it. That's *my* phone. And Lin's name is shining out from the screen at me.

"You took my phone?" I ask wearily. I can feel the outrage trying to build up deep within me, but the emotion vanishes as quickly as it came. Over the last few days, my body has felt like a black hole, swallowing up all emotions before they even have the chance to land.

Nothing really gets through to me; I can't be arsed with anything. Every time I get out of bed, it's as exhausting as if I'd run a marathon; I haven't been downstairs in three days. I hadn't missed a single day of school since I started at Maxton Hall, but now the mere idea of showering, getting dressed, and spending six to ten hours with other people is too much for me. Let alone the fact that I couldn't bear to see James. Just the sight of him would probably make me crumple in on myself like a faded flower. Or burst into tears.

"Tell her I'll call her back," I mutter. My voice is rough because I've spoken so little in the last few days.

Ember doesn't move. "You need to speak to her now."

"But I don't *want* to speak to her." What I want is a little time to get back on my feet. Three days isn't enough to let me face up to Lin and her questions. I sent her a very short message on Wednesday. That's all. She doesn't know what happened between James and me in Oxford, and at the moment, I don't have the strength to tell her about it. Or about what happened after that. If I could, I'd blank out the whole of last week and act like everything's the same as ever. But sadly, as long as I can't even manage to get out of bed, that's not possible.

"Please, Ruby," says Ember, staring hard at me. "I don't know why you're so sad or why you won't talk to me about it, but . . . Lin just told me something. And I really think you need to speak to her."

I glare at Ember, but her determined expression tells me I've lost. She won't leave my room until I've talked to Lin. In some ways, we're far too similar, and stubbornness is definitely one of the traits we share.

Resignedly, I stretch out my hand and take the phone.

"Lin?"

"Ruby, lovely, we have to talk, it's urgent."

Her voice tells me that she knows.

She knows what James did.

She knows that he's plucked my heart out with his bare hands, only to throw it on the floor and trample on it.

And if Lin knows, then the rest of the school definitely does.

"I don't want to talk about James," I croak. "I *never* want to talk about him ever again, OK?"

For a moment, Lin is very quiet. Then she takes a deep breath. "Ember told me that you went off with Lydia on Wednesday evening."

I don't reply, just fiddle with the hem of my duvet with my free hand.

"Did you find out then?"

I laugh tonelessly. "What d'you mean? That he's an arsehole?"

Lin sighs. "Did Lydia really not tell you?"

"Tell me what?" I ask hesitantly.

"Ruby . . . Did you see my message earlier?"

Lin's voice is so cautious that my whole body suddenly runs hot and cold. I gulp. "No . . . I haven't looked at my phone since Wednesday."

Lin takes a deep breath. "Then you really haven't heard."

"What haven't I heard?"

"Ruby, are you sitting down?"

I straighten up in my bed.

Nobody asks that question unless something absolutely terrible has happened. Suddenly, the image of James, totally wasted, in that pool with Elaine is replaced by one that's way worse. James, hurt in an accident. James in the hospital.

"What's wrong?" I croak.

"Cordelia Beaufort died last Monday."

I need a moment to take in what Lin just said.

Cordelia Beaufort died last Monday.

An unbearable silence spreads between us.

James's mother is dead. Died on Monday.

I remember our passionate kisses, his hands running restlessly over my naked body, the overwhelming sensation of him inside me.

No way can James have known about it that evening—that night. Even he isn't that good an actor. No, he and Lydia must have only found out themselves on Wednesday.

I can hear Lin speaking but can't focus on her words. My mind is too busy wondering if it's really possible that Mortimer Beaufort waited two whole days to tell his children that their mother had died. And if so, how shit must James and Lydia have felt when they got home on Wednesday and found out?

I remember Lydia's swollen red eyes as she stood there on my doorstep, asking if James was with me. The blank, emotionless expression on James's face as he looked at me. And the moment that he jumped into the pool and smashed up everything we had created between us the night before.

A painful throb spreads through my body. I take my phone from my ear and put it on speaker. Then I click through my texts. I open the thread shown under a number I don't know. Three unread messages:

Ruby. I'm so sorry. I can explain everything

Please come back to Cyril's or tell me where you are so Percy can pick you up

Our Mum died. James is losing it. I don't know what to do

"Lin," I whisper. "Is that really true?"

"Yes," Lin whispers back. "They put out a press release earlier on, and within about thirty seconds, everyone had heard the news."

More silence. Thousands of thoughts are swirling around in my head. Nothing makes sense anymore. Nothing but this one feeling, which comes over me so suddenly and so violently that the words just bubble up out of me by themselves: "I have to go to him."

———

This is the first time I've seen the gray stone wall around the Beauforts' house and grounds. There's a huge iron gate across the drive with dozens of people hanging around outside it, cameras and microphones in hand.

"Lowlifes," mutters Lin, stopping her car a few yards away from them. Instantly, the reporters swarm toward us.

Lin leans down to lock the car doors from the inside. "Call Lydia and get her to open the gate."

I'm so grateful to have her at my side at this moment, keeping a clear head. She offered to drive me without a second's hesitation, and in less than half an hour from our phone call, she was outside my house. If I'd ever doubted the depth of Lin's and my friendship, those doubts dissolved in that instant.

I pull my phone from my pocket and call the number that's been contacting me so often in the last few days.

It takes a few seconds for Lydia to pick up.

"Hello?" Her voice still sounds as nasal as it did on Wednesday evening when we drove to Cyril's together.

"I'm outside your house. Could you open the gate, please?" I ask while trying to cover my face with an arm. I don't know if it's having the desired effect. The journalists are now standing right next to Lin's car, shouting out questions that I can't really hear.

"Ruby? What . . . ?"

Someone starts pounding on my window. Lin and I jump violently.

"As soon as possible, please?"

"Hold on," Lydia says, then she hangs up.

It takes maybe thirty seconds for the gate to open and someone to come out toward our car. It's not until the person is a few yards away that I recognize them.

It's Percy.

The sight of the chauffeur makes my heart skip a beat. Without warning, I'm plunged into memories. Memories of a day in London that started out nice and ended badly. And a night when James took loving care of me after his friends acted like bastards and threw me into a pool.

He pushes his way past the paparazzi and gestures to Lin to wind down her window.

"Drive through the gates and up to the house, miss. These people know that they'll be trespassing if they follow you, so they won't do it."

Lin nods, and once Percy's moved the press out of the way, she drives into the grounds. The driveway is so long and wide that it's more like a country lane through a park, with frost-covered lawns on either side. In the distance, I can make out a big house. It's square, two stories high, with a gabled roof. The gray slate roof is as gloomy-looking as the rest of the granite-clad façade. Despite its cheerless look, you can tell that rich people live here. I think it fits Mortimer Beaufort to a tee—cold and forceful. It's much harder to imagine Lydia and James feeling at home.

In front of the house, the driveway opens out into a courtyard, where Lin parks behind a black sports car outside one of the garages off to one side.

"Do you want me to come in with you?" she asks, and I nod.

The air is icy as we get out and hurry toward the front steps. Just before we reach them, I grab her arm. My friend turns and looks inquiringly at me.

"Thanks for the lift," I say breathlessly. I don't know what will be waiting for me in this house. Having Lin with me takes some of the fear from that, and that's really good. At the start of term, that would have been unthinkable—back then I kept my private and school lives strictly separate and told Lin practically nothing personal. That's all changed. Mainly because of James.

"Any time." She takes my hand and gives it a quick squeeze.

"Thank you," I whisper again.

Lin nods, then we walk up the steps. Lydia opens the door before we have time to ring the bell. She looks just as messed up as three days ago. And now I understand why.

"I'm so sorry, Lydia," I mumble.

She bites hard on her bottom lip and lowers her gaze to the floor. At this second, I don't care that we're not close, that we barely know each other. I stumble up the last few steps and give her a hug. Her body starts to shake the moment I put my arms around her, and I can't help thinking about Wednesday. If I'd known what had happened and what state she was in, I'd never have left her alone.

"I'm so sorry," I whisper again.

Lydia digs her fingers into my jumper and buries her face in my collarbone. I hold her tight and stroke her back as I feel her tears soak into my clothes. I can't imagine how she's feeling at this moment. If my mum died . . . I don't know how I'd survive.

Meanwhile, Lin has quietly closed the front door. Her eyes meet mine as she stands a few feet from us. She looks as shaken up as I feel.

Eventually, Lydia lets me go. Her cheeks are flushed a deep red, her eyes are bloodshot and glassy. I lift my hand and stroke a few wet strands of hair from her cheek.

"Can I help you at all?" I ask cautiously.

She shakes her head. "Just get my brother back for me. He's totally out of it. I . . ." Her voice catches, hoarse from so much crying, and she has to clear her throat before she can go on. "I've never seen him like this. He's killing himself and I just don't know how to help him."

Her words make my heart pound painfully again. I feel an overwhelming urge to see James and hold him in my arms, like Lydia—but I'm scared of meeting him.

"Where is he?"

"Cyril and I got him up to his room. He passed out just now."

Her words make me flinch.

"I can take you up, if you like," she continues, nodding toward the staircase that curves up to the first floor. I turn to Lin, but my friend shakes her head. "I'll wait here. You go."

"The boys are in the sitting room, if you want to join them. I'll be down in a minute," Lydia says, pointing across the entrance hall to a corridor that leads to the back of the house. Lin hesitates a moment, but then she nods.

Lydia and I walk up the broad, dark brown staircase together. I notice that the Beauforts' house is way friendlier on the inside than it looks from outside. The hall is bright and inviting. There might not be family photos on the walls, like there are in our house, but at least there are no oil paintings in golden frames, portraits of long-dead ancestors, like the ones at the Vegas'. The pictures here are colorful and impressionistic, and while they aren't particularly personal, they at least convey a welcoming atmosphere.

At the top of the stairs, we turn down a dark landing; it's so long that I can't help wondering what's hidden behind all the doors we pass. And how it's possible that a single family lives here.

"Here we are," Lydia murmurs suddenly, stopping outside a large door. For a moment, we both stare at it, then she turns to me. "I know it's asking a lot, but I get the feeling he really needs you."

I can hardly untangle my thoughts and emotions. My body seems to know that James is on the other side of that door—I'm drawn to him like a magnet. And even though I'm not sure that I can help him in the way Lydia is clearly hoping for, I still want to be there for him.

Lydia touches my arm for a moment. "Ruby . . . There was nothing between James and Elaine except that kiss."

I stiffen.

"James came straight out of the pool and collapsed onto a chair. I know he can be awful, but—"

"Lydia," I interrupt her.

"—he wasn't himself."

I shake my head. "That's not why I'm here."

I can't think about that at the moment. Because if I do—if I allow myself to think about James and Elaine—the rage and disappointment will win out, and I won't be able to walk through that door.

"I can't listen to that right now."

For a moment, Lydia looks like she wants to say something else, but she only sighs. "I just wanted you to know."

Then she turns away and walks back down the landing to the stairs. I watch her until she reaches them, a long shaft of light cast over the expensive carpet. Once she's out of sight, I turn back to the door.

I don't think I've ever found anything as difficult as reaching for that handle. It feels cool under my fingers, and a shiver runs down my spine as I hesitantly turn it and open the door.

I hold my breath while I stand in the doorway to James's room.

It has high ceilings and I'm sure it would take up the whole top floor of our little terraced house. On my right, there's a desk and a brown leather chair. To my left, the wall is lined with shelves filled with books, notebooks, and the occasional ornament, which remind me of the statues I saw at Beaufort's that time. As well as the door I've just come in by, there are two more, on either side of the room. They're in solid wood and I guess that one leads to a bathroom and that the other, which is a little smaller, is to James's wardrobe. In the middle of the room, there's a seating area with a sofa, armchair, and coffee table, arranged on a Persian rug.

Cautiously, I cross the room. There's a king-size bed right opposite the door, at the far end of the room. On each side of the bed there are large windows, but the curtains are almost completely shut, so that only two thin strips of light shine onto the floor.

I see James at once.

He's lying in bed, with a dark gray duvet over most of his body. Tentatively, I come closer so that I can see his face.

I gasp for air.

I'd thought James was asleep . . . but his eyes are open. And the expression in them sends an ice-cold shiver down my spine.

James's eyes—normally so expressive—are lifeless. His face is entirely blank.

I take another step toward him. He doesn't react, gives no sign of having noticed my presence. Instead, he stares right through me. His pupils are unnaturally wide, and the stench of alcohol lies heavily on the air. I can't help thinking back to Wednesday evening, but I suppress the memory. I'm not here to muse on my wounded feelings. I'm here because James has lost his mum. Nobody should go through a thing like that alone. Especially not someone who—despite everything—means so much to me.

Resolutely, I cross the last gap between us and sit cautiously on the edge of the bed.

"Hey, James," I whisper.

He winces, as if he'd been falling in a dream and has now landed with a painful bump. The next moment, he turns his head slightly toward me. There are dark rings under his eyes, his hair hangs limp over his brow. His lips are dry and split. He looks like he's been living entirely on booze for days.

When he kissed Elaine, I wished him nothing but ill. I wished for someone to hurt him as badly as he'd hurt me. I wished for revenge for my aching heart. But seeing him this broken doesn't bring me the satisfaction I'd been hoping for. Quite the opposite. It feels more as though his pain jumps over to me and pulls me down into the depths. I'm flooded with despair because I don't know what I can do for him. All the words that occur to me at this moment feel meaningless.

Tenderly, I raise my hand and stroke James's red-blond hair out of his face. I run my fingertips gently over his cheeks, then lay both palms on his cold face. It feels as though I'm holding something desperately fragile in my hands.

I pluck up all my courage, lean down to him, and press my lips onto his forehead.

James catches his breath.

For a moment, we're frozen in that position, neither of us daring to move.

Then I sit back up and pull my hand away.

The next second, James grabs my hips. He digs his fingers into them and kind of plunges forward. I'm so startled by the sudden movement that I freeze. James wraps his arms around me and buries his face in the crook of my neck. His whole body is shaken by a deep sobbing.

I put my arms around him and hold him tight. There's nothing that I can say in this moment. I don't know how he feels in his loss, and I don't want to act as though I do.

All I can do right now is to be there for him. I can stroke his back and share his tears. I can empathize with him and let him know that he doesn't have to go through this alone, no matter what happened between us.

And as James cries in my arms, I realize that I'd gotten the situation totally wrong.

I'd thought that after what he'd done to me, I'd be able to put him right out of my life. I hoped to get over him as fast as possible. But now that I grasp what his pain is doing to me, I know that that's not going to happen any time soon.

James

The walls are spinning. I don't know which way's up and which way's down; all I can tell is that Ruby's hands are there, keeping me semi-anchored in reality. She's sitting on my bed, leaning her back on the headboard, and I'm half lying in her lap. One of her arms is wrapped tightly around me and she's stroking my hair with her hand. I'm focused entirely on the warmth of her body, her even breath, and her touch.

I have no idea how many days have passed. There's nothing but fog when I try to remember anything. Thick gray fog, and two thoughts that get through to me in every brief moment of clarity.

Firstly: My mum is dead.

Secondly: I kissed another girl in front of Ruby.

It doesn't matter how much alcohol I down, or what else I take—I'll never forget Ruby's face at that moment. She looked so shocked and hurt. Like I'd destroyed her whole world.

I bury my face in Ruby's side again. Partly because I'm afraid she'll stand up and leave at any moment. And partly because I'm afraid the tears will be back any second now. But neither of those things happens. Ruby stays and, apparently, there's no more liquid left inside me to get rid of.

I feel as though there's nothing at all left inside me. Maybe my soul died along with my mother. How else could I have done that to Ruby?

How *did* I do that to Ruby?

What's wrong with me?

What the fuck is wrong with me?

"James, you have to breathe," Ruby whispers suddenly.

As she says that, I realize that I have actually stopped breathing. I'm not sure how long ago.

I inhale deeply and slowly let out the air again. There, that wasn't so hard.

"What's happening to me?" Whispering those words is so exhausting that afterward, it feels as though I'd shouted them.

Ruby's hand pauses. "You're grieving," she replies, equally quietly.

"But why?"

Just before, I forgot to breathe—now my breath is coming way too fast. I sit up with a jerk. My rib cage hurts, and so do my limbs, which feel like I've been training too hard, even though I've spent the last few days doing nothing but suppressing the way my life is right now.

"What do you mean, 'why'?" Her expression is warm, and I wonder how she's able to look at me like that.

"I mean, why am I sad? I didn't even like my mum very much."

Even before I've finished speaking those words, I freeze. Did I really just say that?

Ruby reaches for my hand and holds it tight. "You've lost your mother. It's normal to be knocked sideways when someone that important to you dies."

She doesn't sound as confident and sure of herself as usual. I don't think Ruby actually knows how to act in a situation like this. But she's here and doing her best, and that fact feels almost like a dream.

Maybe it is.

"What happened here?" she whispers suddenly, cautiously lifting my right hand.

I follow her gaze. My knuckles are still smeared with blood, and my skin is red and blue with bruises and grazes.

Maybe this isn't a dream after all. Or if it is, it's a highly life-like one.

"I punched my dad." The words come out of my mouth entirely neutrally. I don't feel a thing as I say them. Something else that's wrong with me. Any halfway normal human being knows not to hit their parents. But that moment, when my father gave Lydia and me the news of Mum's death—so emotionless and cold—was the moment when I couldn't take it anymore.

Ruby lifts my hand to her lips and kisses the back of it gently. My heart starts to beat faster and trembling floods my body. Her touch is doing me good, even though her tenderness is killing me. Everything about it feels so wrong and yet so right.

From when I was a little kid, my parents taught me never to show my emotions because doing so allows other people to get to know you, and—up to a point—to get the measure of you. The moment you show weakness, you make yourself vulnerable, and at the top of a big business, you can't afford that. But they never prepared me for a situation like this. What do you do when you lose your mother at eighteen? For me, there was only one answer: Try to drown the truth in alcohol and drugs, and act like nothing even happened.

But now that Ruby's with me, I'm not sure I can go on like that. I let my eyes roam over her face, over her slightly messed-up hair, and down to her throat. I still remember exactly what it was like to press my lips onto her soft skin there. How overwhelming it felt to hold her. To be inside her.

Now she looks just as sad as I feel. I don't know if she's thinking about my mum, or only about how much I hurt her.

But there's one thing I know for certain: Ruby didn't deserve to be treated like that. She's always given me the feeling that I can achieve anything. And whatever might have happened . . . I should never have let Elaine kiss me just to prove to myself and everyone else that I'm a coldhearted arsehole, incapable of feeling a thing, even the death of my own mother. Pushing Ruby away like that was cowardly. And it was the biggest mistake I've ever made in my life.

"I'm sorry," I say hoarsely. My throat feels rusty, and it's a major effort to speak. "I'm so sorry for what I did."

Ruby's whole body stiffens. Minutes go by in which she doesn't react. I think she's even stopped breathing.

"Ruby . . ."

She just shakes her head. "Don't. That's not why I'm here."

"I know how badly I fucked up, I—"

"James, stop it," she whispers fiercely.

"I know you have no reason to forgive me. But I . . ."

Ruby's hand shakes as she pulls it away from mine. Then she gets up from the bed. She smooths out her jumper, then flattens down her fringe. It's like she wants to re-create her neat and tidy appearance—the version of her that I didn't even notice for two years. But too much has happened between us. There's nothing that could make her invisible to me again now.

"I can't do this now, James," she mumbles. "I'm sorry."

The next moment, she walks across my room. She doesn't even turn back to me, doesn't look at me as she goes through the door and shuts it quietly behind her.

I clench my teeth together hard as the stinging behind my eyes returns and my shoulders start to shake again.

═══

I don't know how long I lie in my bed, staring at the wall, but eventually, I pull myself together and go downstairs. It's been dark outside for ages, and I wonder if the lads are even still here. From just outside the sitting room, I can hear their quiet voices. The door's slightly open, and I pause with my hand on the handle.

"This is getting out of hand," Alistair murmurs. "If he keeps on like this, he's going to drink himself into a coma. I don't get why he won't talk to us."

"I wouldn't want to talk if I were him." Keshav. It doesn't surprise me that he's the one who said that.

"But you know your limits. I'm not sure that James does anymore."

"We shouldn't have let it get this far," Wren says. "Until yesterday, I genuinely thought he was just celebrating Oxford."

There's a moment of silence, then Wren goes on, his voice quiet. "If he doesn't want to talk about it, we have to accept that."

Alistair snorts. "And keep watching on as he fucks himself up? No way."

"You can take the drugs and booze off him," Wren mumbles,

"but his mum died. And as long as he won't face up to it, there's nothing we can do, however shit that feels."

An icy shiver runs down my spine. They know. The idea of having to look into their sympathetic faces in a moment turns my stomach. I don't want that. I want this all to be like the old days. But if Ruby's visit has shown me one thing, it's that it's time to face reality.

So I let my neck click, circle my aching shoulders, and walk into the sitting room.

Alistair is about to reply but presses his lips together as he spots me. I head straight for the drinks trolley and pick up a bottle of whisky. There's no way I'll get through what I've got to do next sober. I pour a shot and down it in one. I put the glass down and turn to the lads. Everyone but Cyril is here. Alistair is swirling the last of his drink around his glass and keeping his gaze fixed on the floor. Kesh is watching me, his dark eyes expectant, and so is Wren. Although they already know, it feels important to say the words out loud.

"My mum is dead."

It's the first time I've said it.

And it hurts more than I expected. Not even the booze can help with that. That's exactly why I've avoided talking to them. Words just cause more pain. I turn my face away and stare at my shoes so that I won't have to see their reactions. I have never felt as vulnerable as I do in this second.

Suddenly, I hear footsteps coming toward me. When I look up, Wren is standing right there. He puts an arm around me and gives me a squeeze.

Wearily, I let my head droop onto his shoulder. My arms are heavy as lead and I can't hug him back. But Wren doesn't let me go. A moment later, Kesh and Alistair join us, putting their hands on my shoulders.

There's no need for words in this moment, especially as the lump in my throat won't let me get any out. It takes a while until I've got myself back under control, to some extent at least. Eventually, Wren starts to steer me toward the sofa, and Alistair gets me a glass of water, which he holds out without speaking.

"That's so shit," Alistair mumbles, sitting down beside me. "And I'm so sorry, James."

I can't meet his eyes or say anything, so I just nod.

"What happened?" Kesh asks after a while.

I sip hesitantly from the glass. The cold water tastes amazingly good. "She . . . She had a stroke, while we were in Oxford."

Silence. I don't think any of the lads has even drawn breath. They might have known that Mum had died, but this is clearly new information to them.

"Dad didn't tell us until we got home again. He didn't want us to fuck up our interviews." Remembering the conversation with my father makes my blood run cold. I study my bruised hand, clench my fist, and relax it again.

Wren puts a hand on my shoulder. "We guessed that something bad must have happened," he murmurs after a while. "I've never seen you like that. But Lydia didn't tell us anything, and you weren't in any fit state . . ."

Keshav clears his throat. "This afternoon, Beaufort's put out a press release. That's how we heard."

I gulp hard. "I just didn't want to think about it. About . . . anything."

"It's OK, James," Wren says quietly.

"And I was scared that if I said it out loud, it would make it come true."

At last, I raise my eyes and look into my friends' stunned faces. Keshav's eyes look suspiciously damp, while all the color has drained from Alistair's cheeks. It never even occurred to me that my mates have known my mum since we were kids and so they'd be upset about the news of her death too. Suddenly, I realize how selfish my reaction was. I didn't just ignore reality and hurt Ruby, I pushed my friends and Lydia away too by how I acted.

"You'll get through this. Both of you will get through this," says Wren. I follow his gaze and see Cyril and Lydia standing in the doorway. Lydia's cheeks and eyes are red. I must look pretty similar.

"Whatever it feels like at the moment, you're not alone. You've got us. Both of you do. OK?" Wren insists, clapping me on the shoulder. The look in his brown eyes is steady and serious.

"OK," I reply, even though I have no idea whether I can believe him on that.

Lydia

Percy walks into the front hall just as I'm putting on Mum's pearl necklace. "Are you ready to leave, miss?" he asks, stopping a few feet away from me. "Mr. Beaufort and your brother are waiting in the car."

I don't answer, just do up the clasp of the necklace and check my hair one last time. Then I slowly lower my hands.

I study my reflection. Dad's funeral planner didn't just take care of all the organization, she saw to it that Dad, James, and I were dressed by a stylist this morning. My hair is in an updo and my face is done. "Waterproof mascara—that'll help you get through the day, my lovely," the young woman twittered.

I briefly considered wiping both hands over my eyes while the makeup was still wet, deliberately destroying her handiwork, but Dad's fierce glare held me back. It's only for his sake that I'm looking presentable now. I've got more makeup on than I've ever worn before, even doing photoshoots for new Beaufort's collections. There's delicate eyeshadow and subtle eyeliner, there are three coats of that mascara on my lashes, and she's contoured my face sharply. My cheekbones are a bit more prominent now than they've been in the last little while.

Dad frowned in surprise when the stylist commented on my plump face. I might be able to hide the pregnancy for another month or two—but not much longer.

The minute I imagine my family's reaction to the news, I feel as though someone's constricting my throat. But I can't think about that now. Not today.

After what feels like an eternity, I say "no" in answer to Percy's question, despite which, I turn and stride fiercely toward the door. He follows me in silence. At the cloakroom, he tries to help me with my coat, but I turn away from him. The look in his eyes is so full of sympathy that I can't bear it right now; instead, I slip my arms into my sleeves myself and walk outside. The ground is covered with frost that glitters slightly in the sun. I head cautiously down the steps toward the black limousine parked at the bottom of them. Percy opens the door and I thank him, get in, and drop onto the back seat next to James.

The mood in the car is oppressive. Neither James nor our father, who is sitting perpendicular to us, takes any notice of me. I'm wearing a black sheath dress with long flounced sleeves, and they're both in black suits, specially made for today. The dark fabric is making my brother look even paler than he already is. The stylist did her best to add a little color to his cheeks, but it didn't do much good. The makeup has worked miracles on Dad, though. There's no more sign of his black eye.

I shake my head as I study them both. My family is an absolute wreck.

The drive to the cemetery goes by in a daze. I try to copy Dad and James in keeping my mind somewhere else entirely, but that fails utterly the moment we stop and Percy swears under his breath.

The press are out in force at the cemetery gates.

I squint over to James, but his face is blank as he puts on sunglasses and waits for the car door to be opened. I gulp hard and pull my coat tighter around me. Then I slip my own shades onto my nose. The sight of the barging reporters is making me genuinely sick. The journalists and paparazzi call out to us, but the only words I take in are my name and James's. I ignore them, straighten my shoulders, and hurry past. As we reach the chapel, cemetery staff open the doors for us so that we can walk straight in without waiting.

The first thing I see is the coffin in front of the altar. It's black, and the light from the lamps hanging from the high chapel ceiling is reflected on the smooth, glossy surface.

The second is the woman standing right in front of the coffin. Her hair is as red as Mum's but falls in soft waves to her shoulders. She too is wearing a black coat, which reaches to her knees.

"Aunt Ophelia?" I croak, taking a step toward her.

She turns. Ophelia is five years younger than Mum and, although her features are softer and her expression is less earnest, you can tell at a glance that she's her sister.

"Lydia." In her eyes, I can see the same deep grief that I've been feeling for days.

I want to go to her and give her a hug, but before I can take a single step further, my father takes my upper arm. His eyes are icy cold as he looks at Ophelia and then at me. He gives an almost imperceptible shake of his head. A painful ache fills my body. This is Mum's funeral. They might not have had the best of relationships, but they were sisters. And I'm sure Mum would have wanted us to be there for Ophelia today.

Taking no notice of me or my resistance, my father puts an arm around my shoulders. It's not a loving gesture; it feels more like an unyielding vise. As he steers me toward the row of seats reserved for us, I turn to Ophelia again, but she's vanished into the sea of people in black.

═══

The funeral procession is accompanied by more than a dozen security personnel who walk alongside us and make sure the press don't get too close. Most of them are tactful enough to position themselves along the edge of the path, but some hold their cameras so close to our faces that I could stretch out a hand and touch them.

After a while, I look over to James, who is walking beside me, staring stoically at our father's back. His face looks set in stone, hard and expressionless, and I wish I could see into his eyes. Then I might know what's going on inside him. I wonder if he did any coke or had a drink before we left. In the last few days—since the evening Ruby came round, in fact—he's withdrawn entirely into himself and won't talk to me or to the boys either. I can't blame him. In some ways, we're very similar. I could have done with something to help me through these apparently endless, awful days too.

I tuned out of the eulogy back in the chapel. It seemed to go on forever. If I'd listened to everything the vicar said about Mum, I'd probably have broken down. Instead, I put up an invisible wall between myself and my emotions and focused entirely on not sobbing loudly. I can imagine how Dad would have reacted to that.

I try to conjure that wall back up again now, as we finally come to a stop by Mum's grave. I stare into the black hole that's been dug in the ground and firmly push all emotions away. For a moment, I think it's working. The vicar starts to speak again, but I don't listen to him, don't think about anything.

But as the coffin is lowered into the grave, I suddenly feel like I can't breathe. It's as though there's something huge and dark inside me rising up and sealing my throat so that no air can get through. Every thought I've been trying to suppress for the last few hours fights its way to the top of my mind.

Mum's lifeless body is lying in that coffin.

She's never coming back.

She's dead.

I feel sick. I gasp quietly and press my hand to my mouth, swaying slightly to one side.

"Lydia?" I hear James's voice as if from miles away.

I can only shake my head. I try desperately to remember everything Dad drummed into us before the funeral. Stand up straight, keep the sunglasses on at all times, no tears. He didn't want to give the press any more drama than necessary.

It costs me my last ounce of strength to pull myself together. I try not to think about Mum. That I can never again ask her advice. That she'll never again bring a cup of tea to my room when I've spent too long at my desk studying. That she'll never hug me again. That she'll never get to know her grandchild. That I'm entirely alone, and scared of losing James and Dad too, because our family is falling a little bit further apart with every passing day.

A quiet sob breaks free of my throat. I press my trembling lips firmly together so as not to make another sound.

"Lydia," James repeats, more urgently this time. He moves

closer to me, so that our arms touch through the thick fabric of our coats. Slowly, I raise my eyes. James has taken off the shades and is looking at me, his eyes dark. I can see something in them that I've been desperately searching for in the last few weeks. Something that reminds me that he's my brother and will always stay with me.

James raises his hand hesitantly to my face. It's icy cold but still feels good as his thumb brushes my cheek.

"Fuck Dad," he whispers to me. "If you want to cry, you go ahead and cry. OK?"

The intimacy in his eyes and the honesty of his words finally break down the wall inside me. I let the feelings swirl into a whirlwind because James is there to hold me tight. He puts an arm around my shoulder and holds me close to his side. I bury my face in his chest. He feels like home, and my heavy heart lightens a tiny bit. While my tears drip incessantly onto his coat, we watch on together as the coffin is lowered little by little, until it reaches the bottom.

5

Ruby

On Wednesday, I go back to school. I missed more than a week and now I'm reaping the consequences. Lin brought me her notes over the weekend, but I still struggle to follow the lessons. I'm asked a couple of questions in history but can't answer them sensibly. I stare in embarrassment at my planner, but Mr. Sutton barely seems to notice. He looks like he's miles away, not really with it at all. I wonder if he's thinking about Lydia as much as I am about James.

By the end of the morning, I'm knackered. I'd like to head to the library to do more reading for my next lessons, but my stomach is rumbling too loudly for me to skip lunch.

On the way to the dining hall, Lin hooks her arm into mine. "Are you OK?" she asks, giving me a sideways glance.

"I'm never missing another day ever again," I grumble as we walk toward the dining hall together. "It's the worst feeling in the world not to know what the teachers want from you."

Lin strokes my arm. "You did fine. You'll be caught up again by next week, I'm sure of it."

"Hmm," I say as we turn the corner. "But it was still . . ."

I stop dead.

We're in Maxton Hall's main hall. To my right are the stairs down to the cellar.

The stairs where James first kissed me.

The memory of his hand on the back of my neck and his lips pressed onto mine floods over me without warning. It plays out like a film before my inner eye: his mouth gliding over mine, his hands holding me tight, his self-assured movement making me weak at the knees, when suddenly my face starts to change—it melts and blurs into someone else's entirely. It's not me in James's arms now, it's Elaine he's kissing so passionately.

I feel it like a punch in the belly, and it's a major effort not to crumple.

Then someone barges into me from the side—and I'm back at Maxton Hall. I no longer see the kiss, just the empty cellar steps and people moving toward the dining hall. The cramping pain in my stomach has ebbed away too.

I take a deep breath. School today has been nothing but one long roller-coaster ride. Every time I rise up and reach the top, I think everything's back to normal and I'm going to get through this—then, suddenly, I see something that reminds me of James and I'm plunged back into the depths, into a vortex of pain.

"Ruby?" Lin says beside me. Judging by her worried face, this isn't the first time she's spoken to me in the last few minutes. "Are you OK?"

I force a smile onto my face and nod.

Lin frowns but doesn't ask questions. Instead, she does what she's been doing all morning—she distracts me. On the way to the dining hall, she tells me about the new Tsugumi Ohba and

Takeshi Obata manga series, which she's been devouring. She's so fired up about it that I immediately pull out my bullet journal and make a note of the titles on my reading list.

Once we've finished our lunch, we take back our trays. There's a girl leaning on the wall next to the tray station. I don't know her. She's talking to a boy, but at the sight of me, she goes quiet. Her eyes widen and she nudges him in the ribs—not exactly subtly either. I try to ignore the pair of them.

"Aren't you the girl who got thrown in the pool at Cyril Vega's party?" she asks, coming a step closer.

Her words make me flinch. That bloody pool is bound up with so many horrible memories that I wish I could get it lobotomized out of my brain.

I don't answer, just wait for my turn to put my tray down and get out of here.

"And then James Beaufort carried you out. You know people are saying you're his secret girlfriend? Is that true?" she continues.

It feels like the walls are slowly but surely closing in on me. They're going to crush me any second now.

"If she was his girlfriend, she'd be at the funeral, wouldn't she?" the guy says, just loudly enough that I can hear him.

"Yeah, but that's why it's a *secret*, isn't it. Maybe he doesn't want anyone to know. He's got enough dirty little secrets, you know."

There's a loud crash.

I've dropped my tray.

There's debris everywhere at my feet. I stare at a couple of peas as they roll across the floor but can't even manage to pick them up. My body is rooted to the spot.

"Stop talking bollocks," a deep voice sounds beside me. The

next moment, there's an arm around my shoulder and somebody's escorting me out of the dining hall. I can dimly hear Lin's voice behind me, calling something out, but the person just walks on, leading me out into the stairwell. Only then does their arm leave my shoulder as they turn to face me. My eyes travel up past the beige trousers and dark blue blazer, up to the face of . . . Keshav Patel.

I have to blink a few times before I realize that it's really him standing there. His black hair is tied in a neat bun at the nape of his neck and he's stroking back a stray strand. Then he turns his dark brown, almost black eyes on me.

"Are you all right?" he asks quietly.

I think I could count on the fingers of one hand the number of times I've heard Keshav speak. He's definitely the quietest of James's friends. I've kind of got a bit of an idea what Alistair, Cyril, and Wren are like, but he's still a closed book to me.

"Yeah," I croak in the end, then clear my throat.

I look around and see where we are. This is where I had my first real encounter with James, under the stairs, away from prying eyes. This is where he tried to bribe me and I threw his stupid money back in his face. I can't help wondering whether everything at this bloody school is always going to remind me of him from now on.

"Good," Keshav says. Just like that, he turns, puts his hands in his pockets, and walks away. I watch him until he's out of sight. Less than thirty seconds later, Lin hurries out of the dining hall, her face angry as she looks around for me.

"I'm here, Lin," I say, stepping out from under the stairs.

"I told them what I thought of them," she growls, coming toward me. "Utter idiots. What did Keshav want?"

I wrinkle my brow and look in the direction he disappeared. "I have no idea."

———

The first thing on the to-do list for the events meeting this afternoon is wrapping up the Secret Santa gifts. Over the last couple of weeks, people have been dropping off little presents to us, which then traditionally get handed out in homeroom on the last day before the Christmas holidays.

Normally I love making up parcels of letters and sweets and putting them in bags so that kids in the lower school can take them from class to class. But this time, even the Christmas music we're playing can't lift the mood.

That's probably because an above average number of the letters are addressed to the Beauforts, and we can't decide what we ought to do with them. James and Lydia haven't come back to school, so we can't give these to them in person, and I doubt that they'd appreciate having them sent to them at home. I wish I could just ask the two of them whether or not they want the letters. But that's not an option, so the team votes on it and agrees to hold on to them for the time being. Apart from anything else, we don't know what's in them. Somebody might have gone in for a sick joke.

For the rest of the meeting, I keep catching myself staring at the empty chair where James sat when he was serving his punishment with us. Apparently, everything really is going to remind me of him now, even though I'd love to just forget our time together. Whenever I think of him, it feels as though someone's pushed a hand through my rib cage, wrapped their fingers around my heart, and squeezed hard.

I'm so very angry with him.

How could he do that to me?

How?

Just the thought of letting anyone else get as close to me as he did makes me sick, but he didn't hesitate to kiss somebody else.

And the worst thing is, I'm not only angry with James, I also feel sorrow and sympathy for him. He's lost his mum, and every time I'm filled with white-hot rage toward him, I feel guilty. But I know that I don't have any reason to.

It's not fair, and it's tiring, and by the time I get home, I'm totally worn out by the war all these contradictory emotions are waging inside me. The school day has robbed me of all my energy, and I can't even muster up a cheerful façade for my family. Since Mum found out about Cordelia Beaufort dying, she's treated me like a fragile eggshell. I haven't told her what happened between James and me, but like all mothers, she has an instinctive under-standing of certain things. Like when your daughter is heart-broken.

I'm glad when I can finally fall into bed at night. But despite my exhaustion, I spend over an hour tossing and turning. There's nothing to distract me here. There's nothing left to do, nothing that can force its way between me and my thoughts of James. I lay an arm over my face and screw up my eyes. I want to summon up the darkness, but all I can see is his face. His hint of a mocking smile, the lively glint in his eyes, the beautiful curve of his lips.

I swear, throw off the duvet, and stand up. It's so cold that I get goose bumps down my arms as I walk over to my desk and grab my laptop. I head back to bed and pull the covers right up. I jam a pillow behind my back, open the laptop, and go to my browser.

It feels almost like I'm doing something illegal as I type the letters into the search box.

J-a-m-e-s-B-e-a-u-f-o-r-t

Enter.

1,930,760 hits in 0.5 seconds.

Oh wow.

At the top of the screen are image results. Pictures of James in tailored Beaufort suits, of James playing golf with his father and his father's friends. They make him look respectable. Dressed to kill, like he's got the world at his feet.

But as I open the image tab, I get to see another, less perfect side of him. There's a load of fuzzy phone pictures in which a younger version of James is leaning over a table with a line of white powder on it. Photos of him walking in and out of clubs with assorted women—considerably older women—on his arm. Photos where he looks out of it and off his head. The contrast between this James and the one dressed up to the nines, at fancy galas and parties with his parents and Lydia, couldn't be greater.

I click back to the regular search results. Right under the row of photos there are tons of new articles, mostly about Cordelia Beaufort's sudden death. I don't want to read them. It's nothing to do with me and there's enough of all that in the news as it is. I scroll through more results until James's Instagram account pops up. Without thinking, I click on the link.

His profile shows an eclectic mix of photos. There are books, the mirrorlike façade of a skyscraper, a close-up of a stucco-decorated wall, benches, winding staircases, London from the air through a plane window, his feet in leather shoes on a railway platform, the morning sun shining into a room. If pictures of his friends and Lydia didn't keep turning up among them all, I'd never have linked this account to James.

In group photos with the lads, James is grinning that grin, the one that drives me wild—the breathtakingly arrogant one that's so effortlessly attractive it gives you butterflies all the same.

One photo in particular catches my eye. It's of James and Lydia, and they're both laughing. Pretty rare. I can't remember ever having heard Lydia laugh. But as for James, I only have to look at the picture and I can hear that familiar sound in my ears. The butterflies in my stomach are replaced by a painful tug. I miss James's laugh. I miss the way he is, his voice, our conversations . . . I miss everything.

On the spur of the moment, I download the image onto my laptop. I know that's fucked up, but I don't care. I treat every aspect of my life with rational consideration. I can allow myself to be led by my emotions this once.

Under the photos at the top of James's profile, there are hundreds of messages of condolence. I skim through the comments and gulp hard. Some of them are worse than tactless, they're downright cruel. Does James actually read all this stuff? What would he feel then? If it makes me feel ill, I dread to think what it's like for him.

One comment really stands out for its tastelessness.

xnzlg: for photos of the beaufort funeral check out my profile

My finger hovers over the touch pad and a furious heat floods my cheeks. I click on the link so that I can report it—and freeze.

xnzlg's entire Instagram feed consists of photos of James and Lydia. The two of them, in black, at the cemetery. They're standing side by side, leaning on each other for support. James has an arm around Lydia, holding her close, his chin resting on her head.

Tears fill my eyes.

Why would you do a thing like that? Why would you photograph the worst moments in the life of a family that's already broken and then put the pictures on the internet? Nobody has the right to invade their privacy like that.

I wipe my eyes with my hand. I try to navigate xnzlg's feed and report the account. Then I mark the comments under James's photos as spam until they disappear.

That's all I can do at this moment, and it isn't enough. The photos have stirred up all the feelings that have been building inside me in the last few weeks until I can barely control them. I'm overwhelmed by sympathy for James and Lydia.

I shut my laptop and shove it back into its padded sleeve, then I reach for my phone and open my messages. I decide to text Lydia.

I don't know whether or not she's told her family that she's pregnant, but she definitely needs to know that nothing's changed and that, despite everything, I'm still there for her if she needs me. I open her last message to me and type a reply:

Lydia, I meant what I said. If you ever want to talk, just let me know.

I hesitate a moment, then send it. After that, I stare at the phone in my hand. I know that the sensible thing to do would be to put it away. But I can't help it. Automatically, I open the chat between me and James.

I can hardly believe his first message to me was a little more than three months ago. It feels like years since the evening when James invited me down to Beaufort's in London with him. I remember the moment we'd just put on the Victorian costumes and then his parents turned up unexpectedly. My first thought when I saw Cordelia Beaufort was, *I want to be like her.*

I was impressed by the way her personality filled the entire room—she didn't say or do a single thing, and yet she exuded authority and competence. Despite Mortimer Beaufort's hard face and physical presence, there was no doubting who had the final say in the company. I never properly met her, but I'm still mourning James's mother.

And I'm grieving with James. When I was with him, he said that he didn't even really like his mum, but I know that's not true. He loved her; I could see that very clearly as he wept in my arms.

My eyes flit back to my wardrobe. On impulse, I go over and open the door. Then I bend down. Right at the bottom, on the bottom shelf, hidden behind an old PE bag, is James's hoodie. The one he dressed me in that time after Cyril's party. Carefully, I pull it out and bury my face in it for a moment. It barely even smells of James's detergent anymore, but the soft fabric stirs up memories. I shut the wardrobe door and go back to bed. On the way, I slip the jumper over my head and pull the sleeves down over my fingers.

I don't know how it's possible to be so eaten up with rage, and yet to be suffering so badly with James that I sometimes feel like I can't bear it a moment longer.

Like now, for example.

Indecisively, I pick up my phone again. I twist it in my hands. I want to message James, but at the same time, I don't. I want to console him and to scream at him, to hug him and to hit him.

In the end, I type a brief text:

I'm thinking of you

I stare at the words and take a deep breath. Then I click send. After that, I put my phone down. My eye falls on the alarm clock on my bedside table. It's after midnight now, and I'm still wide-awake. Even if I switch the light off now, I won't be able to sleep, I know that.

I pull my backpack onto my bed and get out my notes from this morning. I'm about to lean back on my pillow again and start reading when my phone buzzes. I hold my breath as I click on the message.

I miss you

I get goose bumps all over my whole body. I don't know what I was expecting. But not an answer like that. As I'm staring at those three words, a second text comes in.

I want to see you

The words blur before my eyes, and even though I'm under my duvet, wearing James's hoodie, I feel cold. So many different emotions are fighting inside me: yearning for James, unspeakable anger at him, and a deep sorrow, as if I'd lost someone too.

I'd love to write that I feel the same. That I miss him too and there's nothing I'd rather do than drive over and be there for him. But I can't. Deep within me, I sense that I'm not ready for that. Not after what happened. Not after what he did to me. It just hurts too much.

It costs me every ounce of strength I can summon to type my reply.

I can't.

Ruby

Christmas is my favorite time of year.

I love all the decorations that turn the whole world into a wonderland. I love the special food, the music, the films—and of course I love all the sweet treats. I love choosing or making presents for my family and then wrapping them up beautifully. Normally, the run-up to Christmas feels magical—as if Father Christmas, or Jack Frost, or whoever, has sprinkled a dusting of glitter over everything.

This year, everything is different.

Although, no. This year, everything is exactly the same as ever. It's just *me* who's different.

The preparations are just no fun because my mind is with James the whole time. I try to take my mind off him, not to think of him, but it doesn't work. Everything that happened over the course of this term keeps replaying in my mind like a depressing film, again and again, until I have to go for a walk to clear my head.

There are days when I wish I could just stay in bed, or that I could go back in time. I'd like to go back and live in a world where nobody at school knows my name, least of all James. Sometimes I lie in bed at night and look at the photo of him laughing, or the Halloween party invitations that feature the two of us. I remember the feeling of his fingers on my hand. Of his kiss. I remember his quiet voice, whispering my name.

I'm more than ready for the holidays. At least this way, I'll have a chance to put a bit of distance between me and Maxton Hall. Because even if James won't be back at school until next term, right now I'm filled with panic every time I turn a corner or walk into a classroom, in case he's there. Which I wouldn't be able to deal with. Not yet.

Luckily, my family is providing plenty of distractions. Mum and Dad spend a lot of time squabbling in the kitchen and regularly need me to rule on whether Mum's latest batch of mince pies tastes better with or without Dad's latest new spice blend that he's added to the filling. In previous years, I've mostly sided with Mum, but to my surprise, I realize that Dad's creations are growing on me.

Ember finds plenty to fill up the rest of my time with. We do what feels like about two thousand photo shoots for her blog, even though I'm sure half the photos turn out rubbish because my fingers are shaking with cold. And this year, she's decided what we ought to give our family for Christmas, when normally, that's one of my favorite things to do. Her ideas are great—we've made a calendar filled with family photos for our grandparents and put together a personalized spa gift set for Mum. For Dad, Ember spotted an ad from someone selling a pretty 1960s spice rack, and I haggled them down to ten pounds for it.

"You're a pretty tough negotiator," Ember says as we wipe it down the best we can in our little garage. She pulls a face as she dusts all the spiderwebs off the back of the thing. "Maybe you should rethink your career goals."

I'm in the middle of spreading out old newspaper so that we can start revarnishing it, but I force myself to grin.

She looks at me searchingly, a pensive frown forming between her eyebrows.

"I don't suppose you want to finally talk to me, do you?"

"About what?" I ask flatly.

She snorts. "About why you're acting like a robot? About whatever it is that's wrong with you?"

Her words make me flinch. This is the very first time that Ember's spoken about the way I've been, rather than acting like it's normal for me to only leave my bedroom when I absolutely have to and barely utter a word to anyone. She hasn't pressured me and hasn't asked questions, and I'm so grateful to her for that.

But apparently, the grace period is over.

She doesn't know what happened between James and me in Oxford, let alone that he then went and kissed Elaine. I feel as though I have to come to terms with that whole thing myself before I can tell anyone else about it. Getting through the days at school is hard enough. But Ember isn't just my sister, she's my best friend. I know that I can trust her. And maybe it is time to stop lugging this burden around all on my own.

I take a deep breath. "I had sex with James."

That wasn't actually the first thing I was planning to say, but hey.

Ember drops the duster. "You *what*?"

Without looking at her, I start unpacking the DIY face masks and laying them out neatly. I fiddle with the elastic straps that go behind your ears.

"A day later, he was making out with another girl," I say, my voice shaking. I stare at the white straps on the dust mask as Ember comes to kneel beside me on the newspaper. "Ruby," she says quietly. Cautiously, she lays a hand between my shoulder blades, and I feel any last remnants of my resistance start to crumble.

Ember and I haven't always been as close as we are now. It was after Dad's accident that we grew together, looking out for each other whenever he was having a bad day, was furious with the entire world. We understood why he felt like that, but it wasn't an easy time for us. We only got through it together.

The bond we've shared since then is different from anything I'll ever have with anyone else, and as Ember squeezes my shoulder, the words just burst out from me. I tell her everything: about the Halloween party; about James's father and the expectations he puts on his son, and how hard that pressure is for James to deal with; about Oxford and everything that we shared with each other then. About the evening when Lydia came round to ours and drove me to Cyril's. About James, who'd done cocaine and then jumped into the pool. And about Elaine Ellington.

As I speak, the whole gamut of emotions flits across Ember's face: sympathy, outrage, incredulity, excitement, and, finally, deep anger. Once I've finished, she spends a minute just looking wide-eyed at me, then, without a word, she takes me in her arms and gives me a hug. It's the first time in days that I haven't felt the urge to cry. A warmth fills me, settles over my stormy feelings and seems to soothe them, a tiny bit at least.

"I just don't know what to do now," I mumble into Ember's

shoulder. "On the one hand, it's so awful that this has happened to him. I wish I could be there for him. But on the other hand, I don't want to see him ever again. Not after what he did to me. I want to go over there and scream at him, but I can't because I know how shit things are for him."

Ember pulls away from me and takes a deep breath. She brushes my hair off my cheek and behind my ear. Then she gently strokes her warm hands over my head. "I'm so sorry, Ruby."

I gulp hard and pluck up all my courage to say, "I hate him for it."

Ember's green eyes are full of empathy and affection. "So do I."

"But I keep asking myself if that's even allowed."

She frowns and shakes her head. "You have every right to feel that way, Ruby. You're acting like there are set rules for a situation like this, but there aren't. You just feel the way you feel."

"Hmm," I grumble uncertainly.

"And if there are days when you want to give James a slap, that's totally legitimate—whatever things are like for him at the moment," Ember continues, her voice insistent. "You can't make your feelings dependent on his, just because he's going through a shitty situation. He acted like an arsehole, and if you ask me, you're entitled to tell him that. What am I saying? You're entitled to shout it from the rooftops."

It takes me a moment to process Ember's words. "I just get the feeling," I begin slowly, after a pause, "that nothing's going to change, whatever emotions I allow myself. It's either going to hurt because of his mum or because he cheated on me. So that's why I'm trying . . ."

". . . not to feel anything at all," Ember finishes my sentence quietly.

I nod.

"That doesn't sound very healthy, Ruby."

I stare at my hands as silence expands between us.

After a long time, Ember sighs. "I just can't believe he actually did that. I mean, I know what people say about him, but . . ." She shakes her head.

"I seriously thought it was a nightmare. He was . . . like a whole different person."

"It sounds so horrible."

"The other thing I don't understand is why he didn't just come to me. He could have told me about everything. We could have . . ." I give a helpless shrug. I have no idea what I would have done if James had come to me. But at any rate, none of this would have happened. I'm sure of that.

"I expect he probably wasn't in the mood to talk that evening," Ember suggests hesitantly. "It sounds to me like he was trying to destroy even more of his life, without thinking about the consequences."

I take a jagged breath.

"Anyway, I get why you feel this way. It's totally OK. And I hate him too for what he did to you."

Ember flings her arms around me again and this time I hug her back, just as tight. "Thanks, Ember," I whisper.

After a long moment, she shoves me back and gives me a warm smile. "Shall we get started?" She points to the spice rack.

I nod, glad not to have to speak any more about my feelings. We put on the face masks and search for suitable music. Ember picks the Michael Bublé Christmas album and together we start on varnishing.

"Oh, and I've hit six hundred," she says after a while.

I cheer and pretend to bow down to her. "You're a queen."

"I'm considering applying to some of the London fashion houses in the summer holidays." Ember won't look at me as she says that, just focuses her entire attention on the top corner of the spice rack, even though that's been finished for ages now. The mask is covering most of her face, but I'm pretty sure she's blushing.

"Do you want any help with the applications?"

Ember pauses and now she plucks up the courage to glance in my direction. "So, do you think it's a good idea?"

I nod encouragingly. "You've known for years that you want to go into fashion. So I'd say the sooner you get started, the better."

She keeps on working in silence.

I study her thoughtfully. "What's wrong?" I ask.

Ember only hesitates a moment. "I really wish I could do an internship at a firm that makes ethical, eco-friendly, and stylish plus-size clothes," she explains in the end. "The trouble is, it's really hard to find anything that ticks all those boxes. So I guess I'll just have to apply to anyone that's offering anything. But it doesn't seem like there's much point working for people who don't even make clothes in my size. D'you see what I mean?"

I nod. "Yes, but work experience is important. And you'd be able to see what they do and figure out how you're going to do things differently one day."

"But I feel really uncomfortable about it." She sighs. "I keep asking myself, should I trust my gut instinct, if it's telling me not to go there?"

"It might just be nerves. Remember how many good people have your back. Your blog has so many readers. They all believe in you and your vision."

"That's sweet of you."

"I'm not just saying it to be sweet. I mean it. I'm one hundred percent certain you're going to start your own fashion empire one day, and get off to a flying start."

Ember grins from ear to ear—mask or no mask, I can tell by her sparkling eyes.

"During the holidays, we can make a list of possible companies, maybe?" I suggest, running my brush over the inside of the rack.

"That's a great idea. I've made a start because I've been wanting to put together a guide to ethical plus-size fashion."

I'm about to tell her it's a plan when there's a knock on the garage's side door.

"Ruby?"

Ember and I freeze. We can't let Mum see what we're doing here. She is absolutely incapable of keeping a secret, especially when it comes to presents for Dad. We've experienced that more than once over the years.

"Don't come in!" Ember yells in alarm, taking a hasty step in front of the spice rack so that Mum wouldn't be able to see it if she stuck her head around the door.

"I wasn't going to," she says, her voice muffled. "Ruby, you've got a visitor."

Ember and I look at each other in confusion.

"Lin?" she asks.

I shake my head. "No, she's spending the holidays in China with her mum, visiting family out there."

Ember's eyes widen. "Do you think it's . . . ?" She doesn't say his name, but my heart still skips a beat.

"Who is it, Mum?" I call.

"Any chance you could come out? I have no desire to have a conversation through the door."

I roll my eyes and pull one loop of the face mask off my ear so that it partially hangs down, making me feel like a surgeon taking a break in the middle of a major operation. I open the door a crack and squeeze out. Mum looks at me and the mask with raised eyebrows, and I spot her standing on tiptoes in an attempt to peek round the door. I hastily shut it behind me.

"Who is it?" I ask quietly.

In an instant, Mum's face is serious again. "It's the Beaufort girl."

My heart plummets. I've got déjà vu for the evening when Lydia came here looking for James. Surely there can't have been another disaster.

Not again. Please, not again.

"Where is she?" I ask.

Mum nods toward the hall. "In the living room. Your dad and I are in the kitchen if you need us."

I nod and take the mask off completely. I walk down the hall toward the living room with cautious steps. This time, I'm bracing myself, Ember's wise words still fresh in my memory.

Lydia is sitting on our old, flowery sofa, her hands clasped in her lap, her eyes fixed on the coffee table. She's wearing a loose, floaty chiffon blouse with a black pleated skirt, and her hair is in a ponytail, as usual. Not a strand is out of place. As ever, Lydia gives the impression of having everything perfectly under control.

But the apathetic expression in her eyes tells a different story.

"Hi," I say quietly, not wanting to startle her.

Lydia looks up and sees me in the doorway. She summons up the energy for a weary smile. "Hi, Ruby."

For a moment, I'm not sure what to do, but settle for sitting down next to her on the sofa. I resist the urge to make small talk, to ask her how she is, or if everything's OK. I just wait.

After a while, Lydia swallows. "You said I could ask you if I needed any help."

For a moment, I'm confused, but then I nod hastily. "Yes, right. Anything at all."

She glances uncertainly toward the living room door, like she's keeping an eye out for someone. She's probably afraid of my parents or Ember coming in or overhearing us. I budge over a fraction toward her.

"What is it?" I ask.

Lydia exhales audibly. Then she straightens her back and sits up tall. "I've got a checkup tomorrow, and I need someone to come with me."

It takes me a second or two to realize what she just said. "You want me to go with you?" I ask in surprise.

She takes a shaky breath, presses her lips tightly together, then nods. "You're the only person who knows."

"Is there something wrong? Does it hurt or something?"

Lydia shakes her head. "No, it's just routine. But I . . . don't want to go there alone."

I wonder how hard it was for her to come here and ask me that. This is the first time I've really understood how lonely Lydia must be. I'm the only person she can ask to go with her to an appointment that must be scary, and nerve-racking.

There's only one answer to her question, and I give it like it's the most natural thing in the world.

"Of course I will."

———

The only word to describe the room is "sterile." The walls are white and there's only one picture up. On the left-hand side, there's a desk in front of a wide window with closed blinds; to the right, there's a pale blue curtain screening off one corner. I presume Lydia's going to have to undress behind there soon.

We're sitting on the two chairs in front of the desk, watching Dr. Hearst as she types on her computer at lightning speed.

At first it was weird to be here with Lydia. But the moment she was asked by a nurse to pee into a little cup, I realized that we were long past the point of embarrassment.

Now Lydia is fiddling with her tartan scarf and squinting at the door. Maybe she's toying with the idea of getting up and running away. As her eye catches mine, I give her a reassuring smile—or try to. I don't know exactly what my job here is, so I try to act the way I'd want her to if our roles were reversed. It seems to work, because Lydia's shoulders relax a tiny bit.

Once Dr. Hearst has finished with the computer, she rests her hands on the desk and leans toward us slightly. Her face is friendly, however severe the bun holding up her dark hair may be. She has lots of laugh lines; warm brown eyes; and a pleasant, calm voice.

"So, Lydia, how are you doing?" she asks.

I watch Lydia as she looks back at the doctor.

Suddenly, she makes a kind of hysterical sound that was probably intended to be a laugh. But she quickly pulls herself together and clears her throat as if nothing ever happened. "Not too bad, I think."

Dr. Hearst gives an understanding nod. "Last time, you said the sickness was very bad. How is that going now?"

"It's better. I haven't been sick at all for a week. But sometimes it really hurts when I stand up after a long time sitting down. Is that normal?"

Dr. Hearst smiles. "That's nothing to worry about. The ligaments in your womb are under a lot of strain now, making room for the baby. I can prescribe you magnesium, which should help with the pain."

"OK, that sounds good," says Lydia with relief.

After the conversation, Dr. Hearst sends her behind the curtain to undress. I stay in my chair, staring at the painting over the desk, while she examines her. I'm trying to figure out what the shapes and colors are meant to represent but stand no chance. It's one of the weirdest pictures I've ever seen, all in yellow, red, and blue. I wonder if it was done by a child.

I hear Dr. Hearst say, "Everything is as it should be. The cervix is nicely closed, and so long as you have no cramps or bleeding, it should all be fine."

Lydia murmurs something that I don't catch, then she's allowed to get dressed again. I sigh with relief. We've got through this part.

"You can join us now, Ruby."

Lydia is now lying on a bed with her blouse pushed up. Her fingers are resting on her bare belly, and I realize that you can see a clear bulge now.

I smile nervously back at her as I sit on a chair beside her. The doctor is bringing over something that I presume is an ultrasound machine.

"So, are you ready to see your baby, Lydia?"

Lydia nods, but she's clearly tense, so I scoot a bit closer to her. The doctor rubs a transparent gel onto Lydia's belly and then presses the tip of the scanner to it. I stare in fascination at the screen, but at first, I can't make anything out at all in the fuzzy black-and-white image. Dr. Hearst moves calmly over Lydia's skin and, after a while, the picture changes. It gradually comes more and more into focus and . . .

I catch my breath. Beside me, Lydia gasps an "oh" of surprise.

I'm pretty sure there's a little head on the screen, over to the right.

"There you are," says Dr. Hearst, pointing to the screen with her finger. As she moves the scanner, the baby becomes clearer to see. Now I can make out tiny arms and legs. This is so, so cool—far and away the most fascinating thing I've ever seen in my life.

"Wow," I whisper, and the doctor smiles at me.

I dare to glance at Lydia. Her eyes are huge as she stares at the screen in disbelief.

"Hold on," Dr. Hearst says suddenly, leaning in a little closer. For a moment, the black-and-white chaos is back, but then the little bubble comes into view again.

"Is everything OK?" Lydia asks anxiously. I put my hand on her shoulder. The doctor's hesitation is making me nervous too. The baby moved, I saw it very clearly. She can't give us bad news now—not now. Lydia wouldn't cope.

"Ms. Beaufort, may I introduce you"—Dr. Hearst is beaming at Lydia—"to Baby Number Two!" She points to a dot on the screen. "They're slightly hidden behind their little brother or sister, so it's harder to make them out."

Lydia gasps. She stares incredulously at the monitor as Dr. Hearst zooms in on the second little bubble and enlarges the image. I can't see anything myself, but I know she's telling the truth.

Twins.

Lydia is not expecting one child but two.

I can't imagine what's going through her head right now. I pat her shoulder a little awkwardly, desperately trying to think what to say, when Lydia suddenly throws back her head and laughs.

Dr. Hearst and I exchange glances that say we can't blame her. Lydia must be in shock. After everything she's been through in the last few weeks, I wouldn't be surprised if she ended up having a breakdown.

"That's crazy." She giggles after a while, turning her head toward me. "That's just . . . I don't know what to say."

Dr. Hearst presses a few buttons on the machine and smiles at Lydia, and then at me. "They're non-identical twins and both well-developed. Everything looks fine. Do twins run in your family, Lydia?"

Lydia nods and shakes her head all at once, still staring at the screen.

"She has a twin brother herself," I answer quietly for her, trying to suppress the image of Lydia's twin. James has no place in my head right now.

"There's nothing to be afraid of." Dr. Hearst is trying to reassure Lydia, but I don't get the impression she's taking any of it in. "We'll keep a slightly closer eye on you from now on, and I'd recommend a glucose tolerance test to rule out gestational diabetes.

You can make an appointment at reception . . ." She gives a brief lecture on healthy eating and the next checkups, but I can tell that Lydia isn't listening.

I study her pale face. She really needs something soothing about now. And I've got a pretty good idea of what.

7

Ruby

Smith's Bakery doesn't look like much from the outside. It's part of a row of shops with flats above them, between my favorite thrift store and a takeaway pizza place that's been closed every single time I've walked past. They refresh the front every year, but it gets so weather-beaten that the paint barely lasts a few weeks before it's looking tatty and unloved again. There's a sign with fancy lettering in green and gold over the big front window that displays the day's freshly baked treats to every passerby. Everything is made in the shop, from soft white bread, scones and rolls, to Bakewell tarts, to pies—everything your heart could desire.

"I always come here when I'm feeling down," I tell Lydia, who is looking a little doubtfully at the shopfront. I go up the steps to the bakery and hold the door for her. The delicious aromas waft out from the ovens toward us, and the smells of fresh bread and cinnamon fill my nose.

"My favorite smell," I say, turning to Lydia. "If there was a perfume that smelled of fresh bread and cinnamon, I'd buy the entire stock and then bathe in it until I'd never smell of anything else ever again."

Lydia's lips twitch ever so slightly. Still, it's the first sign of emotion she's shown since we left the doctor's office.

Phil, my mum's colleague, is serving a customer as we approach the counter. There are wooden shelves on the wall behind him, filled with loaves and baguettes. On the counter, there are two little baskets with free samples of buttered bread. I take a couple in passing and hand one to Lydia while I pop the other into my mouth.

"Have a taste," I say through a mouthful. "The bread here is so good."

Lydia follows suit, somewhat hesitantly.

The bakery is small and cramped. The space isn't really designed for settling down with a coffee, but they've squeezed in a couple of tables and seats anyway. One's by the kitchen door, where they make the dough, and the other is so close to the counter that you can't help getting a bit jostled by other customers when it's busy.

I gesture toward the little bench and battered table at the back of the shop. Lydia squeezes in, looking around her. She doesn't seem to know what to make of this place. There's an air of skepticism about her that reminds me of her mum and the way she studied me the only time we met.

I shake the memory out of my head. "Do you know what you'd like?" I ask.

Lydia squints past me, her head to one side as she eyes the array of cakes. "What would you recommend?"

"The Bakewell tart is my favorite."

"I'll go with that, then."

I nod and smile, and walk up to the counter just as Mum emerges from the bake room. She beams at the sight of me and wipes her hands on the apron she's wearing over a striped shirt, embroidered with the bakery logo.

"Hi, Mum, I'm here with Lydia," I say hastily, gesturing with my thumb back to our table. "She's had a tough day and I thought a Bakewell tart and a hot chocolate would be sure to make her feel better," I add in a whisper, hoping that Lydia can't hear me.

"There's nothing that a Bakewell tart and a hot chocolate can't cure," Mum replies with a conspiratorial wink.

"Thanks, Mum."

I go back to Lydia and sit on the wobbly chair opposite her. She's resting her chin on her hand. "How long has your mum worked here?"

"Since before I was born. She started here straight from school."

She smiles slightly. "Must have been cool as a kid."

"There were always biscuits," I say, waggling my eyebrows.

Lydia's smile broadens.

"Do you know what you want to do, one day?" I ask after a while.

Now her expression darkens. "What do you think?"

"Lydia, just because you're having a baby, that doesn't mean your entire future is screwed up."

She lowers her eyes and runs her finger over the dents in the tabletop. "Babies," she murmurs after a long time.

"What?" I say, confused.

"My future isn't screwed up just because I'm having *babies*. Plural." The smile is back, more restrained this time, but I can't help returning it.

I don't know what happens next, but suddenly we both start laughing, hesitantly at first, and then louder. Lydia claps her hand to her mouth like she can't quite believe what she's doing. But that just turns her laugh into a semi-muffled snort, which sets us both off again.

Just at this moment, Mum comes over with a tray. "What's so funny?" she asks as she sets the steaming mugs in front of us, followed by the cake plates.

Lydia presses her lips together and shuts her eyes until she's got herself back under control. Then she looks at Mum and says, perfectly calmly: "Ruby and I were just laughing at how weird life can be, Mrs. Bell." She leans in to sniff the hot chocolate. "This smells divine, by the way."

Mum blinks in surprise, then gives Lydia a gentle pat on her arm. She knows that she lost her mother not so long ago, and I'm sure she wishes there was more she could do for her than just bring her cake and hot drinks. "Enjoy it."

Lydia watches Mum as she walks back to the counter to serve the next customer. Then she sighs softly, pulls the mug of hot chocolate closer, and wraps both hands around it.

"I always wanted to be a designer for Beaufort's," she says, answering my question after all.

"But surely you . . ." *still can*, I want to say, but one glance from Lydia is enough to cut me off.

She picks up her spoon and stirs the hot chocolate for a while. "Once upon a time, I dreamed of bringing my creativity to the firm, but Mum and Dad considered my ideas too modern, not traditional enough," she goes on. "I kept getting into rows with them because I wanted a bigger role than they were planning for me. Unlike James, I really would like to take the company on.

But for them, it was all about him. Ever since we were born. Regardless of what either of us wanted." She pulls the spoon from the mug and slips it into her mouth. "Mm." She sighs with delight.

"I hate how much pressure you were both put under. Still are. It must be so hard," I mumble, turning my attention to my own drink. The warmth is doing me the world of good, and my cold fingers are gradually thawing out.

Lydia looks so sad and hopeless that I wish I could give her a hug. "Anyone looking at our family from the outside would get the impression that Mum and Dad love us more than anything, and just want the best for us. Wanted. Whatever." She clears her throat. "I can't complain about having grown up like that. I don't have any right to. I don't know how much James told you, but . . . there are things that just went wrong and can't be put right again."

I can't help wondering if she means her father. And whether he only gets violent with James the minute he doesn't get his own way, or if he's rough with Lydia too. If so, then I'm even more worried for her.

"He only told me a few things," I say evasively.

I know that Lydia knows him better than anyone else in the world, but I still can't talk to her about the things he confided in me. Even after everything that's happened, I couldn't betray him like that.

"He's doing better, by the way. He's stopped drinking since the funeral. Now he's working out obsessively instead."

I remember the blank look in his eyes. James's tears. The way he clung on to me. The cuts and bruises on his hand.

"And things between him and your dad . . . ?" I ask cautiously.

"You know they had a fight?"

I nod.

"Dad acts like nothing ever happened. He's practically never at home, and when he is there, he orders James into his office to brief him for Beaufort board meetings."

On the one hand, I'm glad that James's relationship with his father hasn't escalated any further, but on the other hand, I know what James feels about the company and what a weight it must be on his shoulders to work for the firm. I'm so sorry for him, especially seeing that that's all kicked in sooner than he was expecting.

"I hope you two can get through this, Ruby."

I look into Lydia's turquoise eyes. Her eyes that look exactly the same as James's.

Wearily, I shake my head. "I don't think we can. To be honest, I don't even want to."

It's the first time I've said that aloud. But it's the truth. I don't think you can ever just get over a thing like this. Everything James and I have gone though. And I really don't want to. Especially not when I think about everything I'm going to face in the future. It feels like there's a shadow lying over all my dreams, and only because I confided them in James, and then he hurt me so badly.

"You could try," Lydia suggests gently, but I shake my head again.

"I understand that the news about your mum knocked him sideways, but . . ." I shrug helplessly. "That doesn't change anything. I hate him for what he did."

"But you were still there when he needed you. That has to mean something, doesn't it?"

I stir my hot chocolate and take a deep breath. "I still have feelings for him, yes. But at the same time, I've never been this angry with anyone in my whole life. And I don't think that anger is just going away."

Neither of us speaks. The oven seems to be beeping louder now than a few minutes ago, and the bell over the door and the coming and going of other customers are louder too.

"Would it have been better if I'd gone to my appointment on my own?" Lydia asks out of the blue.

My head snaps up. "No!"

There's a blush on Lydia's cheeks and she suddenly looks almost shy. I wonder what's going on in her head right now.

"If I'd known how you were feeling, I'd never have taken you up on your offer. I—"

"Lydia," I interrupt her in a gentle voice, reaching across the table to take her hand. Her eyes widen and she stares at our interlinked fingers. "I meant what I said to you. I'd like to be there for you. Our friendship has nothing to do with James. OK?"

She looks back at me, and I think I can spot a glimmer in her eyes. She doesn't reply to my words, just gives my hand a quick squeeze. And that's more than enough.

James

The raw guitars of Rage Against the Machine have been filling my ears for more than an hour, and it feels as though my whole body is in flames. But it's still not enough.

I'm standing at the gym, gripping the short bar that's hooked to the top. I hold my elbows close to my body and let my forearms ride up, then stretch them down, working my triceps over and over again. Sweat drips from my brow onto my T-shirt and my muscles are shaking, but I don't care. I just keep going. Eventually, I'll reach the point of total exhaustion, where there'll be room for nothing in my head but a loud, meaningless roar, and all thoughts of Beaufort's, Mum, and Ruby will be silenced. Once I've done my arms set, I sit down on the seat and grab the chest press handles. I push them forward slowly and as my arms move back, I feel the burn in my pecs.

I only realize that the door to the fitness room has opened when Lydia pops up in front of me, arms akimbo. My sister is staring down at me, saying something, but with the din in my ears, I can't hear her. I don't let her put me off, just keep on doing my reps. Lydia leans down so that I have no choice but to look at her. Her lips slowly form another word—and I don't need to hear this one to understand it.

Idiot.

What have I done now? I've barely left the house since the funeral and I haven't touched a drop of booze. Which has been hard, especially in the moments when I can't stop the dark thoughts. But I stuck to it, partly for Lydia's sake, after her trembling body at Mum's funeral reminded me that my job as a brother is to be there for her. So I'm not entirely sure why she's currently standing red-faced in front of me, apparently giving me a torrent of abuse. Although I have to admit that her open-mouth-close-mouth act looks kind of funny while the music thumps in my ears. It's almost like she's lip-synching.

Suddenly, Lydia steps closer and flicks out one of my earbuds. "James!"

"What's wrong?" I ask, taking the other one out too. The sudden quiet seems almost threatening. Lately, I've needed sound around me all the time, otherwise I start to think.

"I wanted to talk to you about Ruby."

I take my hands off the grips and reach for my towel. I wipe it over my face and neck, where the sweat has pooled. I avoid looking at Lydia.

"I don't know what you—"

"Cut it out, James."

It feels like I'm wearing a tie that's too tight, constricting my throat. I cough. "I don't want to talk about her."

Lydia looks at me, shaking her head. The corners of her lips are turned down and she's crossed her arms over her chest. In this second, she reminds me so much of Mum that I have to turn away for a moment. I stare at the towel and wipe my hands on it, even though they're long dry.

"I really wish I could help you. Both of you."

I can only laugh bitterly at that. "There is no *us*, Lydia. And there never was. I fucked it up."

"If you explain—" Lydia starts again, but I cut her off.

"She doesn't want to hear my explanations. And I can't exactly blame her for that."

Lydia sighs. "I still think you have a chance. I wish you'd take it instead of holing yourself up here and wallowing in self-pity."

I remember Ruby's message:

I can't.

Of course she can't. I kissed another girl, and that's unforgivable. I've lost Ruby forever. And Lydia waltzing in here and trying to convince me of the opposite is the last straw. I wanted to switch off and distract myself, but that's not possible anymore. Slowly but surely, the rage crawls back into my body. Rage at Mum's death, rage at my father, rage at myself—and the whole world.

"What's it to you?" I ask. My fingers clutch at the towel.

"You both matter to me. I don't like seeing either of you miserable, for fuck's sake. Is that so hard to understand?"

"Ruby doesn't want me back, and there's no way I'm going to force it. I don't want you intruding on her either." I stand up, intending to head over to the two treadmills set up in front of a huge panoramic window that looks out onto our gardens. But I don't get far. Lydia pulls me back by the elbow. I spin around, glaring angrily at her.

"Don't look at me like that. It's time you got your shit together," she snarls. Then she jabs a finger into my chest. "You can't push everyone and everything away forever."

"I'm not pushing *you* away," I mutter through clenched teeth. "James . . ."

I try to summon up the mask of inapproachability that was always my second face at school and official meetings with my family. But this is Lydia in front of me. I've never had to hide anything from her and so I just can't do it. Frustrated, I throw the towel down to one side.

"What do you want me to say, Lydia?" I ask feebly.

"That we'll get through this together. You and me. Like always." She swallows and touches me gently on the arm. "But if you can't be honest with me, and keep hiding away like this, then that won't work."

I snort in disgust. "You're acting like you always tell me everything, like *you're* the open one out of the two of us. I've always had to squeeze everything out of you. I only found out about your affair with Sutton because you got caught." I push her hand away and stare coldly into her eyes. "Just because Mum died, it doesn't mean that it has to be us two against the world from now on. Don't make us into something we never were, Lydia."

She flinches and stumbles back. Without deigning to look at her again, I turn and shove my earbuds back in. If my sister says anything else, I don't hear it. The loud guitar riff drowns out the ugly reality of my world.

Ruby

The memory of James is so strong that, even after weeks of no contact, everything still feels like it happened only yesterday. I'm sleeping badly. I delete his photos from my laptop, only to download them again a day later, and run my fingers over his smiling mouth like a psychopath. At the same time, I feel like a liar because I told Lydia that I don't want him back, when my body is clearly not of the same opinion.

I miss James.

It's absurd.

Absurd and insane.

And I could slap myself for it. He broke my heart, for God's sake. I really shouldn't miss a person who does a thing like that.

Christmas comes and goes and, for the first time in my life, I can't enjoy it. The films we watch seem dull and all the songs we listen to sound the same. I know that Mum and Dad have been cooking flat-out, but the food tastes bland. And to top it all off, my relatives keep asking me why I'm so down and whether it has anything to do with the boy who gave me that lovely bag for my birthday. After a while, I can't take any more of it and crawl off to my bedroom alone.

Once we get to the end of the year, I decide that I can't go on like this a minute longer. I'm sick of feeling like this. I've always been a positive person who looks forward to new beginnings. I refuse to let James take that mindset away from me.

So I jump up and have a shower, dress in one of my favorite outfits—a tight tartan skirt and a flowy cream blouse—grab my new bullet journal, and go downstairs, firmly resolved to announce my New Year's resolutions to Ember and our parents.

But as I walk into the living room, I stop in my tracks.

"What are you doing here?" I ask in surprise.

Startled, Ember whirls around to face me, and so does Lin, who was in the middle of slipping colorful mini umbrellas into an array of glasses. Lydia pauses in mid-movement too, but the streamer in her hand takes on a life of its own and unrolls itself. We watch in silence as it ends up in a sad little heap on the floor.

Then Ember plants herself crossly in front of me. "Why did you pick today of all days to emerge from your shell?" she snaps. "We've been able to set our watches by the times you come out of your room, but now—right when I've been planning a surprise girls' night for you—you have to come down early. That's just . . . bloody hell, Ruby!"

I look at each of them in turn. Then a slow smile spreads over my lips.

"We're seeing the new year in together?" I ask cautiously.

Lin smiles back at me. "That was the plan."

As the realization truly sinks in, I give Ember a firm hug.

"Thank you," I mumble into her shoulder. "I think this is just what I need." And Ember had guessed that, which shows me yet again that she knows me better than anyone else in the world.

"I thought it might help cheer you up a bit," my sister whispers, stroking my back.

I nod. For the first time since the whole thing happened with James, I feel truly happy. "Thanks," I say again, to Lin and Lydia, hugging each of them too. "I can't wait."

After that, I help them put up the rest of the streamers and to scatter the rose-gold confetti. Ember hooks up the ancient pair of speakers we bought at some flea market to her laptop and tells me the plan for the evening while hunting for a suitable playlist. She's obviously had a lot of ideas and planned everything down to the tiniest detail, which makes me want to fling my arms around her neck again. But I refrain, and just listen from my spot on the sofa.

"I thought we could start by writing down our favorite moments from the last year and then sharing them with each other. Then we can watch a film—we'll pick one in a minute—and polish off this mountain of popcorn." She points to a bowl on the coffee table. Dad normally uses it for taking enormous salads to family parties. Now it's filled to the brim with popcorn, and the sweet, buttery scent of it is wafting across the whole room, making my mouth water.

"Then we can have dinner," Ember continues. "Dad's made us quiche for the main course, and there's pudding too, and then we'll get to what I suspect will be Ruby's favorite part of the night."

Lin holds up a translucent bag, in which I can make out little books and pens.

I don't even pretend to think about it. "Writing our New Year's resolutions!"

Ember nods and laughs. "And at midnight, the dancing starts—unless we're all in a food coma."

"One or the other, definitely," says Lydia, taking a handful of popcorn. She flicks the first piece into her mouth, and a slight smile plays around her lips. "Sounds like a nice plan, doesn't it, Ruby?"

"Nice? It's the best plan I've heard in ages. Thanks, everyone."

After that, we settle down on the floor around the coffee table. Lin smuggled out of school a couple of the huge sheets of paper we normally use for brainstorming at committee meetings and we spread them out in front of us, a Keaton Henson playlist playing in the background.

"OK." Ember starts things off. "One of my biggest highlights of the year was my work on my blog and getting so many new readers." She jots that all down on her paper.

"So, a high point for me was my mum's gallery finally breaking even. We're doing really well at the moment and I hope it'll be the same next year," Lin says, her attention focused not on us but on the pen in her hand. I'm surprised that she's shared something that personal.

She and Lydia don't know each other all that well, and I could understand them finding the situation awkward. But neither of them seems to, and that's really nice.

"I went to your gallery once," Lydia says suddenly. "With my mum."

Lin looks up in surprise. "Really?"

Lydia nods. "It's lovely, so stylish. I'll cross my fingers for you for things to go better still next year. I know how tough it can be, especially when you're starting from scratch."

The two of them smile at each other, then Lydia clears her throat. "I had a mini-break in the Alps with Mum in January. We went to a spa hotel and really spoiled ourselves—just the two of us. It was the first time in ages we'd done anything like that. I think that's my nicest memory from the year."

"It sounds gorgeous," I say quietly, resting my hand on her knee for a moment. I don't know what else to say, but want to show her how much I appreciate her honesty.

"How about you, Ruby?" Lin asks.

For a second, my mind's a complete blank and I have no idea what I could write on my paper. But then I scan through the year, a month at a time, and realize that overall, it was good. Despite how sad I've been since the thing with James, so much has happened, just since September, that I can be grateful for.

I'm events team leader, my grades are good, and I got an interview at Oxford. I've got to know Lin better, got closer to Ember, and I've even made a new friend. And, for the first time in my life, I've fallen in love.

However badly it ended for James and me . . . when I think back over our conversations, our phone calls, and our shared memories, I regret nothing. On the contrary, even that experience is one of the highlights of my year. Even if it's all over.

I gulp hard and stare at the white paper on the table in front of me.

"I don't even know where to start. I think the Oxford visit was the best. I've spent so long dreaming of strolling around there with my family. And actually being there . . . I'll remember it forever," I say hoarsely, forcing myself to smile.

"It looked like something out of a fairy tale," says Ember.

I nod, draw a little bubble, and write *Oxford trip* inside it.

That seems to have broken the ice. We share even our tiniest and weirdest memories of this year. Like the time Lin won a bouquet of flowers in a supermarket for being their thousandth customer, or the time an old lady slipped Lydia a pound coin and told her to buy herself a treat.

Soon, the mood is much more cheerful than when we started out. We laugh together, and it feels like the four of us have been friends for ages. Around eight, Mum and Dad say goodbye and drive round to some friends. I can see how relieved they are that I've ventured out of my room this evening and I'm spending the night with friends.

After that, we watch *How to Be Single*, which was one of Ember's Christmas presents—she loves Rebel Wilson—and two hours later, when the credits start to roll, I get why. Even Lydia laughs out loud in some places, although every time that happens, she looks like she can hardly believe it's her making that noise.

Before the end of the credits, we launch into Dad's quiche.

"You're so lucky, Ruby." Lin's holding up a forkful of quiche and studying it closely. "To have a baker for a mum and a chef for a dad. If it were me, I'd be in seventh heaven. I miss our cook at home."

"You used to have a cook?" Ember asks, wide-eyed.

"Yeah," says Lin, shrugging her shoulders as if it was the most natural thing in the world. "But then everything changed at home and I had to learn all the basics. Mum's cooking skills were kind of rusty too, but she's taught me lots of great Chinese recipes that she got from her gran. These days, we really enjoy cooking together."

I take a bite of quiche and let it melt on my tongue.

"The only thing I can cook is scrambled eggs," Lydia says pensively. "That must have been such a drastic shock to you and your mum."

For a moment, Lin seems surprised by Lydia's words, but then she smiles slightly. "I've learned never to look back, only forward." She puts her fork down on her empty plate and wipes up the last crumbs with her finger. Then she picks up one of the bags. "We should do these now. It's almost ten."

"Oh, how pretty," I say as Lin passes round the little notebooks. They're very plain with black covers and accents picked out in gold, speckled creamy-white pages, and two ribbon bookmarks—just what I like best.

"This is going to be my first bullet journal," says Lydia, staring at the notebook and then looking at us in slight confusion. "What do I have to do?"

Ember piles up our plates and puts them to one side, then she puts her laptop in the middle of the coffee table so that we can all see the screen. "It's really simple," she says. "Every New Year's Eve, we write down our resolutions." She opens her book and points to the first page. "And before that, we have to decide on a heading."

Together, we search the internet for fonts we like and try to copy them, or to be inspired by them. For the most part, we work in silence, the only sounds being our pens on the paper and the soft background music.

But as I focus on the last details of my heading and circle the date of the coming year in a pale gray, I suddenly feel heavyhearted again. By this time next year, everything will have changed.

In seven months from now, I'll do my A levels. And—hopefully—I'll pass. And after that I'll leave Maxton Hall College and—hopefully—be at St. Hilda's. I'll have new teachers and new classmates. I'll have a new room in college and new surroundings and new friends.

An exciting new life.

A life without James Beaufort.

The idea takes me by surprise and hurts more than I'd have thought possible, but I try to push it away. I grab a pen and start writing:

Resolutions:

- *Get A level grades I need*
- *Oxford*
- *Keep in touch with Mum, Dad, and Ember*
- *Make at least one new friend*
- *Stop worrying so much about what other people might think of me*

But as I make a note of each point in turn, I realize that it doesn't feel right. This list isn't honest enough, and if I really listen to my heart, I know why.

In the last year, I fell in love for the first time—and my heart was broken in the cruelest way. I can't just erase that fact. I'm going to need quite a while to work through it. Because heartache doesn't stop just because we've rung in a new year.

Until now, I haven't wanted to see James. I'd hoped that eventually, I'd start to forget him. But now I realize that I can't write my resolutions while things are still up in the air between us. There's way too much that I want to say to him. And I don't think I'll be able to start the new year without doing that. I won't be able to start again while James is still taking up so much space in my thoughts, my feelings, and my life.

"Ruby?" I hear Lin's voice as if from a great distance.

I look at her and make a decision.

But before I put it into action, I'm going to party with my friends.

James

Normally, New Year's Eve with my friends is legendary. In the past, we've rented a lakeside villa or thrown parties in London that are booked up months in advance. We've kept drinking into the small hours and forgotten everything around us.

This year, I spend New Year's Eve at home alone.

Where's Dad? Not a clue. The staff have the night off and Lydia's out with a friend. She didn't tell me who. Since our fight a couple of days ago, she's been ignoring me, only speaking to me when she has to.

Wren tried to talk me into going away with him and the lads this year too, but I couldn't get my arse into gear. Just the thought of being stuck in some London club with all the deafening music and champagne makes my hair stand on end. I can't keep on acting like the old days. Not after my life has turned one-eighty in the last three months. Not when nothing inside me looks the same anymore.

I spend the evening watching wildlife documentaries about the Kenyan savannah on my laptop and eating takeaway kebab and chips out of cardboard boxes. Sometimes I succeed in taking my mind off things for five minutes straight. But most of the time, I'm thinking about Ruby.

Over the last few weeks, I've realized to my frustration that we didn't collect enough shared memoires. There are no photos of us, nothing to remind me of what we experienced together. All I have left is the bag I had made for her birthday. It's still standing there beside my desk, mocking me day in, day out. I can't count the times I've picked it up and looked inside, just in case Ruby left anything in it. A note, or anything to hint that she really used it and liked it.

I feel as though my memories are slowly starting to fade. The sensation of Ruby's skin on mine, our voices, her laugh. Everything is growing mistier and less tangible, even the day she was here, consoling me. The only thing that I can still see clearly, that still replays over and over again in my head, is the expression on her face when she saw me with Elaine. I'll never forget that. And I'll never forget what it did to me—even through the haze of alcohol and drugs. At that moment, and every day since.

My original plan was to sleep through into the new year, but it's after one now and I'm wider awake than ever. On the spur of the moment, I decide to go down to the fitness room. Maybe an hour on the treadmill will not only tire out my body but also get my head to shut up.

I put on my shorts and T-shirt, pull on my running shoes, and grab my iPhone, which has been sitting, ignored, on my bedside table since this afternoon. My headphones are still plugged in and, as usual, I have to untangle them first. I'm about to put them on when I hear someone walking down the landing.

Presumably Lydia's back.

I open the door to wish her a happy new year—and freeze.

My sister is not alone there.

I rub my eyes because I think I'm dreaming. But no. After I've lowered my hand again, I can still see two people.

Ruby is standing on our landing.

There's a dark blue bundle jammed under her arm. It doesn't take me much thought to work out what it is. It's my jumper. The one I put on her after Cyril's party. The one I didn't mind missing from my wardrobe because I liked the idea that Ruby had it.

Ruby is saying something quietly to my sister, who nods. Lydia glances briefly at me, but looks away again at once, then vanishes into her room. Good to know that I've pissed my sister off so thoroughly that she can't even bring herself to wish me a happy new year.

"Can we talk?" Ruby asks.

I swallow hard. I haven't seen her, or heard her voice, for so long, and now she's standing only a few feet away. Being this close to her is making my heart beat like wild; I long to cross the gap between us and take her in my arms. But I just nod, turn, and walk back into my room. Ruby follows me hesitantly. I click the light on and sigh. It's definitely looked better in here. My checked pajama trousers that I just took off are lying in the middle of the floor, there are magazines everywhere, and the bed is unmade and probably stinks of greasy takeaways.

And to top it all off, Ruby's bag is standing in plain sight on my desk.

Ruby looks around, her expression indecisive. In the end, she sits on the smaller of the two sofas. My hoodie is in her lap.

Why the hell does my room suddenly feel so warm? I feel in urgent need of a glass of water.

"Do you want anything to drink?" I ask.

"No, thank you."

I pour myself some water but as I lift the glass, I notice that my hand is shaking. So I put it down on the desk and look at Ruby instead.

She says nothing.

After a minute or two, I make a desperate attempt to break the silence between us. "Have you had a good evening?"

Ruby contracts her eyebrows. "Yes," she says.

That's all.

I've never found it harder to know the right thing to say than I do in this second. I feel like I've forgotten how to put a coherent sentence together. After I've spent so long thinking about everything I want to say to Ruby, there's now a black hole in my head, getting bigger with every moment we spend sitting opposite each other in silence. All I can do is look at her. I'm overwhelmed by the longing to sit next to her. But I resist it and pull my desk chair over to the sofa so that I can sit opposite her and we can see each other.

"We were writing our resolutions earlier," she says eventually.

I wait for her to go on.

"And I realized that there is still so much that hasn't been resolved between us. I can't feel good about going into the new year like this."

My pulse starts racing. I definitely wasn't prepared for that. I clear my throat. "OK."

Ruby lowers her gaze to the jumper in her lap. She strokes the soft fabric absentmindedly. Then she takes it in her hand and lays it on the little round table between us.

She looks up and our eyes meet. I can make out all kinds of emotions in her face: Sorrow. Pain. And, last but not least, a spark of anger that grows bigger the longer her eyes rest on me.

"I'm just so disappointed in you, James," she whispers suddenly.

My chest clenches painfully. "I know," I whisper back.

She shakes her head. "No. You don't know what that felt like. You bloody ripped my heart out. And I *hate* you for that."

"I know," I repeat, my voice husky.

Ruby takes a deep breath. "But I love you too, and that's making the whole thing way harder."

"I . . ." It takes a few seconds before I realize what she just said. I stare speechlessly at her.

But Ruby's still talking, as though her words hadn't meant a thing. "I don't think it would ever have worked out between us. It was nice, even though we only had such a short time together, but now I have to—"

"You love me?" I whisper back.

Ruby jumps. Then she sits bolt upright. "That doesn't change anything. The way you treated me . . . You kissed another girl, the day after we slept together."

"I'm so sorry, Ruby," I say insistently, even though I know my words aren't enough.

"And it doesn't change my resolution to start the coming year without you," Ruby continues.

The pain her words cause me takes my breath right away. I know Ruby. Once she's set herself a goal, she pursues it and won't let anyone steer her off course. She's here to finish things with me.

"That'll never . . . I'd never do anything like that again," I gasp breathlessly.

"I very much hope so, for your next girlfriend's sake."

I sense panic rising within me. "There won't be another, for God's sake!"

She just shakes her head. "It would never have worked out, James. Let's be honest."

"Why would you say that?" My voice is shaking with despair. "Of course it would."

Ruby stands up and strokes her hands down her checked skirt a few times. "I have to go home; my parents will be waiting." She goes to the door, and the knowledge that I can't stop her is almost killing me. I stare at her, unable to move. The moment feels like a final goodbye, and I'm not ready for that. "I need a clean ending. Can you understand that?" she asks, looking back over her shoulder, her hand on the door handle.

I nod, though every part of my body is screaming the exact opposite. "Yes, I understand that."

Ruby has given me so many chances already. I know I have no right to another.

"I . . . Happy New Year, James." The pain that's paralyzing my body is reflected in Ruby's eyes.

"Ruby, please . . ." I force the words out.

But she opens the door and leaves.

Lydia

James and I have to go back to school on the first Monday of term after the Christmas holidays. Dad says that after nearly a month, it's time to get back to normal. But the situation at home is anything but normal. Without Mum, who used to keep building bridges between us, dinners with Dad are absolute torture. And things are still tense between James and me. We're hardly talking and avoid each other most of the time. When normally, he's the person I feel most comfortable with.

Now we're both staring silently out the window as Percy drives us to Maxton Hall. Having to go back there feels like a massive waste of time to me. After all, I already know I'm not going to get to uni, even if I'm still able to do my A levels. So what's the point?

Once Percy's pulled up outside the entrance, he rolls down the screen and turns toward us. "Is everything OK?"

I nod without a word and try to smile. I sometimes wonder if my smile still looks the same as before. Before all this happened.

"If you need anything," he says in his deep, calm voice, "you only have to give me a call. And if any journalists turn up, let the head know about them. He's well aware of the situation and will make sure they don't bother you."

His words sound almost like he'd learned them by heart.

I've long suspected that Percy is finding Mum dying harder than he's letting on. After all, they'd known each other for more than twenty years. He rarely makes jokes now, and sometimes, when he doesn't think anyone's looking, there's such a sad, forlorn expression on his face that my own heart aches for him.

"All right," I say, tapping two fingers to my forehead in salute.

At least that makes Percy give me a weary smile before he turns to James. "You take care of your sister, Mr. Beaufort."

James blinks and looks around. His face turns to stone the moment he realizes we're outside the school already. Without a word, he picks up his bag and opens the door. I glance apologetically at Percy before following James out. He's halfway across the parking lot before I catch up with him. Cyril, Alistair, Kesh, and Wren are waiting on the front steps.

"Beaufort!" Wren grins broadly, holding out his fist. "About time you put in an appearance around here."

James pulls the corners of his lips up a fraction and bumps his fist against Wren's.

"It's not the same without you," Kesh adds, taking James's face in both hands. He gives him a friendly slap on the cheek.

Meanwhile, Cyril comes to give me a hug. "Lydia," he murmurs into my hair. I gulp. He smells so familiar that I wish I could spend the whole school day standing like this with him. But that's not an option, so I cautiously pull away.

"Good morning," I say tiredly.

Cyril's ice-blue gaze roams inquiringly over my face. Then he puts an arm around my shoulders and we go up the stairs with the others and through the huge double doors into Maxton Hall.

Our friends have lined up around us in an odd formation, presumably to shield us from people's questions, but there's no need. Nobody will speak to us. James looks back at me over his shoulder and we both respond the same way. We straighten our backs and stride through the school the way we've always done.

Assembly drags on forever, same as ever, and eventually, my neck starts to ache from staring fixedly straight ahead. We're sitting in the back row, and not a minute goes past without someone turning round to us and then whispering to the person sitting next to them. I ignore them all. I can't breathe properly until Lexie declares the assembly over and we can file out of Boyd Hall.

"Did you hear?" Alistair asks as we go up the stairs in the main block. "George crashed his car the day after his eighteenth."

"George who?" I ask.

"Evans," Wren and Alistair answer at the same time. "You know, the football captain?"

"Oh. Is he OK?"

"Just a scratch on his forehead. More luck than brains, that guy."

"Oh, and Jessalyn got off with Henry at Cyril's party. Apparently, he fell asleep mid-shag," Wren says, determined to fill us in on all the gossip.

"Can't have been exactly amazing sex, then," James says drily.

Everyone looks at him in surprise. That was exactly his old tone—bored, with a touch of arrogance. Almost the old James.

"Well, to be honest," Cyril breaks the silence. "I nearly fell asleep once myself."

"Cyril." I pull a face. I might have ended up in bed with him more than once in the past, but I really don't want to think about that. "Too much information."

"I hope for your sake you were drunk," says James.

Cyril grins. "Not just drunk."

"Guys, we're at school. Can we keep the conversation a bit less X-rated?" I suggest.

Alistair turns toward me, eyebrows raised. He shakes his golden curls out of his face and walks backward for a couple of steps. "Lydia Beaufort, is that really you? You're worse than the rest of us put together."

"Hmm. Not worse than James, if you ask me," Kesh muses.

"Or me." Wren raises an eyebrow.

"You two come in joint second place." Alistair digs him in the ribs and Wren laughs out loud.

I shake my head with a grin. I love the boys for acting totally normal. It almost makes me feel like nothing's changed. And it's taking my mind off things, which is exactly what I need right now. My first lesson of term is about to start, and it's with Graham—the thought of how things will be between us is making me edgy. I haven't spoken to him since that horrible phone call just after Mum died.

I hoped that my longing for him would fade over time, but the opposite seems to be true. It hurts more with every day and my only consolation in the last few weeks has been not having to see Graham on top of everything else. But the grace period is over.

Before we say goodbye outside the classroom door, James gives me a hard stare. It's as difficult as ever to tell what he's thinking, but I can't help noticing a trace of worry in his eyes. We might not have spoken for days, but he knows how scared I am of being face-to-face with Graham again.

"I'll be OK," I croak.

James eyes me a moment longer, then nods. "Message me if you need anything," Cyril murmurs, giving me another hug. "See you at lunch."

I shut my eyes and allow myself to enjoy the sensation of being held, of not being alone, for a moment or two. He lets go of me and steps to one side.

And then I see Graham.

He's standing right behind the lads, who are blocking the corridor outside his classroom. His hair has a slight wave and it's a bit longer than in my memory. He's wearing a checked shirt under a cardigan, and he has a huge pile of papers in his hand. He looks between Cyril's and James's heads, and his golden-brown eyes, which always fascinated me, stare straight into mine.

A shudder runs through my body. The moment seems frozen in time, and I don't dare to move for fear of losing control. But suddenly, Graham tears his eyes away from me and looks at Cyril instead. The expression on his face is one I've never seen before. It's a mixture of relief and coldness, something I don't understand and can't make sense of.

"Come on," says James, who's been looking from me to Graham and back again. He nods down the hallway to where he and the others are heading for class. The boys wave, then walk away.

Now I'm alone in the corridor with Graham. He shifts the pile of papers in his arms, fiddles about as if to straighten them up, but they're already as tidy as can be. Our eyes meet again.

"Lydia . . ." he says hoarsely, sounding so sad that my throat constricts.

I shake my head. "Don't."

Then I turn away, walk into the classroom, and sit in my seat. I spend the whole ninety minutes staring at the wood grain in the desk in front of me, just so as not to have to face the front.

James

School is just dragging on and on today. If I weren't so worried about Lydia, I'd have skipped off by now. Lessons go at a snail's pace, and I couldn't care less what the teachers are saying. At break and lunch, people are practically queuing up to offer me their condolences, which I'm sure are kindly meant, but after a while, it starts pissing me off so much that I tell poor Roger Cree to shut the fuck up and leave me alone. After that, word gets round that it's safer not to get too close to me just yet.

The worst point of the day comes at the start, though, when I bump into Ruby before first period. We both freeze—her on one side of the corridor and me on the other—and look at each other.

I hate you for that. But I love you too, and that's making the whole thing way harder. I remember what she told me.

She's the first to look away. Without a word, she walks past and disappears into her classroom. The whole encounter lasts ten seconds max, but it feels like a lifetime.

From then on, all I can think of is Ruby and what she said on New Year's Eve.

She loves me.

She fucking *loves* me.

It feels like there's a gaping wound in my chest that just won't close up. I want to respect her decision, but seeing her and knowing that I've lost her is killing me.

After school, I can't get out of the building fast enough. Hands in pockets, I hurry outside, eyes fixed straight ahead.

Percy opens the car door for me and I mumble "thanks" as I get in.

Lydia is already there, looking exactly how I feel.

I let myself sink back, shut my eyes, and lean my head against the seat.

"Tiring, huh?" I hear Lydia say quietly.

I hate how cautious her voice is. Like she's afraid even to speak to me. I know that that's my own fault, but at the same time, I'm aware of how screwed up it is that my own sister no longer dares talk to me. I eye the minibar. I've gone a long time without a drink, but after that shit day, the need to numb my senses—no matter how—is taking hold.

I don't answer, just reach forward and open the little door. But before I can reach for the bottle, Lydia grabs my wrist.

"You're not getting off your face now just because you've had a crappy day," she says, keeping her voice deliberately calm.

She's right; I know that. But I ignore her and try, gently but firmly, to prize her hand away. No such luck. She's got her fingers dug into my arm. I jerk it away from her. Lydia slips forward, catapulting her bag onto the floor of the car.

"Idiot," she snarls, immediately starting to pick up her stuff, which is now all over the place.

I sigh and bend down to help. "Sorry. I didn't mean for that to happen."

Lydia presses her lips together as she gathers her belongings, her movements jittery. I pick up a couple of pens and hold them out to her. She takes them without looking at me. Then I pick up her planner, a few tampons, and a round white plastic tub that looks like it's got chewing gum in it. The lid has come loose and I'm about to close it properly when I catch sight of the label.

Prenatal Vitamin Supplements: Folic Acid, Omega-3 DHA, Calcium, and Vitamin D

Lemon, raspberry, and orange flavor

It also features a picture of a woman's silhouette as she holds her rounded bump.

It feels like Percy's just driven straight over a pothole, but we're still in the parking lot. Blood roars in my ears.

"What's this?" I croak, looking up from the tub to Lydia, then back again.

All the blood drains from my sister's cheeks and she stares at me, wide-eyed.

"What is this, Lydia?" I repeat, my voice firmer this time.

"I . . ." Lydia just shakes her head.

I read the label again and again. I understand all the words, but they don't make sense. I look back at Lydia and open my mouth to ask the same question again when . . .

"They're not mine," she blurts.

I breathe out fitfully. "Whose are they, then?"

Now she presses her bloodless lips together. She just shakes her head; the shock in her eyes is enormous. I really don't want to pressure her, but I need her to know that she can trust me.

"Whatever's happened—you know you can tell me anything, Lydia. I'm there for you," I say insistently.

Tears pool in her eyes. She claps her hands to her face and starts sobbing. At that moment, I know. I sense the truth without Lydia having to say a word. Deep inside me, I feel shock, panic, and fear rising up all at once, but I push them down again and breathe in deeply.

Then I come to sit closer to Lydia. "They're your vitamins, aren't they?" I murmur.

Her shoulders shake so hard that I can hardly make out her stammered "yes." And then I do the only thing that makes any sense to me in this situation. I take her in my arms and just hold her tight.

James

Lydia is sitting on her bed fidgeting about with the pillow in her lap. I'm trying for the hundredth time to sneak an unobtrusive look at her belly. After half an hour walking up and down in my bedroom, trying to get my pulse under control, I'm now slumped on one of the sofas in hers.

I'm trying to find the right words, but my thoughts are whirling, so messed up that I can't even get one sentence out.

How?

How the hell are we meant to look after a baby?

How can we keep it a secret from Dad?

How can you take a baby with you to Oxford?

"I didn't want you to find out this way."

I look up. There's no mistaking how tense Lydia is. Her cheeks are flushed; her shoulders are stiff as a board.

"I . . . I don't know what to say."

I feel so utterly stupid. At the same time, I'm realizing how egoistic I've been in the last few weeks. I've spent the whole time bemoaning my own fate, my loss, my guilty conscience, my broken

heart, when the whole time, my sister knew that she was pregnant and thought she couldn't tell me. Of course there are things
we keep from each other, but not something like this. Not a thing
this huge and life-changing.

"You don't have to say anything," Lydia whispers.

I shake my head. "I'm sor—"

"No," she interrupts. "I don't want sympathy, James. Not
from you."

I dig my fingers into the armrest to stop myself from jumping
up again and marching around the room. The fabric crunches
under my unyielding grip.

The chasm that opened between Lydia and me when I hurled
those unforgivable words at her feels unbridgeable. I'm not sure
what I can ask her and what I can't. Plus, I know absolutely nothing about pregnancy.

I shut my eyes and rub my hands over my face. My limbs feel
tired, like I've aged from eighteen to eighty in a few hours.

In the end I clear my throat. "How did you find out?"

Lydia looks up in surprise. She hesitates for a moment, then
starts to tell me. "My . . . uh . . . cycle is never very regular anyway, so at first, I didn't think anything of it when my period was
late. But after a while, I got suspicious because I was feeling really
weird too. In general." She shrugs. "So I bought a test. When we
were in London. I did it in a restaurant loo and nearly fainted
when it was positive."

I look at her, shaking my head. "When was that?"

"In November."

I gulp hard. Two months ago. Lydia's been keeping this secret
for two months, probably shit-scared, and feeling totally alone.
The news has really knocked me for six, so how must she have

been feeling all these weeks? On top of everything else that's happened.

Suddenly, the thing I want most in the world is to overcome the distance between us. "I can't imagine what that must have been like for you."

"I . . . I've never felt so alone. Not even after the business with Gregg. I never thought that being with Graham could ever be worse than that."

"Does he know?" I ask cautiously.

"No."

Lydia is clearly trying not to break down, but I can see how hopeless she feels. She must have spent the last two months constantly pulling herself together, constantly focused on keeping her secret and never showing anyone her real feelings. I hate myself for having left her in the lurch like this. All I've thought about has been myself.

That's over now. I have no idea what lies ahead of Lydia in the next few months. But at this second, I'm one hundred percent clear that she's not going through them alone.

I take a deep breath and stand up.

As I sit next to her on the bed, I push everything aside—the grief, the pain, the rage I've been feeling. Cautiously, I reach for her hand.

"You're not alone," I assure her.

Lydia swallows hard. "You're just saying that. But the next time you lose your temper, all you're going to do is yell unkind words at me again." Tears run down her cheeks and her body shakes as she suppresses a sob with all her strength. Seeing her like this is killing me.

"I really mean it, Lydia. I'll be there for you." I take a deep breath. "The person I was after Dad told us what had happened—that's not me. I don't *want* to be that guy. It was just . . . It was too much for me. I wasn't strong enough, and I'm sorry."

"You're squishing my hand," Lydia murmurs.

For a moment, I'm confused, but as I follow Lydia's gaze, I catch on and let go. "I'm sorry for that too." I smile apologetically at her.

"Oh, James." Suddenly Lydia leans into me and rests her head on my shoulder. I breathe out. "What you said really hurt me."

I gently stroke the back of her head.

We used to sit like this often. When we were five, Lydia would climb into my bed if there was a thunderstorm, and when we were ten it would be because Dad had screamed at us over grades that weren't good enough. Even at fifteen, after the Gregg thing, she knocked on my door some nights and then lay down in my bed next to me without a word. I always used to stroke her hair and tell her that everything was going to be fine, even if I was never convinced of that myself.

I wonder if she's remembering those times too, or if that's a part of our past that she's repressed. Repression is one thing we Beauforts are pretty good at.

"What I said wasn't true. You're the most important person in my life, Lydia."

Beside me, Lydia freezes, and with every second that she doesn't react, I feel more and more exposed. I'm desperately searching for something I could add to lighten the mood but can't think of a thing. So instead, I decide to ask one of the questions that have been buzzing around inside my head for more than an hour.

"Have you been to the doctor? I have no idea how it all works.

Is everything OK? What are those vitamins for—do they mean you're short of something, or what?"

I notice the tension gradually easing from Lydia's body. She takes a deep breath and then turns her head to look at me from the side. I return her gaze. In the moment that a slight smile starts to spread over her lips, I know that we've made it. The gulf between us has been bridged.

"I got the vitamins straight after the first checkup—nearly everyone takes them to start off with. And last time, everything was totally fine." She pauses. "Except, there was one tiny surprise."

I raise an eyebrow. "Another one?"

"It's twins."

I stare at Lydia in disbelief. "You're kidding me."

She shakes her head and pulls out her phone. She opens the gallery and shows me a photo where you can see the pale outline of a tiny body against a dark background. Then she pulls up the next picture. It actually looks exactly the same—except that you can clearly see a second outline next to the first.

Something skips in my stomach and I suddenly feel really weird. At the same time, I laugh with disbelief. "That's too crazy to be true."

Lydia grins. "I couldn't help laughing at first either, because I couldn't believe it. Well, saying that . . . I actually laughed and cried at the same time. Ruby must have thought I was having a nervous breakdown."

At the sound of Ruby's name, I automatically straighten up a little. "Ruby was with you at the appointment?"

Lydia avoids my eyes, studying the phone in her hand intently. "Yes. She's known for a little while."

I rub my hand over my chin. My throat suddenly feels dry.

"I asked her not to tell anybody. Please don't be pissed off with her."

I can only shake my head. Then I sink back and cross my arms over my face.

Ruby knew.

Ruby was there for my sister. After everything I did to her, she didn't leave Lydia in the lurch. Unlike me.

I can't breathe.

"James?" whispers Lydia.

My arms are shaking, but I can't lower them. I'm so ashamed. Of everything. All the mistakes I've made as a boyfriend and a brother fall on me like a ton of bricks, until I can hardly bear it.

My sister pulls my arms away and looks at me in concern. Understanding spreads over her face. After a while, she drops down beside me and together, we stare up at the chandelier in the middle of her room.

"Lydia," I whisper into the silence. "I've fucked up."

Lydia

I've never seen my brother like this before.

I knew that the break with Ruby had affected him, but I had no idea how badly he was hurting.

Now that he's dropped the mask, I can see the shame in his eyes, as well as the deep sorrow and pain that it's caused him. It's the first time he's openly showed me how he's doing inside.

I feel a desperate longing to do something for him and Ruby.

Because it's clear that they both have feelings for each other and that they're both miserable.

"Why didn't you do anything to show her how sorry you are?" I ask cautiously, after a while.

James turns his head to me. "I tried to apologize to her," he says, his voice shaky. "She said she couldn't."

For a moment, neither of us speaks.

"I can understand that," I begin eventually, which makes James flinch, barely perceptibly. "But then again . . . I don't know. I just so wish you two would get it together."

"Ruby doesn't want that, and I have to respect her wishes." He sounds so resigned as he says those words that I suddenly feel an urge to shake him.

"Since when have you been the type to give up, just like that?"

James snorts.

"What?"

"I didn't give up, *just like that*. I'm thinking about her all the time, and I'm pretty damn sure I'll never have feelings for anyone else. But if she doesn't want me, then . . ."

I grab one of the sketchbooks off my bedside table and whack James over the head with it.

He sits up with a jolt. "Ow, what the . . . ?"

I sit up too, ignoring the black dots dancing before my eyes. "You have to *show* her, James! Show her how important she is to you and how much you regret it."

"You didn't see the way she looked at me on New Year's Eve. Or hear what she said . . ." He shakes his head. "She's determined to begin this year without me—I can't go bothering her with what I feel for her. In her opinion, we have nothing in common and it would never have worked out."

"I'm not telling you to go and shower her with declarations of love. But until she knows how sorry you are for what you did, she won't be able to forgive you."

I see the cogs starting to turn in his mind and add another thought. "You have to show her. Not just with words. With actions. If she says you've got nothing in common, convince her that that isn't true."

He gulps and breathes out heavily. He's fighting a battle with himself; I can see that.

I remember the drive back from Oxford together. The morning before everything changed. James looked so happy. And he was exuding an inner peace that I'd never seen in him before. Like it was the first time he was at one with himself. Like the invisible burden he always carries had disappeared. I want him to get back to that.

Even so, there's one extra thing he needs to know. "James," I say, waiting patiently for him to look at me. "If you kiss anyone else who isn't Ruby ever again, I will personally cut out your tongue."

James blinks in surprise. Then he slowly shakes his head. "I don't know how I never clocked that you're spending a lot of time with Ruby these days."

I'm tempted to laugh but I restrain myself. "I meant what I said. I really would love it if you two got it together again."

James exhales audibly. "I want that too. More than anything."

"Then bloody well fight for her."

He doesn't say a word for some time, just stares at the ceiling with a strangely engrossed expression. I wish I could read his mind and see what he's thinking right now.

"I'm going to," he says quietly, in the end.

I put a hand on his shoulder and give it a quick squeeze. "Good."

One corner of his mouth twitches up slightly. It's such a minimal movement that probably no one else would even have noticed it.

"But first, I need a plan."

12

Ruby

"D'you think Beaufort's been crying?" is the first thing I hear upon walking into the library study center on Wednesday afternoon. The events committee meeting isn't for another half hour, so I'd been planning to use the time to borrow a book that's been on my Oxford reading list for months.

But I regret the decision the minute I hear the loud giggling.

"He's welcome to cry his eyes out on my shoulder any time he likes."

I stand on tiptoes to peek through the books on the bookshelf. I can see two girls sitting side by side at a desk, their heads together over a book. They're plainly not working though. They aren't even bothering to keep quiet.

"Apparently he's not averse to offers of consolation." The first girl gives a suggestive grin.

"He must be even richer after his mum died, and that makes him even hotter." The other sighs. "Maybe I'll give it a go."

Fury bubbles up inside me. One, we're in the library; and two, they have no right to speak that disrespectfully about James; but on top of that, I can't go anywhere in this school without hearing his name, and that's doing my head in.

On my way here, I passed three groups of kids who were chatting about him, and it's been like that all week.

It's not like there isn't any other gossip they could be getting their teeth into—Alistair was caught in the boys' loos, kissing some bloke who doesn't even go to this school. And Jessalyn is now seeing the boy who—allegedly—fell asleep in the middle of doing the deed their first time. I still don't know whether to believe that part, especially considering the beaming smile plastered across her face the whole time these days. There's also a rumor that after their mum's death, Lydia fell into Cyril's arms and they're now more than just good friends. I really doubt that one, though, and she has more important stuff on her mind anyway. On the other hand, after I heard the story, I glanced over at Cyril in maths, and he was looking so smug that for a brief moment, I wasn't sure *what* to believe.

But despite all that, everyone always wants to talk about James. Always and everywhere.

Did you see those photos of James Beaufort?

I felt so sorry for him.

Is he really going out with that Ruby?

It makes my throat dry out and my heart start thumping every single time. How am I ever meant to forget him when he's the number one topic of conversation and I can't even get away from that in the library?

Abruptly, I pull the book off the shelf and walk around into the study area. The girls jump as they realize that they're not

alone. As I march toward them, I wonder whether to say anything, but I don't have the energy. I glare scornfully at them and
walk past, in the direction of our group room.

As I get there, I shoot through the door as fast as I can, then
lean my back against it. I shut my eyes, rest my head against the
door, and try just to take a few deep breaths for a moment.

"Hey."

My eyes fly open.

James is sitting on the other side of the room. On the same
chair he always sat on last term, when Mr. Lexington made him
join the events committee as a punishment.

He looks different. There are dark rings under his eyes and
there's a hint of a shadow on his jaw to show that he hasn't shaved.
His hair is even messier than normal, probably because it's grown.

I wonder if I look different to him too.

Seconds pass and neither of us moves. I don't know how to act
in his presence. I've been blanking him in corridors between lessons, but now we're the only people in this room.

"What are you doing here?"

My voice is hoarse. But the last thing I want to do is give him
the idea that he still has an effect on me. No, he needs to think I'm
totally unfazed by being around him.

"Reading." He holds up a book—wait, it's a manga. I read the
title with a frown, even though I've already recognized the picture
on the cover.

James is reading *Death Note*. Volume three.

I once told him that's my favorite.

I look at him in confusion.

"It's our team meeting in a minute, so if you'd kindly find
somewhere else to read . . ." I push myself away from the door and

walk over to my place, as if my pulse isn't thumping in my ears right now.

I slowly unpack my things and spread them out on the table, then I go to the whiteboard and write the date in the top right-hand corner. I wish there were any other jobs to do, but Lin has both the laptop and our notes in her bag. So I sit down and pretend to be engrossed in reading my bullet journal.

Out of the corner of my eye, I see James put the manga down on the table in front of him. His movements are slow. It almost feels like he doesn't want to startle me. I feel his eyes on me and find myself holding my breath.

"I'd like to rejoin the events committee this term."

I freeze. Not looking up from my planner, I say: "What?"

"If you and Lin don't mind, I'll run it past Lexie."

I look up in disbelief. "You can't be serious."

James stares calmly back at me. Now I know what seems so different about him. He still looks tired, but that look of despair I saw in his eyes at New Year's is gone. It's been replaced by a calm that, in that moment, really gets to me. I can be strong when he's messed up. It's when he's quiet that I get edgy. Is that what people mean when they say people complement each other? Or do we just knock each other off-balance?

"I enjoyed it here, even if I didn't expect to at first. I want to be part of the team again."

I can't stop staring at him. "I don't believe you."

"You said yourself that I'm a good organizer and that the team wouldn't be the same without me. And the training schedule for this term means that lacrosse and the events team only clash once a week. The coach is OK with it."

I pick up my backpack and start digging around in it, just so that I don't have to keep looking at James. I have no idea what this means.

I'm not an idiot—James isn't here because he's rediscovered his love for Maxton Hall events. It definitely has to do with me. But what he said is true. Thinking back to last term and the effort he put into the Halloween party, I have to admit that James's presence was anything but a drawback for the team. His ideas and hard work helped make the party a total success.

If I chuck him out now, I'll have that on my conscience for the rest of the year, especially when we could do with an extra pair of hands, or someone else's opinion. My duty as team leader is clear—plus, I'd have to explain everything to Lexie if I turn James away.

"So long as everyone else agrees," I say in the end.

"OK."

I gulp hard. Even if James does want to get involved on the team again, that doesn't take away from what I said at New Year's. Keeping school and my private life apart always used to be my specialty. And even if I let a few boundaries get blurred last term, that's not going to happen again.

"I'll be voting against," I continue, giving him a hard stare.

He leans his arms on the table and meets my eyes just as firmly. "I know."

━━━━

It takes less than five minutes for the others to vote to readmit James as a new/old member. Meanwhile, I sit at the front, my cheeks burning, and try not to let on how much the idea of spending three afternoons a week in this room with him from now on is getting to me.

Lin distributes handouts and gets straight down to business.

"Can someone bring Beaufort up-to-date with our plans for the charity gala?" she asks.

I let my eyes wander over everyone in turn. These meetings have been routine for me, but I guess that's a thing of the past. James just being here is a total distraction, setting off an avalanche of memories that makes my entire body tremble. I remember the feeling of his hands on my legs, my stomach, and my breasts. The way he whispered my name. His mouth, and what it felt like on my lips and my skin.

I feel my face flush even redder and try desperately to suppress the thoughts. This isn't the time or the place. It's time to keep my personal life strictly out of school again.

"The charity gala is happening in February," Jessalyn says in answer to Lin's question. "The PTA has decided to raise money for the Pemwick Family Center. They want to expand their mental health work and they're really short of cash for that."

"It's going to be as fancy as every year," Kieran adds. "Black-tie, and we've got a huge budget to play with. Lexie is expecting us to butter everyone up so they'll donate loads of money." I jot down *fancy party* and *huge budget*, which is utterly pointless because I'm perfectly well aware of both facts, but it gives me an excuse to look down and away from James's eyes.

"It's going to be in Boyd Hall. There's a drinks reception with canapés first, then a banquet by a chef from a five-star hotel. He's had firsthand experience with the Family Center and their work, so he's doing it for free. So we've got more to spend on décor and entertainment," Lin explains. "We've hired a pianist from London for background music, and Camille's family recommended a troupe of acrobats for the grand finale."

"Some of them used to be in Cirque du Soleil." Camille sounds very pleased with herself. I'm about to write *Cirque du Soleil* when I clock how silly I'm being. I can't spend an hour and a half sitting around staring at my notebook just because James is here. I put my pen down again and look at Camille as she takes over. "They're going for a mystic vibe."

Next to me, Lin sighs. "But we still have the same old problem of finding sponsors who want to come to the gala and make a donation. We can't just invite parents. And we need people to make speeches. It would be ideal if the Family Center had helped them in the past, because that would make it sound really authentic."

"Last week, we said we'd keep asking around," I say, finally able to speak. "Did anyone get anywhere?"

I just have to look at the discouraged faces of my team to know what they're going to say.

"No one answers my emails, and if I phone, they either say maybe next year, or just come straight out and tell me to leave them alone," says Kieran. "Nobody wants to talk about their past problems. Least of all at Maxton Hall."

The others nod.

"Maybe we need to think outside the box a bit," suggests Jessalyn. "Maybe we don't need people to have used *this* Family Center, just something similar."

"Good idea," I say. "We could also ask the local universities if anyone in their relevant departments would be prepared to speak." My smile is more confident than I feel. "We'll get there. We've got a while yet."

Murmurs of agreement.

"Now that you're back on the team, it would be great if you could take charge of décor, and arrange things with the company and Mr. Jones," Lin suddenly says to James. "He can always use a hand getting the hall ready."

I pluck up the courage to glance at James.

He blinks in mild confusion, but just says, "Sure."

I'm trying really hard not to grin at that. Cleaning the hall with the caretaker is a nightmare job—no one wants to get stuck with that, so it makes me laugh that Lin has just delegated it to James. And it's further proof of what a great person she is.

The rest of the meeting goes to plan, but I'm glad when the ninety minutes are up. Lin and I divide up the jobs we have to do, while everyone else says their goodbyes and leaves the room—except for James and Camille, who seem to be packing their stuff extra slowly. I try to pay them no attention but without much success. I hear every word of condolence that Camille is murmuring. My stomach clenches, but I remind myself that I'm not going to feel hurt *by* James anymore, and certainly not *for* James. I don't intend to feel *anything* when it comes to James Beaufort from now on.

"See you later," I mumble to Lin.

She nods and shoos me away. I pick up my backpack and head to the door, staring straight ahead. At the very moment I reach for the handle, a hand closes around it so that mine ends up on top. I look up into James's face. We're only inches apart. I take in his familiar smell, spicy and a bit like honey, and the warmth of him.

"Ruby," he whispers.

I pull my hand away like I've burned it. Then I look at him with the expectation of him either moving his own hand or opening the door. He hesitates a moment, then turns the handle.

I exhale. "Bye, Lin," I say, hurrying out of the room.

I walk to the bus stop faster than ever as his voice echoes around my head and through my whole body.

Lydia

"I don't believe it." James sighs with frustration. He pushes his laptop away and turns on his chair to face me. "Another two have turned me down."

I eye my brother from my spot on the sofa. When he first told me about his plan to rejoin the events committee, I was surprised. But the longer I think about it, the more I like his decision.

Ruby loves working on that team. Showing her that he doesn't just get her passion, he shares it, is a good first step. Besides, last term, James discovered how much he enjoyed organizing those parties—even though he'd never admit it.

"You have to be persistent. Appeal to their consciences, not their wallets. Then they'll turn up at the gala," I say, sipping from the mug of fruit tea I've wrapped my cold fingers around. I think the housekeeper knows I'm pregnant. She brought up the teapot unasked and gave me a knowing look as she whispered that she was sure it would do me good.

James nods absentmindedly and pulls his laptop a bit closer again. At the same moment, there's a quiet ping as a new email pops in. James squints as he reads it, and I reach for a biscuit. A few crumbs drop onto the sofa as I nibble on it, but luckily, he's too busy typing a reply to notice—he hates crumbs.

"Have you spoken to Ruby?" I ask after a while.

I hear the sound of an email being sent, then James turns back to me. "No." He rubs his face with his hand. "At the moment, she can't even bring herself to look at me."

"You can't force her, obviously. But sooner or later, you two will have to have a conversation," I say gently. "The longer you leave it, the bigger the gap between you will grow. Believe me."

My brother gives me a long look. Clearly, he can put two and two together. "You still haven't spoken to Sutton, then?"

I shrug my shoulders. "What is there to talk about? We both know that it's better this way."

"Yeah, but he doesn't know you're pregnant. That changes everything."

"He doesn't want anything more to do with me." I shove the rest of the biscuit into my mouth and chew. "He's told me that more than once. Besides, for one thing I have my pride . . ."

"And for another thing . . . ?"

I look back at James. "Besides, I'm scared to tell him. I don't want to know how he'll react. I have to get my own head around it first, and then I'll have space to work out what to do if he doesn't respond the way I'd hoped."

"Lydia . . ." James's phone rings. He doesn't go to answer it, just keeps looking intently at me.

"Pick up!" I insist. "I bet that's a potential sponsor."

He hesitates a moment. Then he picks up his phone and glances at the screen. He takes the call. "Owen," he says loudly. "Thanks for getting back to me."

I pretend to vomit. Owen Murray is the CEO of a telecoms company and one of Dad's best friends. Neither James nor I can stand him, and I'm pretty sure the feeling's mutual.

"Not too bad in the circumstances," says James. Suddenly, his voice is firm and businesslike. "No, I'm not calling on Beaufort's business but on behalf of Maxton Hall. We're holding a charity gala for the Pemwick Family Center in early February and we're looking for sponsors."

I can hear a quiet murmur on the other end.

"Of course. I'll send you the details. That would be amazing, Owen, thank you."

James ends the call and types something into his phone.

"If you don't tell Sutton, you'll never know *how* he'll react."

"So you think I should tell him?"

He nods. "Yes. And I think he has a right to know."

I stare into my cup. I peer at the rest of the bright fruit tea and try to make out a pattern in the sludge on the bottom.

Don't call me. We agreed.

Even if he decides to be there for me and the twins from now on—what does that even mean? That he feels guilty, nothing more. But there's nothing I want more in the world than to be with Graham because *he* wants it too. By choice and not because the pregnancy has forced his hand.

James's phone rings again. He holds up a finger to tell me that our conversation isn't over, then he takes the call.

I finish my tea and put the empty mug down on the table. Then I pull out my own phone and tap on my messages. I still have Graham's number saved. I just couldn't bring myself to delete it. Just having it there and knowing that I could text him if I wanted to is enough.

I scroll to the top of our chat. It's not just everyday texts and photos; we shared our deepest anxieties and worries. Any normal person would have deleted those messages, rather than keeping them and constantly flicking through them like an old photo album.

Apparently, I'm not a normal person.

This is all I have left of him. And I'm just not ready to let go of him forever. To be honest, I don't know if I ever will be. I miss him so much. I miss our phone calls, him laughing at bad action comedies, our fingers intertwined beneath a café table. Knowing that I can't get that back is driving me almost out of my mind.

"That sounds great," James says. His voice sounds so enthusiastic that I raise an eyebrow at him. "Yes, of course. No, thank *you*, Alice. Speak to you later." James sighs with relief and stretches both arms over his head.

"Alice? Alice Campbell?" I ask.

He turns to me. "She owes me a favor."

"I'd rather not know why."

He smiles with embarrassment. "Ruby really admires Alice."

Hardly surprising. Alice Campbell set up her own cultural foundation while she was still at Oxford.

"You're really pulling your finger out," I remark, instantly regretting it as James's face grows serious.

"Don't change the subject," he says, but I shake my head.

"I can't tell him. How am I meant to sit through his history lessons after that?"

"You could switch teachers."

"That would look really weird."

James shrugs his shoulders. "There are all kinds of reasons to switch. I don't think it would be that weird. If you came into my class, we could say it'll help us revise together."

"I don't know," I mumble.

"Well, whatever you do," James says, "I'll help you." He gives me another long, serious look, then turns back to his laptop.

I feel a slight tingle in my stomach and put my hand on it to tell if it's one of the babies. I can feel them moving a tiny bit now—almost like having butterflies.

Now that James knows, I'm feeling a lot better about things, but it still doesn't change the fact that I'm having two children, I'm going to be a single mum, and I will probably have to leave school without A levels. Although . . . maybe I can get them done before everything comes out.

I force myself to take three deep, calm breaths. I can't get caught up in thinking about the future when it's all up in the air anyway. I have to take each day as it comes. Because if I spend my whole time worrying, that won't do anyone any good—least of all the little beans inside me that have to be my priority from now on.

"Fuck," James exclaims suddenly. He's linked his arms behind his head and is staring wide-eyed at his monitor.

"What's wrong?"

James is rigid. Anxiously, I get up and walk over to his desk. I stand behind his chair and hold on to the leather back. Then I lean down a little.

The first words I see are *University of Oxford*.

Glancing down a little further, I see *Dear James . . . and many congratulations . . .*

"You got in!" I blurt out.

James still isn't responding, so I turn his chair round to face me. His face is a picture of sheer shock.

"James, you got in. That's amazing!" I grab him by the shoulders and pull him up to give him a hug. He stumbles and it takes him a moment to hug me back.

"Fuck," he repeats.

I don't know whether he's pleased or freaking out. As I hold him, I wonder whether I've got an email too. The old Lydia would be running to her phone now, like a woman obsessed, to see if she'd been accepted too. The new Lydia, on the other hand, doesn't want to know if she's just been handed a future that she can't go through with either way.

I squeeze James a little tighter, happy that things are going to plan for at least one of us.

James

"I don't need to tell you that we have been through a difficult period lately. But from here on, we can look forward, not back. Because that's what Cordelia would have wanted."

I suppress the urge to roll my eyes. My father has no idea what Mum would have wanted. Certainly not this performance that he's putting on right now.

It's his first official speech as CEO to the Beaufort board and heads of departments, and he's got them all eating out of his hand. There are twelve men and women in total, hanging on to his every word with hopeful faces, while I'm sitting here on one side of the long conference table, wondering how I can sneak out my phone without attracting attention.

"If we all pull together, we can help each other out of the

depths of our emotions and put Beaufort's on the front foot once more. There will be a few changes to face in the months ahead, and I am counting on you all for support. And at this point, I would like to offer you my thanks in advance. Because you are our most crucial asset, it is more than ever important to me that, in the months ahead, I will be able to draw on your expertise."

I slip my hand into my trouser pocket and pull out my phone. Over the last couple of hours, the lads have been bombarding me with messages, trying to get me to come out for a drink this evening. It's my first day on the Beaufort board and, in their world, that's something worth celebrating.

But I'm not in the mood to party. I know that I should make the most of my friends while they're all here because in the future we won't have so many opportunities. And they're already pissed at me for only training twice a week now.

All the same, there's only one person I want to see tonight.

And that person has been ghosting me for weeks because I pushed her away.

OK, so I see Ruby at school all the time, but I miss her.

I want her to be able to look at me again without the pain making her flinch.

I want to be able to talk to her, whenever and wherever.

I want to know if she got an offer from Oxford.

"Nothing about the corporate culture of Beaufort's will change after the death of my wife," my father plows on. "She is the foundation that our success is built on. When Cordelia and I first met, she told me what it meant to join this company, and it is my intention to honor her memory."

Applause rings out. I clap my hands twice, then sneak a

glance at the message that's just come in from Cyril. **We're at Wren's. When tf are you coming?** He adds a photo of them all sticking up their middle fingers.

Looks like I don't have a choice. I've got to join them after this meeting. I've ditched them too often lately, and it won't hurt to take my mind off things. Off this situation. And, mainly, off Ruby. Whatever I do, she's always in my head. She's the only person who'd get how I hate sitting here and listening to Dad talk about how he'll manage Mum's life's work. I told Ruby everything that night in Oxford. Those are thoughts I won't even let myself think, and it was the first time I'd ever said them out loud.

Ruby understood. She didn't talk about my sense of duty or what my name means. She listened to me and encouraged me. Encouraged me to think about a future of my own.

The longer I sit here, the more I long to see Ruby. And the more often I tell myself that it's impossible, the stronger that yearning gets.

I have to see her.

I just have to.

"I am not just speaking for myself here. My son, James, who, as of now, will be learning the ropes for his future position at Beaufort's and, incidentally, received an offer from Oxford this week, also shares my ambitions."

I look up at the sound of my name and the subsequent applause. There are some friendly nods, but other board members are very well aware that I've got my phone in my hand under the table and are pulling disapproving faces. I stare coolly back at them, not putting my phone away.

"Would you like to say a few words, James?" asks my father.

I look at him, trying not to reveal my surprise. He didn't mention anything before the meeting about me making a speech. His expression is unwavering and as cold as ice. If I don't speak up now, there'll be hell to pay.

Fucking arsehole. He knew perfectly well that I wouldn't have come if he'd told me in advance that he was planning to parade me like a racehorse. So he just threw me under the bus.

I stand up slowly, slipping my phone back into my pocket. I squint at my untouched glass of water and regret not having drunk anything earlier. As I look around the room, my throat is tight. I've known some of these people since I was a kid, but there are others I only met at Mum's funeral.

I clear my throat. It feels like my mind and body are totally separate as words that mean nothing at all emerge from my lips.

"If my mother were here today, she would be proud to see the drive and determination that you are putting into our company."

I haven't a fucking clue if Mum would have thought that. I didn't ever really know her.

Something in my chest clenches. For a moment, I consider running out, without another word, but I can't. The only way out of here is to get through the next hour. Whatever it takes.

"I am looking forward to a future where I can follow in Mum's footsteps, doing what she loved and devoted her life to. I can never fill her shoes, but I can at least do my best."

My gaze meets my father's. I wonder if he can see the lie in my eyes, and if he clocks that I'm just putting on a show here. Because that's all it is. A show where everything is rehearsed and nothing is real.

There doesn't seem to be enough room in my chest for oxygen—it suddenly feels so tight that it's hard to breathe. Again, I think about Ruby. Ruby telling me that I can do what I want.

Ruby, who made me believe in a life where I have options and can choose my own path.

"I can say with true conviction that with all of you as colleagues, the future will surely be crowned with success."

I nod to everyone around the table and sit down. Some of the disapproving glares have softened during my speech, and they all clap again.

I dare to glance at Dad and a shudder runs through me. He gives me a nod, clearly satisfied with my words. I've never felt more like a puppet.

Ruby

I read the email once.

And again.

And then a third time.

I read it again and again until the letters start to blur together and I have to blink.

"Mum," I say.

Mum makes an inquiring sound. She's sitting next to me at the kitchen table, flicking absentmindedly through a homeware catalog.

"Mum," I repeat, more urgently this time, pushing my laptop toward her, the email open.

Now she looks up. "What?"

I hold my breath, pointing fiercely toward the computer. Mum's gaze follows my finger. Her eyes flit over the screen. She pauses and looks at me, then back to the screen. The next moment, she claps her hands to her mouth. "No way," she breathes quietly.

I nod. "Yes way."

"No!"

"Yes!"

Mum jumps up and flings her arms around me. "I'm so proud of you!"

I hug her back and shut my eyes. I try to do what I always did when I was little—I concentrate really hard so that I'll always remember this moment. I drink in Mum's scent, the sound made by the oven, the aroma of baking scones, and the immeasurable joy that floods through me as I realize that my most heartfelt dream has come within touching distance.

"I'm so happy," I mumble into her shoulder.

Mum strokes my back. "You deserve it, Ruby."

"I need to start applying for bursaries and a student loan," I say, not letting go of her.

Her embrace is firmer than ever. "There's plenty of time for all that. You don't have to think about it all at once. Now—"

She's interrupted by the doorbell.

"Will you get that?" she asks, pulling away. "Ember must have forgotten her key. Then you can tell her your good news right away."

I nod and take the corner into the hall so fast that the rug skids over the wooden floor and I hit my shoulder on the coat-rack. But even that can't stop me from flinging open the door, a grin on my face . . .

. . . that immediately freezes to ice.

James is on the doorstep. He's in the middle of running a hand through his hair, and—just like me—he stops dead in mid-movement. His cheeks are slightly flushed, and his breath is forming little clouds in the icy winter air. It looks like he's on his way to an important meeting, or one's just finished.

I want to slam the door in his face.

And I want to hug him.

Maybe it's just as well that I'm incapable of doing anything. I just stare at him, feeling my heartbeat quicken at the sight of him.

"I . . ." he begins, but his voice dies away.

I remember the day he turned up under the pretense of bringing me the dress for the Halloween party. Then I could see him fighting an internal battle with himself, and it's the same now—his innermost feelings want to be set free, but he can somehow never quite let that happen.

"I can't go on like this, Ruby," he suddenly bursts out. He shakes his head and looks up at me. "I can't go on like this."

He sounds tired and broken. Sad and shattered. Like something's happened from which there's no going back.

It's clear that he can't be on his own right now. But at the same time, I'm annoyed that he's here. I'm the last person he should come to if he's got problems. Why does he have to wreck this moment for me? I've just got an offer from Oxford, for God's sake. I should be dancing around the house, not letting his pain get me down like this. The thing between us is over—*he* ended it. And we shouldn't be taking two steps back, desperately clinging on to something that no longer exists.

"You can't go on like what?"

"I've just been at a Beaufort's board meeting. Lydia's pregnant. And I got into Oxford. I . . . I'm fucked up right now."

James's chest is rising and falling frantically, like he's been running a marathon. And it probably feels that way to him. I know how much he hates the pressure his dad puts on him, and just at the moment, it looks like he's about to buckle beneath it.

I take a deep breath. "I get how bad that must be for you.

But . . . I'm not the person you should turn to when you're down," I reply as gently as possible.

He hurries up the steps to the front door, until he's standing right in front of me. His eyes are dark; his expression is desperate. I've never seen him like this.

"I can't keep away from you any longer. You're the only person who truly understands me. I need you. And I'm going to fight for us, because I'm yours. I'll always be yours, Ruby."

I grip on to the doorframe and stare at him in total disbelief. My body is flooded with hope, pain, and rage all at once, a chaotic blend that sets my heart racing and my thoughts whirling wildly.

I can't believe he just said that.

I can't believe he's trying again, having another go at knocking my life off course.

Suddenly, I'm furious. How dare he rejoin the events committee? How dare he wreck this moment for me?

"No," I say with an effort, shaking my head. "No."

"Please, Ruby, I—"

"Do you know what *I* need, James?" I interrupt him. "I need peace. I need time for myself, to get over you. I really wish for you to be happy one day, and that you won't let your dad run your life for you. But I can't help you with that."

He shakes his head. "I feel better when you're with me. Then I am just . . . happy."

"It's not my fucking job to make you happy!" I scream.

James flinches and takes a step back. He slips off the top step, and for a moment it looks like he's going to lose his balance, but he catches himself at the last second. He stares at me and the unspeakable shock in his eyes takes my breath away.

"James," I croak.

He shakes his head. "No, you're right. I . . . I shouldn't have come here."

Without another word, he turns away and walks down the steps. He hastily crosses our front garden until he reaches the low wooden gate. He opens it, steps through, and then looks back at me again. His eyes are glassy, like they're full of tears, but I can't tell if that's because of what I said, or just the cutting wind. Before I can say anything, he turns and leaves.

James

The bright lights of the club dance to the beat over my friends' faces and the bass thumps in my ears, shaking my whole body.

I'm sitting in the lounge on one of the comfy sofas, watching Alistair, Kesh, and Cyril as they dance with a group of girls, not far from me. Wren is sitting out too. I think the lads took one look at my face and decided that they couldn't leave me on my own this evening. Like I'm a little kid, for fuck's sake.

"You OK, bro?" Wren yells suddenly in my ear.

I raise an eyebrow. Normally, Wren would be the last person to talk about emotions. Seriously. We've both spent years perfecting the art of bottling up our problems. It's one of the reasons we're best mates.

"Don't give me that look. I'm just worried about you."

I can hardly hear what he's saying, but his expression speaks louder than words anyway. The moment I set foot in this club, everyone clocked that something must have happened. Cyril handed me a G&T without a word, but even now, a good hour later, I haven't touched it. I could down it in one. The urge is strong. Maybe that would finally drown out Ruby's words, which have been playing in my head on a constant loop.

It's not my fucking job to make you happy!

I understand why she's angry—she has every right to yell at me. Driving over to hers was a knee-jerk reaction that I can't explain, looking back at it.

I hate this situation. I hate that I went to Cyril and not her that Wednesday, and not a single day goes by when I don't wish for a time machine to make it all unhappen. Because I could have talked to Ruby, when my friends and I have always had the motto "oblivion at all costs."

I turn away from Wren and stare at my glass. The pounding music isn't enough to shut down my thoughts and I wrestle with myself for a moment. I look over to the others. Cyril and Alistair are dancing with a couple of girls, while Kesh is leaning against the wall beside them, sipping his drink. For a moment I wonder about getting up and joining them, but it feels as though there are lead weights hanging from my body. It takes me almost every ounce of strength I possess to lean forward and put my glass down untouched on the low wooden table in front of me.

"My whole fucking life is a wreck," I say in the end. I don't know if Wren heard. The music is deafening and he's several drinks in. But his dark brown eyes watch me closely as I continue. "And there's nothing I can do about it."

Apparently he did hear, because he leans in a little, grabs my shoulder, and gives it a squeeze for a second. "You'll do what you've done all your life, bro."

"What's that?"

Wren's mouth twitches into a grim smile. "You'll keep on going. If there's one thing I've learned from you in the last few years, it's that."

I gulp hard.

"Anytime I'm close to giving up, I remember that. It's really helped me lately," he adds.

Again, my eyes rest on the full glass of gin and tonic. What does "keep on going" mean in this case? Forget Ruby and act like none of this ever happened? Or fight for her?

"I know you're going through a lot at the moment, but it's your turn to ask me what's been up with me lately," he says.

Wren's words make me look up. "What?" I ask, confused.

He frowns back at me. After a while, he breathes out hard and rubs the back of his neck. "Doesn't matter. Forget it." He stands up and nods toward the dance floor, toward our friends, who are bathed in blue and purple light. Their movements are relaxed, like they haven't a care in the world.

As long as I can remember, that's been our specialty. Acting like we don't give a damn about anything or anybody. Like life's just a game where nothing matters, nothing lasts. Over the last few weeks, I've realized that we've been under an illusion. Everyone is vulnerable; everyone has something to lose.

I shake my head, but Wren doesn't take no for an answer. He grabs my hand, pulls me up off the sofa and onto the dance floor. The boys cheer as they see us and open up their circle so that we can join them. I spend a while trying to move to the beat, but it's not working.

I'm about to apologize to the others and tell them that I'm leaving when someone dances up to me and wraps an arm around my waist. I turn around with a frown—and find myself looking into Elaine Ellington's face.

"James!" she screams over the music, smiling at me. Her honey-blond waves frame her flushed face. As fast as I can, I push her arm away and leave the dance floor to head back to our lounge. When I get there, I feel strangely out of breath. I order a water and drop onto the sofa.

The sight of Elaine felt like a punch in the guts. I carry the memory of the evening in Cyril's pool around with me twenty-four seven at the best of times, and in that instant, it was so fresh that I felt a wave of nausea wash over me.

But I'd reckoned without Elaine. After a while, she comes over and sits down beside me, one leg crossed over the other.

"That's not a very nice way to say hello," she says, running her hand through her hair. Her eyes sparkle with amusement. She's sitting so close to me that we're almost touching. She budges a fraction closer. My whole body freezes as the scent of her perfume reaches my nose.

"I just wanted to tell you how sorry I am about what happened to your mum. If you ever want to talk or anything—I'm always here for you." She puts her hand on my leg and runs it slowly up the fabric of my trousers.

"Elaine, stop it," I say firmly, pushing her hand away. I shift to the side and look seriously at her.

"Did I do something wrong?" she asks in surprise.

I shake my head. "No. I'm the one who got everything wrong," I reply.

Elaine raises an eyebrow. "What's the matter?"

I shrug my shoulders but don't speak.

For a moment she just looks at me, then she shakes her head. "Yeah, you've been better."

"Sorry," I say. "But I can't do this anymore."

She slides away from me a little. "Pity," she says, standing up. "We've always had fun together."

She pauses there for a moment, as if she's waiting for me to stop her from leaving. When I don't move, just stare straight ahead, she walks back to the dance floor without another word.

I let myself sink back into the sofa and stare up at the ceiling. I've never noticed the little lights up there before, which are presumably meant to look like stars. I find my hand reaching into my pocket to pull out my wallet. Shakily, I open it and take hold of the slip of paper hidden behind my driving license. I've avoided looking at the list in the last few weeks, for fear that it would make me feel even shittier than I already do. I hold it up so that the little ceiling lights are almost shining through the paper. Point by point, I read through what Ruby and I wrote together. I swallow hard and notice how rough my throat feels all of a sudden.

Never in my life has anyone taken an interest in me the way Ruby does. I've never had anyone be my first thought when I wake up and the face I see before my eyes when I go to sleep. And there's never been anyone who wanted to make my dreams come true.

With those thoughts in mind, I fold the list up again and hold it tightly in my hand as I leave the club.

15

Ruby

"Here's to Ruby!" Dad calls out.

"And to Lin," I add, grinning at my friend.

It was Dad's idea to have a little Oxford party with Lin at home and to raise a glass to our success. When Mum and I first told him, he refused to believe a word of it until he'd seen the email for himself. As he read it, he kept murmuring "no," but then he hugged me so hard that my ribs are still slightly achy four hours later.

"I can't believe they made us both offers," I whisper to Lin over the rim of my champagne glass.

"Me either."

The idea of spending the next three years still with my friend sets off a whole wave of excited butterflies in my stomach. I'm so happy that it feels kind of unreal.

"We really have to put the work in now, Lin," I say.

"Can't you two just enjoy the moment for one evening?" asks Ember.

Mum and Dad laugh, while Lin and I give each other a guilty

smile. "You're right," I say. "But there's still a lot that can go wrong!"

Lin puts her glass down on the coffee table and takes a nacho—the only nibbles we could conjure up at such short notice. "It's a conditional offer, though—we still have to get three A's to get in."

"And I need to get a bursary too," I add quietly, trying to suppress the rising panic. The careers adviser at Maxton Hall has assured me loads of times that I have an excellent chance of getting one and that I really have no need to worry. But that's easier said than done.

Lin's cheeks go pale and she puts the half-eaten tortilla chip down next to her glass. "What if I don't make the grades in one of my subjects? Grandma says she'll support me through uni, but I bet she wouldn't then."

"Girls, you should be celebrating, not worrying yourselves sick!" Mum is sitting opposite Lin and me on our flowery armchair, looking at us with a shake of her head.

Lin and I exchange worried glances again but then pick up our glasses and have a big swig of the champagne.

"I guess you wouldn't even have gotten in if you weren't like this, huh?" Ember muses with a grin. She wasn't surprised by the offer and is trying to be pleased for me, but I can tell how sad she is that I'll be moving out. Oxford isn't that far away, but it's very different having a two-hour train journey between us instead of the width of the landing. Ember hates change, and I'm pretty sure if she had her way, we'd all carry on living at home together for the rest of our lives.

Although her mood has rubbed off on me slightly over the day, and the thought of leaving home is making me a little sad, that can't outweigh my happiness at being accepted. And since James turned up here, I'm even more determined not to let anything or anyone rob me of this joy.

Once we've finished the champagne, Lin and I leave my parents to watch TV and go up to my room.

"Oh shit," Lin mutters as I shut the door behind us. Her eyes are fixed on her phone and she sits on my desk chair without even looking up from her screen.

"What?" I ask.

"Nothing."

Her reply is so quick that I prick up my ears. "What's wrong?"

She shrugs. "Looks like Cyril got in too."

I hesitate a moment, then whisper: "So did James."

"Really? Looks like half the Beaufort clique is going to be in Oxford, then. Alistair and Wren have put it on their Instas too." Lin is typing something. I glance at the screen and see a lad with his top off—I'm pretty sure it's Cyril.

OK, I can't hold back any longer. I've been suspicious for months that there's something going on between Lin and Cyril that nobody else knows about. The way the two of them act around each other speaks louder than words. I thought for ages that they hated each other, but now I'm pretty sure there are sparks flying between them when they get into an argument.

"What are you doing?" I ask cautiously, sitting down cross-legged on my bed.

She looks up guiltily. "Nothing."

"That was too quick, and it's the second time you've said 'nothing' in a couple of minutes. I don't believe you."

Lin bites her lip and looks back at her phone. Her cheeks are fiery red.

"Lin, come here," I say, patting the spot on the bed beside me. She dubiously eyes the place where my hand is resting but slowly gets up and walks over. She leans her back against the headboard, crooks up a knee, and hooks both arms around it. I watch her settling in and turn toward her expectantly. She strokes a strand of her black hair back behind her ear. I get the impression she doesn't know where to start.

"I know you don't like talking about this stuff," I say gently. "But if there's something on your heart, you can always tell me."

Lin gulps hard. "There's not much to tell," she whispers.

She looks almost shy—the opposite of the Lin I know. She's such a strong, self-confident person who always stands up for herself and says what she thinks without worrying what other people might think about it. Seeing her like this makes me suddenly uneasy.

"I've been into Cyril since I was thirteen."

My eyes widen. "Seriously?"

She nods slowly. "When I started at Maxton Hall, Cyril and I sat next to each other in a few subjects. He . . . wasn't always the way he is now. Back then he was considerate and sweet. He really made me laugh. I can't describe exactly why he fascinated me so much, but I liked him right away."

For a moment, she says nothing, just stares at her knee. I'd like to say something encouraging, but I hold back. This is the first time she's told me anything about her love life and I have to give her the time she needs, without interrupting.

"But the whole time I've known Cyril, he's been in love with Lydia, so I always knew that we had no chance. I was still really upset when they got together though. There was never anything official, but you know how stuff like that gets around at school.

After she dumped him, I . . . comforted him. One thing led to another and . . ." She shrugs awkwardly, and her grip on her knee tightens.

She looks so sad that I wonder how I didn't notice all this.

"Was it just a one-off, or something more?" I ask cautiously.

Lin shakes her head and gives a breathless laugh. "We've been having sex every couple of weeks for two years."

My mouth drops open. And shuts again. I can't believe she's kept that secret from me for so long. "I . . . Does *anyone* know about this?"

Lin shakes her head again. "No. I'm well aware that as far as Cy is concerned, there's only Lydia. And I'm OK with that, but I don't want it getting out. I want to keep a bit of my dignity at least, and we've never been a couple or anything." She hesitates a moment. "Anyway, it's probably ended by itself."

"What do you mean?"

"He hasn't contacted me since Cordelia Beaufort died. Probably because he's too busy consoling Lydia." She shrugs her shoulders. "He's ignoring my messages and now he's always hanging around with her at school."

"I . . ." I cut myself off, shaking my head. "Was it weird for you to spend New Year's Eve with Lydia?"

Lin gives a narrow smile. "I like Lydia. And she can't exactly help the fact that I happen to be into the lad who's hopelessly in love with her."

"I don't know what to say."

"It doesn't matter, Ruby, seriously. I just wish he'd be honest with me for once. I don't think I deserve to be ghosted like this. He could have just told me that Lydia's given him another chance."

"I don't think she has."

She shrugs yet again. "I shouldn't even care. It's not like I'm in undying love with him."

Her voice is light, but the sad look in her eyes contradicts her words.

"Cyril's a pig if he's ghosting you and you don't know where you stand," I say furiously.

"I know it must sound like that. But we both knew what we were getting into. He never made me any promises and nor did I to him. And he can be really great—self-assured, funny. And tender . . ." Lin blushes and buries her face in her hands.

"That sounds like more than just a physical thing, Lin."

"I know!" She groans, peeping out from between her slightly spread fingers. "I didn't realize that until now when I haven't spent any time with him outside school for ages. I *miss* him."

Her last words sound so revolted that I have to grin.

"Have you ever talked about it? Properly, I mean?" I ask gently.

She shakes her head and goes bright red. "Cyril and I never spend much time talking when we see each other."

Oh wow.

"We've been friends for so long and I had no idea. I feel like a really bad best friend right now."

"You're a great friend. I just didn't want to tell anyone because . . . oh, God knows. There was something exciting about keeping it a secret. But now that the whole thing's clearly over as far as he's concerned, it's killing me." She sighs deeply. "We're both exactly the same, Ruby. Neither of us wanted to get into anything serious before Oxford."

One of the many things that Lin and I have in common.

"And now both James and Cyril have got offers too," I mumble.

"Yeah."

For a moment we're quiet, each lost in our own thoughts. When I moved to Maxton Hall, I lost all my friends from my old school. After that, I decided that I'd keep all my friendships really superficial. I didn't want to put my energy into anything that wasn't going to last.

But that changed when I met Lin. OK, so I'm still scared that this might be another temporary thing, but I'm prepared to take that risk—this conversation now is showing me that again.

I take Lin's hand and give it a gentle squeeze. "You can always talk to me, Lin. Always. I want you to know that."

I've never said that to her before, and I find it surprisingly hard to get those words through my lips. Not because I don't mean them, but because they mean so much to me.

"Thanks. You can too," Lin says, her voice husky with emotion. She turns her hands so that we can link our fingers together. "I mean that. You can talk to me about James anytime. Or about anything else."

I chew the inside of my cheek and think about the moment this afternoon when James was standing on the doorstep, telling me all that stuff.

I'll always be yours, Ruby.

His words made the ground wobble beneath my feet. He looked so determined, like nothing in his life mattered more than winning me back.

"James was here this afternoon," I begin after a while.

Lin keeps holding on to my hand as she looks inquiringly at me. "What did he want?"

I shrug my shoulders. "He said that he needs me. That I'm the only person who understands him. And that he could be happy with me."

Lin takes a sharp breath. "And?"

I shrug again.

I meant what I said to him. It's not my job to make James happy. Even so, I regret yelling it at him like that. He was clearly struggling, and I'm probably the only person who gets why. When we were in Oxford, he told me that he'd never told anyone about his fears of the future, and I can imagine how he must have been feeling after the Beaufort board meeting and getting into St. Hilda's. But . . . we split up. He can't put all that on me. I can't be the only thing that gives his life meaning. That's not what a relationship is meant to be about.

"I want to be there for him, but at the same time, I don't know if I can," I whisper.

"I get that," Lin replies. "But . . . I also see the way he looks at you in team meetings. I think he really does want to win you back."

I shake my head. "That's what he wants right *now*. James is so fickle—in another two weeks, I'll bet something else will happen to shake up his life, and then he'll vanish or freak out or do something else to sabotage us, and I'm not having it. I'm not going to let him hurt me like that again."

I blurt out the last words so fiercely that Lin looks at me in surprise.

"That's just what I admire about you."

I blink in confusion. "What is?"

She smiles slightly at me. "I could see exactly how the thing with James messed you up. How much you suffered for him and his family. You were there for him after he hurt you so badly—and now you're staying strong and focusing on yourself. I think that's amazing."

When she puts it like that, it all sounds more heroic than I feel. I breathe out shakily. "I yelled some really nasty things at him earlier."

"Do you still have feelings for him?" Lin asks unexpectedly.

Now it's my turn to flinch.

I remember what I said to him at New Year's. I can't just stop loving James. These emotions won't go away, however much I wish they would.

"Yes," I whisper.

Lin gives me a sad smile. "Shame we can't just switch it off, isn't it?"

I mumble in agreement. "Anyway. I think it's time we got back to what this evening's meant to be all about—we're celebrating."

She nods vigorously and presses my hand one last time before she lets it go. "You're right."

I grab my laptop and find the Oxford website. We spend the next hour looking at the college accommodation, clicking through student pages, and making lists of the stuff we want to do together once we start there.

But however hard I try not to think about them, I can hear James's words echoing in my head all evening long.

16

Ruby

I spent the whole weekend alternately being happy about my offer from Oxford and wondering whether James would come to the events team meeting on Monday—and how I should act if he does. At this point, I have to admit that my New Year's resolution to make a clean break has failed. James is everywhere. Either in person or in my thoughts—and I don't see any way of changing that in the future, especially as remembering his words, even two days later, still sends an excited tingle through my body.

And I feel that exact same tingle now as Lin and I walk into the meeting room after lunch and see James in his usual place, with a book in hand, which is normal for him lately. I glance over, curious to see what it is this time—the new John Green novel—then hastily look away and ask Lin to go through the agenda with me again before the others arrive.

The minutes stretch out like chewing gum, but eventually, Camille strolls in last, and we can get started.

"Doug," Lin says. "The posters are looking great. We've had loads of compliments on them already."

Doug flashes Lin a fleeting smile, which is still more than anyone else has gotten out of him in recent meetings.

"They might even attract the attention of a potential sponsor or two."

I nod. "The guest list is much healthier now too. Although we still need some speakers, which is worrying me. We don't have much time left," I say. "Kieran, did that professor ever get back to you?"

"Yeah," he replies, but he doesn't look too thrilled, so I can guess what's coming next. "He's too busy, I'm afraid. But he did say he'd make a decent donation."

"OK, well, that's that. Better than nothing." I give him an encouraging smile. "Has anyone else made any progress?"

Nobody speaks.

"All right, fine, then—"

James clears his throat.

For a moment, I'm in two minds. I don't want to look at him. But I can't ignore him either. That would just make the others ask questions that I don't want to answer. Can't answer.

"Yes, Beaufort?" Lin jumps in for me.

"Alice Campbell says she'll make the closing speech."

My head jerks up.

James meets my eyes. It's only now that I see how pale his face is. And there are dark circles under his eyes, like he hasn't slept since Saturday.

I still regret yelling those words at him. He didn't deserve that, and I wish I could talk to him again calmly and explain why I got so angry when he turned up on my doorstep.

My guilty conscience must show on my face, because James's eyes narrow before he carries on like nothing ever happened.

"The Family Center really helped her and her family to get back on their feet a few years ago. She'd be happy to help out with the gala. I told her that you'd be in touch to discuss the details."

I stare at him in disbelief. It's only when a small but satisfied smile spreads over his face that I realize this is no coincidence. He actually remembered that I once mentioned in passing how much I admire Alice Campbell and her work.

I don't know what to do with this information. The longer I think about it, the more I want to have a quiet conversation with him.

I'm desperately wondering how I can ask him to wait a moment after the meeting.

"That's amazing, Beaufort," Lin says when I've gone too long without answering. "Thank you. If you have anyone else we could contact, please let us know."

James coughs again. "And Boyd Hall is all sorted. I've booked the décor firm for next Friday at four, and let Mr. Jones know."

For a moment, there's total silence in the meeting room.

"Considering how much you hated this team at first, you're really putting the work in now," Jessalyn remarks.

James doesn't reply, just looks at me again, in a way that gives me goose bumps all down my arms.

"That's straight after our meeting," Lin says. "So I suggest we all go over there together, OK?"

Mumbles of agreement fill the room.

"The next thing on the list is the photo booth," Lin continues, dragging me back to the present.

Suddenly, I have a flash of inspiration. It's risky but thrilling. It'll give me a chance to speak to James and apologize to him. Safely away from Lin's critical eyes and Camille's curious ears.

"Right." I clear my throat. "My parents say I can borrow their car on Saturday, so I'll pick it up then. But apparently, the parts are pretty heavy."

I pluck up all my courage and look back at James.

"James," I say, my voice steady, "would you help me get it all in the car?"

For a split second, his eyes glitter with surprise.

But then he nods and says, "Yeah, sure," like I didn't ask him anything special.

I ignore both Camille's quiet gasp and Lin's speaking glance and spend the rest of the meeting staring at my planner and asking myself what the hell I just got myself into.

━━━

James is waiting for me as I drive into the Maxton Hall parking lot on Saturday. He's wearing jeans, a black coat, and a gray scarf. He's blowing on his hands to warm them up, and I can't help wondering how long he's been standing there.

As he sees me, he lowers his hands and smiles uncertainly at me. I have no idea how to read it. It's a new smile. One where his body is rigid and his eyes are sad. One that appeared after we split up—after his mum died, and after everything that's happened since.

I miss his old smile.

I push that thought down as I pull up in front of James. If today is going to be even moderately successful, I have to get myself together.

"Morning," he says, dropping into the passenger seat of our people carrier. It's an old car and kind of beaten-up, but it goes, which is the main thing. Luckily, Ember and I cleaned it yesterday evening, because I'm now realizing that there's something weirdly intimate about the way James is looking around.

His eyes rest on the Yankee Candle scent tree dangling from the rearview mirror as I start the engine again.

"My mum loves those things," I explain. "She adores floral scents and that really winds my sister up. Ember hates the smell of roses and Mum loves it."

I need to stop babbling. It's not like I didn't have a reason to ask James to come along with me today. But I'm finding it hard to direct the conversation straight back to our failed relationship. Especially considering how long we still have to be in this car together.

"My mum always loved the scent of flowers too."

It's a real effort to keep my eyes on the road and not turn abruptly toward him. Evidently James has no problem with skipping the small talk.

"Do you miss her?" I ask quietly.

It takes him a moment, then he says, "Yeah, actually," in a kind of growl of agreement. "Things are different without her."

"In what way?"

Out of the corner of my eye, I see his shoulders twitch. "There's no buffer between me and Dad anymore. Lydia wants to take that role, but I'm doing my absolute best not to let that happen. I don't want her to get stuck in the middle—least of all now."

"How is she? I've hardly seen her this week."

"Pretty good. I think." He hesitates a moment. "I wish she'd just tell Sutton. But at the same time, I get why she doesn't want to."

"The whole situation is just total shit."

"Yeah." For a moment, he's quiet, then he clears his throat. "So, how are you?"

I really don't understand how a conversation can feel so normal and so weird at the same time.

"Good. I . . . um. I got an offer from St. Hilda's too."

"I knew it. They'd be total idiots if they didn't take you," he replies. "Congrats, Ruby."

I glance at him in surprise. He looks seriously back at me.

I don't know how he keeps doing this. One day he's crushed, standing shivering on my doorstep, and the next he's back at school, finding the strength to act like nothing happened. And now he seems totally unfazed, even though I know that last Saturday had an effect on him.

"Thanks," I mumble. For a moment, I try to find the right words for what I want to say to him next. I've had since Monday to think about it, but right now, my mind has gone totally blank. "I'm sorry about what I said to you last weekend," I start. "That was—"

"Ruby." James tries to interrupt me, but I shake my head.

"I want to get over you," I say quietly. "But being mean to you won't make that any easier. I really am sorry. And it's important to me that you know that."

I feel his eyes on me. "There's nothing for you to apologize for," he whispers.

I don't know how to answer that. The words sound bitter as he says them and I want to contradict him, but on the other hand, I'm scared that that will turn the conversation in a direction I'm not ready to go. I wanted to say sorry, and I've done that. At the moment, I don't think I have the strength for anything more.

So I stay quiet and accelerate. The silence between us gets more and more awkward the longer it goes on, and after a while I can't bear it any longer and turn on the radio. The cheerful pop

music on Mum's favorite station is in stark contrast to the oppressive atmosphere between James and me. We spend the remaining
fifteen minutes of the drive in silence, but I'm aware of his presence for every second. I hear his quiet breathing and sense when
he moves beside me. And the heater might not be up very high,
but just the thought that I'd only have to stretch out my hand to
touch him makes me burn up.

I'm really glad when we get to the old business parking lot and
I can finally get out of the car. The cold air feels so good on my
flushed cheeks.

"It's over that way," I say, pointing to a unit with a colorful
sign over the doorway. James comes to stand beside me and, as
we set off, my arm brushes against his.

We're both wearing thick coats.

But even so, the touch feels like an electric shock.

I take a step to the side as subtly as possible and hurry toward
the door. I push it open and step into the small warehouse.

I look around. It looked way more inviting online. The pale
yellow light offers the bare minimum of illumination, and the low
ceilings are covered with spiderwebs. There are various electronic
gadgets lying around, but most of the space is taken up by photo
booths—at least twenty of them. There are small speakers playing garage music quietly, and a balding guy who's sitting at a desk
behind the narrow counter is nodding his head to the beat.

"Wow, nice shop you picked out," James whispers, but before
I can reply, the man sees us and gets up with a smile.

"You must be Ruby," he says, coming over.

"That's me," I reply with a nod, taking his outstretched hand.
"And this is James."

They shake hands too.

"I'm Hank, and I'll show you quickly how the photo booth works first. D'you want to come round?" He beckons us around the counter and then points at one of the booths.

"This is the one you went for, right?" he asks as we stand next to it.

I study the thing. It has black walls and a red curtain over the door. To one side, there's a thin slit with a light-up sign above it labeled *Photos*. Next to the door, there's a little blackboard telling you about the various filters you can put on your pictures. The chalk-style lettering is lovely, with looping handwriting.

"Can I personalize that with stuff about our event, Hank?" I ask, pointing to the board.

He nods. "Of course. I'll give you a spare marker pen."

I smile at him. "Perfect. Thank you."

"So, here goes. There's a built-in SLR camera in here, which you work via the touchscreen. It's really easy to use—you just have to press on the camera symbol. Then you get three seconds to pose before the picture is taken. After that, you can use the filters or, if you don't like it, you can delete it and take another."

I move the red curtain aside slightly and study the screen. "It looks pretty foolproof."

"Want to give it a try?" asks Hank, grinning like a little kid.

Before I can say no, James replies. "Yes, please."

I raise an eyebrow, but he pays no attention and steps into the box. He holds the curtain back and looks expectantly at me.

"What are you waiting for? In you get!" says Hank beside me.

Just like that, I step into the little booth and eye James skeptically. Meanwhile, he's concentrating on the screen. "We have to make sure everything works, don't we?" he asks quietly.

I'm irritated that I didn't think of that myself because I was too busy keeping an arm's length from James.

"Ruby, you're blocking the camera."

Back to the wall, I squeeze along until I'm standing behind James, who's sat down on the little stool in front of the camera.

"Look into there," he says suddenly, pointing to the small black hole over the touchscreen.

I bend down so that I can see over his shoulder, into the camera. Now I appear on the screen too, but I can hardly focus on the blurry image of our faces.

A strand of James's hair is tickling my cheek and my nose is filled with the familiar scent of him. I'm suddenly far too warm in my coat. Beside me, James has frozen, and I think he's even stopped breathing. I slowly turn my head and look at him. I'm so close to him that if I wanted to, I could brush his skin with my lips.

At that moment, James clicks the button.

The quiet sound plucks me out of my trance with a jump. I suddenly remember what we're actually doing here—and realize what I was about to do.

"All seems to work," says James, as if he never even noticed the chemistry crackling between us for a few seconds just now.

Did I just imagine how hot that was?

As fast as I can, I push my way out to where Hank is waiting for us, the strip of photos in his hand.

"A funny pose, but you seem to have figured out how to operate the camera," he says, pressing the four little pictures into my hand.

No, I definitely was not imagining things.

In the photo, my face is turned toward James, while he's looking straight into the camera. And his expression . . .

I give a dry gulp.

I know that look. And the curl of his lips there.

James must have felt it too. In this second, I'm absolutely sure of that.

"Nice," I croak. I'm about to hand the photos back to Hank, but before I can, James takes them from me. Without even looking at them, he slips the strip into his coat pocket.

"Where do we sign?" he asks, in the same businesslike tone he used that time we went to Beaufort's.

Hank leads us back to the counter, where I fill out three forms, and he gives me a little instruction book. After that, the three of us carry the box out to the boot of Mum's car. I'm glad to be back out in the fresh air. It's gloriously cool on my hot cheeks.

On the way back, I put the radio on again, a little louder this time. Why on earth did I think it would be a good idea to ask James to come along? I should have realized how hard it would be to be this close to him for such a long time.

Out of the corner of my eye, I can see James unbutton his coat and unwind his scarf.

"If you're too hot, I can turn the heater down a bit," I say with an effort.

"Ruby." The way he whispers my name is so familiar.

I grip the steering wheel, trying my hardest to focus on the road. The air between us feels more highly charged than ever, but I'm desperately fighting that down.

The lights ahead of us turn red, and I slowly brake, rolling the car up to the stop line. Then I dare to glance in his direction. James looks at me and I can see countless emotions in his eyes, which make me long to reach for him, to hug him, to hold him tight.

"I just wanted to say that I'm—"

"Please don't." I cut him off pleadingly, shaking my head.

He clenches his teeth so hard that a muscle in his jaw starts to twitch. We look at each other for a moment, and there are so many unspoken words between us.

But I can't talk to him now. It's just not possible. Not when I get the feeling that I'm about to cave in.

The next moment, James turns his face away again and looks straight ahead. "It's green."

I put my foot down. The drive to school has never felt longer.

Ruby

"I think I'd prefer it a bit mintier," Ember says thoughtfully.

I drag the cursor further left and upward over the color field, lightening the moss green and taking it in a bluer direction. "Like this?"

My sister gives a grunt of agreement. I save the color and click on preview in WordPress so that we can admire our handiwork.

Ember has been rebranding her blog, *Bellbird*, with a new logo, a more modern WordPress theme, and a fresh color palette. Her latest post is right at the top—a guide to ethical plus-size fashion—and below that are three smaller windows with thumbnails showing her most popular articles. On the right-hand side are links to her social media profiles and a photo of her that I took last summer. She's standing in a meadow of flowers, wearing a floral, summery maxi dress with a plunging neckline. I remember the exact moment a grasshopper jumped onto her and I snapped her screaming and trying to shake it off—it was hilarious. Sadly, she didn't choose that one as her profile picture; she went for one where she's laughing happily and stroking a strand of hair off her face. Beneath it, she's written:

> Hi, I'm Ember! I'm a plus-size fashion blogger who loves words and cake, and I find inspiration in everything beautiful. I hope you enjoy reading my blog!

"It looks great," I say, impressed. "Really professional."

"You say that every time," Ember replies, scanning the page with narrowed eyes. When it comes to her blog, she's as much of a perfectionist as I am with my bullet journal.

"I know, but it's true." I browse her latest outfit posts. Even though I took the photos myself, I could look at them again and again. Ember looks so beautiful. For the zillionth time, I wish Mum and Dad weren't so critical of social media. They're worried that Ember might reveal too much personal information, but she takes an impressively professional approach to *Bellbird*. These days, she even has a couple of brands that she works with regularly who send her clothes.

"Oh, by the way," my sister says suddenly, "I saw a dress that could have been made for you. You still need one for the gala, don't you?"

I nod. "Show me."

She turns the laptop toward her slightly and her tiny desk wobbles dangerously. I hastily grab my glass of orange juice to stop it tipping over. We've been sitting here side by side, working on her blog for two hours now, with Frank Ocean's melodic voice coming from the little speakers in her laptop.

Ember opens one of her bookmarks and we watch together as

the page loads slowly, eventually revealing a dress that makes me breathe a sigh. It's black, with a V-neck, and it's in some flowing fabric, fitted at the waist and then falling in soft waves from the hips.

"Are there any more pictures?" I ask, but at that moment I catch sight of the price. "Oh, God. It costs over two hundred pounds," I stutter, raising a finger to shut the window. "Why would you show me a thing like that?"

Ember catches my hand and grins at me. "Not for us, it doesn't. The company is offering me a collaboration."

I hesitate. I know that Ember gets a lot of offers of collaboration with shops these days, but that doesn't mean she has to accept every one of them.

"You've been looking for ages," my sister continues. "And this would be perfect for a fancy occasion like that, wouldn't it? I could ask them."

I shake my head at once. "No, I can't accept that."

"Why not?"

I give an uncertain shrug. "Dunno. Isn't it kind of off to get stuff for free?"

"Do you think actors pay for the designer dresses they borrow for premieres and awards ceremonies?"

"I've never really thought about it, to be honest," I admit.

"Well, now you know," Ember says. "They offered me the chance to try three dresses, and they'll even pay me if I write an honest review of the fit and so on. All I'd like to do is take a photo of the two of us wearing the dresses and publish it—if you don't mind."

I look back at the dress. I click through the other pictures, falling deeper in love with the sweeping skirt, the soft-looking fabric, and the little appliqué details on the neckline with every photo. I've never worn such an elegant dress—apart from the one the Beauforts lent me for last Halloween.

"I don't even need to ask, do I?" Ember says suddenly, and as I turn my head to look at her in confusion, she won't meet my eyes. Her smile is resigned. "You presumably still don't want me tagging along."

"Ember." I sigh, taking a deep breath to give my automatic reply. But then I pause.

Ember's been there for me day and night in the last few weeks. She's taken care of me and hasn't breathed a word about what happened with James to Mum and Dad—no matter how insistently they asked her.

I know how much Ember longs to come to one of our school events. And now that I come to think about it, the charity gala is probably a more suitable occasion than any of the other Maxton Hall parties. It's the one event of the year where everyone's on their best behavior. There will be too many celebrities and VIPs around for anyone to want to make a bad impression. So there's a more sedate atmosphere, and the chances of anything bad happening to her are relatively low.

Ember watches me attentively. She doesn't move a muscle, as if she's scared that the least twitch would provoke a negative answer.

"I'll take you," I say in the end.

Ember's eyes grow wide. "Do you really mean it?" she asks in disbelief.

I take a deep breath. These are our last few months together and I want them to be as nice as possible. Soon we won't be seeing each other every day, and however much I'm looking forward to Oxford, that's still a scary thought.

"On a couple of conditions," I add in a firmer voice, because I want Ember to know that I'm serious. She waves to me to go on. "You have to stay with me the whole evening. And only talk to people I know and say are OK. I really don't want you getting messed about by some creep. Deal?"

Ember flings her arms around my neck and hugs me so tight that I almost fall off the chair and have to cling on to her desk.

"You're the best! I won't leave your side for a second," she declares. I hug her back and close my eyes for a moment. A wave of worry washes over me and I ask myself if I'm doing the right thing. After all, I know more than her about what can happen at these parties. But on the other hand, Ember's nearly seventeen. She's clever and self-confident and knows what she wants. I should probably just have more faith in her.

I'm certain that I've made the right choice when Ember pulls away from me and beams at me, eyes shining. "This means we can now officially start dress shopping. And I've got an event to wear it to! Plus, this is going to be the best blog post of all time. I can't wait!"

I smile back at her and feel her excitement and genuine joy spill over to me. It's the first time in ages that I've felt this at peace. "I'm happy that you're happy."

As I speak, my sister's smile suddenly fades.

"What's wrong?" I ask.

Ember avoids my eyes. She starts to click on random web pages, like she isn't really focused on what she's doing. "Nothing. It doesn't matter. I just can't believe that these are our last few months together."

"I'm only going away to university. It doesn't mean we'll never see each other again, Ember," I say gently.

Ember keeps staring at her laptop screen. "It does, and you know it."

I shake my head fiercely. "Things won't be exactly the same, but that definitely doesn't mean we'll never see each other again. I'll come home every weekend and I'll keep working with you on your blog. We can chat and FaceTime, and I'll send you cringey pictures of my lunch and tell you the books I'm reading and—"

She laughs and interrupts me. "Promise me, Ruby," she says, her voice deadly serious.

I put an arm around my little sister's shoulder and pull her to my side. "I promise."

James

The week before the gala is one of the most stressful of my life.

I still have all the schoolwork that Lydia and I missed before Christmas to catch up on, and there's so much to do for the event that I don't know whether I'm coming or going. Ruby and Camille decide on Monday to swap the lightbulbs in Boyd Hall for ones with a softer, more atmospheric light, so I have to buy the bulbs. On Tuesday, the pianist suddenly announces that he wants to be paid way more for hardly any music, so Kieran and I have to go to see him and bring him round. As we drive over there, Kieran talks me into coming to listen to the school choir rehearsal on Wednesday and checking their song list because Ruby's too busy and Lin doesn't appreciate the finer points of classical music (his words). But the absolute highlight comes on Thursday when the entire team is called in to polish the silver cutlery (not my favorite job) and to fold napkins into miters (sheer hell). I always thought I was reasonably good with my fingers, but apparently I'm incapable of following simple instructions on napkin-folding.

The lads give me funny looks when I turn up at lacrosse training already knackered, or have to skip it altogether, but they don't ask questions. I wouldn't even know how to explain what's up with me.

It feels like I'm clinging on to a straw, refusing to let go. On our way back to school, Ruby made it very clear that she still isn't ready to hear what I have to say. And I respect that. But that moment in the photo booth—when we were so close, Ruby's lips less than an inch from my jaw, when I could feel her ragged breath on my skin . . . At that moment I realized that I'm not fighting in vain.

And I'm not giving up as long as there's even a single glimmer of hope for us. I've never been a particularly patient person, but when it comes to Ruby, I have all the time in the world—or I'll make it. Ruby is worth it.

Even so, I breathe deeply as I pull on my jersey on Friday and finally get to run out onto the field. The coach has us doing brutal circuit training, but the physical exertion is doing me good and taking my mind off things. Right now, we have to give each other piggyback rides across the playing fields. Alistair is pretty strong, but after ten minutes, he gives way beneath my weight and we both crash to the ground.

"Fuck," I growl, rolling onto my back. It's February now, so spring is within touching distance, but it's still bloody cold out here, and the ground is fucking hard. I'm pretty sure I've just scuffed up both my knees.

"Don't stop!" Mr. Freeman roars, blowing hard on his whistle.

"Up you get," says Alistair, clapping his hands.

He crouches down in front of me again as Kesh runs past, Wren on his back.

"No, it's my turn," I retort, patting myself on the back. Alistair rolls his eyes but does as I say and jumps onto my shoulders. The next moment, I sprint away, past my teammates, as fast as I can, until every muscle in my body is burning and the gap to Kesh and Wren is shortening.

When we're level with them, Wren groans. "Not again!" He slaps Kesh on the side to spur him on. "Get moving, bro."

Kesh picks up speed, his face grim, and I follow suit as Alistair yells. I'm already missing a session every week, so I'm under scrutiny. Not just from my mates, but from the coach too. I can't let myself down now, even though my chest burns like fire with every breath.

In the end, Kesh and I finish almost neck and neck. I'm so out of breath that it's a major effort not to drop onto all fours. Kesh holds out his fist and I bump it with mine, while Wren gives me a shove. "You're a beast. How the hell did you catch up that fast, Beaufort?"

"Good work today, lads!" shouts Freeman, clapping his hands. His gaze roams over each of us in turn, then a smile spreads over his lips. "You've definitely earned a reward. It's my round."

We cheer. Yes, the circuit training is brutal, but it's only twice a term, and he generally then takes us down to the pub near the school and treats us to burgers and chips—after which we always forget how he made us suffer in the previous few hours.

"What's Lexie doing here?" Cyril asks suddenly, his eyes on the edge of the field.

The whole team turns to look. I don't think I've ever seen the head teacher down here on the training grounds before.

"Have you guys been fucking around again?" I hear someone ask behind me as the coach heads toward Lexington and has a brief conversation with him. He means me and the boys, obviously, but none of us answers. My mind is racing. Something must have happened for Lexie to be here right now. But I have no idea what.

A moment later, Freeman jogs back toward us and claps his hands. "Change of plan, boys! You're needed in Boyd Hall. The events committee need your help setting up for the gala tomorrow evening."

I freeze. It's six o'clock. The décor firm should have finished ages ago.

Everyone grumbles, and the coach's face darkens. "Didn't I make myself clear? Boyd Hall. Now."

Ruby

I don't think Lin or I have ever been as close to a nervous breakdown as we were today. We arrived at Boyd Hall at four, like we'd discussed with James and the others, to help the décor company get everything ready for tomorrow evening. But the only person we found there was Mr. Jones, the caretaker, who was swearing loudly and colorfully into his phone, before subsequently informing us that the firm had accidentally double-booked themselves and decided to honor the more lucrative contract.

I just stood there in shock for a couple of minutes, then turned to Lin. The moment I looked into her eyes, I could tell that she was already mentally running through every option still open to us.

Mr. Jones added that after a bit of back and forth, the company had eventually agreed that they would at least drop off all the stuff we'd ordered from them at some point in the next hour. Even so, there weren't enough of us to get everything set up and looking good in the time available.

To top it all off, Mr. Lexington suddenly turned up out of the blue and looked around the bare, undecorated hall in disbelief, at which point I wished the ground would just open up and swallow me. I explained contritely what had happened, expecting him to shake his head in disappointment and start looking for a new chair for the events team. But to my surprise, he just gave me a firm look and announced that he was going to find people to help.

Not long after that, the doors to Boyd Hall opened and the entire lacrosse team trooped into the room. Without even glancing in our direction, James marched directly over to Jonesy, his expression grim, and then, as I looked on in amazement, Mr. Lexington got the attention of the rest of the team, pointed to Lin and me, and announced that all further instructions would come from us.

I then switched to autopilot, trying to dish out the jobs to be done among the boys in as organized a way as possible. That was an hour and a half ago now, and since then, I've pulled back from the brink of a breakdown, the same as Lin.

"It's taking shape, don't you think?" she says beside me as we work together to unroll a cable from the stage across Boyd Hall to the sound desk.

I look up and around me. Most of the decorations have already been put up, the stage is nearly built, and between them, Alistair and Wren have set up all the little tables on the floor in front of it.

"A bit further right, Ellington," I hear the coach say suddenly, and take a closer look at how they've arranged them.

Oh no. There's not enough room between the tables. I walk over to them and smile diplomatically at the lacrosse coach. "Thank you so much for your help, Mr. Freeman, but we need to make sure that people can get through between the tables."

He blinks in surprise. Then he clears his throat and pulls his cap further down over his face. He takes a step back and beckons me forward with the other hand.

"Alistair," I say. "Wait a moment." I explain how much space we need between the tables so that guests have room to move. "The first row can't be too close to the stage either. We can't expect people to donate if they've been sat so close to the speakers that they're deafened by the end of the evening."

I give a friendly yet determined smile and look expectantly at them until Alistair shakes his head with a sigh. "You're hardcore, Ruby."

While Wren and Alistair shift the tables into the right places, Lin and I start to check that all the cables on the sound desk are working.

"If we keep this up, we will actually be ready," Lin says, but I hardly hear her because, at that moment, James comes through the huge main doors.

He's carrying a table and glances at the plan Jessalyn is holding out to him. He looks around, then heads straight for the edge of the hall, where he puts the table down exactly where it needs to go. Then he wipes his forehead with the back of his hand.

Alistair wasn't exaggerating when he said he couldn't feel his arms anymore—the whole lacrosse team looks absolutely shattered. They were doing the dreaded circuit training this afternoon. After way less effort than they've been putting in, I really feel my muscles the next day, so I can't imagine how sore the lads will be tomorrow.

I watch James as he takes a water bottle from Doug and swigs. My stomach feels weirdly jittery. With his damp hair and flushed cheeks, in his lacrosse uniform, James really doesn't look half bad. Nuh-uh. I gulp. Suddenly, I'm remembering the last time I saw him breathless, sweaty, and red-faced. That time, he was naked, whispering sweet nothings into my ear and kissing me until I lost my mind.

"Earth to Ruby?" Lin breaks into my trance. "Can you pass me that wire?"

"Yeah." I hurriedly look away and try to steer my thoughts back to safer ground.

===

We don't finish getting everything set up until well into the evening. It seemed to take hours to drape the panels of fabric over the windows, and we needed several attempts to get the lighted columns mounted next to the stage. At one point, part of the stage came down, nearly hitting Doug—fortunately, he got away with nothing worse than a shock and a grazed arm, which Camille patched up for him with surprising care.

We had to make a few compromises—like not being able to decorate the ceiling—but all in all, the results are respectable. Especially now that it's dark and the chandeliers are filling the hall with their warm light.

All the round tables have been fully set. There are white tablecloths with silver runners over them, silver candlesticks, carefully folded napkins, and fine porcelain plates. Jessalyn crafted the table numbers to help people find their seats. There's a screen on either side of the stage, and the presentation about the Family Center that Doug put together is playing on the left, but the one on the right doesn't seem to be working. Still, I've got plenty of time to sort that out, and if necessary, I can get one of the technicians to come and have a look at it tomorrow morning. The light-bulbs that James bought at the beginning of the week bathe parts of the room in a bluish-purple hue, and there are projectors throwing little circles of light onto the walls.

OK, so it all took twice as long as if the professionals had put everything together, and it's not as absolutely perfect as I'd have liked, but I'm still proud of what we've achieved.

I can picture the atmosphere tomorrow evening—the elegant guests, the delicious-smelling food, the classical music, and the head teacher smiling with satisfaction.

I look around at the boys, who are all knocking back huge gulps of water. We could never have managed without them. I make up my mind, walk over, and clear my throat. Twenty heads turn toward me. I can tell by the tingle on the back of my neck that James's is among them.

"Thank you for your help," I begin, looking each of them in turn in the eye. Except James. I'm still shocked by the thoughts that bubbled up in me earlier at the sight of him, and I don't want to risk blushing beetroot red in front of the whole team. "We really owe you."

"How about you buy us all a drink tomorrow? Here at the gala?" Cyril suggests with a grin. "That would be . . . fun."

"My offer from earlier still stands," interjects Mr. Freeman. He turns to me. "We were about to head to the pub to toast their hard work at training."

"Great idea, coach," says Alistair, clapping his hands. "So, back to the original plan? Black Fox?"

All the lacrosse lads cheer.

"And the first round's on me," says the coach, straightening his cap. "And of course the events committee is invited along, Miss Bell. You've been putting hard work in too."

"I wouldn't go that far," mutters a guy I've never seen before in my life. "They'd have been screwed without us . . ."

"Shut it, Kenton," says James with quiet menace.

Kenton presses his lips together.

"Let's go," Freeman says, nodding toward the doors.

The others head out with Doug, Camille, and the rest of my team following on behind. Never in my wildest dreams would I have thought the lacrosse and events teams would go out for a drink together by choice.

Lin nudges me in the ribs. "I'm gonna talk to Cyril for once," she whispers, her expression determined. "So I at least know where I stand."

I nod. "Good idea."

"You're not coming, are you?"

I shake my head, and the firm look fades from Lin's eyes.

"Then neither am I," she says, nodding toward my clipboard. "I'll help you."

"Don't be silly," I reply, hugging it to my chest so that she can't see the things still to be ticked off. "A chance like this isn't going to come around again. Go, and try to find out why he's been ghosting you. And if he acts like a dick, give him hell."

Lin hesitates a moment longer, but I point firmly toward the doors, so she eventually turns and runs after the others. I hear her soles click through the hall, then a loud bang as the door slams shut behind her.

Now I can turn back to my list. I sigh with the realization that the feeling I've been carrying around for weeks—in my chest, my stomach, and my whole body—has gotten stronger, not faded. I wonder if it will ever stop. I shake off the thoughts and get to work, ticking off the jobs.

First I head to the grand piano to the right of the stage and polish away each of the fingerprints left by our helpers on its glossy black surface. Then I play music quietly on my phone, which I slip into the back pocket of my jeans. As I listen to the soothing tones of Vancouver Sleep Clinic, I check that the name labels and place settings are right on every table.

"You didn't come to the pub," says a voice behind me suddenly.

I whirl around and see James standing in the doorway to Boyd Hall. He's still wearing his training jersey and has his hands deep in the pockets of his joggers. I can't read his expression.

"I've still got a few things to do," I reply, waving my clipboard.

James walks in and my heart skips a beat, even though he's still several feet away from me. "Can I help?"

Automatically, I shake my head. "No, there's no need. Thanks though." Then I turn back to the table beside me, even though I'm pretty sure I've already checked that one.

"You don't have to do everything yourself." His voice sounds a little closer than before. "I'm already feeling bad because the décor company let you down."

"It's not your fault," I mumble.

I don't know if I can be alone in a room with him. With James standing in front of me, glowering at me, even the massive Boyd Hall feels tiny. Like the fifteen feet between us are only a fraction of an inch. My whole body feels drawn to him, and there's nothing I can do about it.

I know that even now, after all these weeks and everything that's happened, I'll feel so much better if I just turn and walk toward him, but I fight the impulse down. I take a deep breath and stare at my clipboard. If James has got it into his head to help me, it won't be easy to shake him off. He's proved that much in the last few weeks.

"The projector needs checking. There's no picture on the right-hand screen," I say after a while, risking a glance in his direction.

He's still looking at me with that expression that I can't interpret. In the end, he nods. "OK."

He walks to the desk in the middle of the hall and I follow at a slight distance. God, why am I so uptight? Things shouldn't be like this between us. But I don't know myself exactly how things *should* be instead.

What we had is over.

Over. Over. Over.

I just have to convince my heart of that. And my body.

James walks behind the mixing desk and studies the various plugs and switches. He focuses his attention on each wire in turn, following it up with his hand to see where it goes. Then he checks the back of the projector on the right. He pulls a cable out and plugs it back in again, switches it on and off, and furrows his brow when nothing happens.

Then he looks back at me.

"Ruby, I have to tell you something," he murmurs.

My heart leaps again. "What's that?" I ask, barely audibly.

James picks up the cable and wiggles it. "This wire is dead."

I blink several times and look at the wire in his hand. And, yes, I can see where it's broken. There's a place where the colored wires are peeking through the plastic coating. "Oh."

James lowers it slowly. "That almost sounds like you expected it to be something else."

That tone of voice. So deep and velvety and pleasantly calm. I

get goose bumps, but shake my head. But before I can say anything, James continues. "Because if you're finally ready to hear
what I have to say, I can get it off my chest at last."

I hold my breath. I can only stare at James—at this moment,
I'm incapable of anything more.

"I'm sorry," he blurts.

"James . . ." I whisper.

"There's so much that I want to tell you," he replies just as
quietly, closing the gap between us slightly. I don't think he's even
really aware he's doing it; his body moves toward mine as if drawn
by a magnet.

Me too, I want to say. James is filling all my senses, just by
standing there and looking at me like that. My knees suddenly
feel very weak; the ground is melting beneath my feet.

There's so much that I want to say to him too, so many words,
but I can't utter a single one while he's looking at me like that. My
throat is dry and I have to cough. "We're here for the gala. For
the events committee. Not to chat."

"But I *have* to talk to you. God, Ruby, I can't go on like this
another second." His words are passionate but his voice is still
endlessly soft. Like he's afraid that any increase in volume would
scare me away.

I can see his thoughts whirling behind his blue-green eyes.
Soon he'll form them into words. I can feel it—the air between
us crackles with electricity.

"Please, Ruby. You don't have to say anything. Just listen to
me, please," he begs.

I can't move. I just stand there, shoulders stiff and hands
shaking, as he comes another fraction closer. Now I have to put
my head back to look up at him.

His moody eyes roam over my face and it feels like his fingers are stroking my skin. His skin on my skin, his fingertips running over my cheek, my nose, and my mouth. My body remembers the touch of him perfectly.

"I'm sorry," he whispers.

"For what, exactly?" I reply hoarsely after a couple of seconds.

On New Year's Eve, I resolved to close the chapter entitled "James Beaufort," but now . . . now it feels like we're on the point of breaking everything open again.

"*Everything.*" The answer is instant. "Absolutely everything."

My breath quickens. How does James manage it? Make me feel lost and found at the same time? His words are turning my world upside down. I should be focused on the gala. Not on these emotions. Not on the fact that I feel as though I've been transported into a fairy tale with the hall so beautifully deco-rated, standing face-to-face with the boy who means so much to me.

"I'm sorry," James repeats. His eyes are remorseful and full of pain, but it's the first time since everything happened that his expression is fully open. At this moment, James is holding noth-ing back—I can see hope and affection in his eyes, and something that makes me gasp sharply.

This is my James.

My James.

Whatever happens between us, he will always be a part of me, and I will of him.

The thought shakes me and tugs at my firmly closed-up heart.

"I acted like an idiot," he whispers, lifting his hand to my face.

All the words that are on the tip of my tongue vanish as I feel the warmth of his hand on my cheek. The moment is so over-whelming that I have to shut my eyes.

"When my father told me about Mum's death, it felt like the world came crashing down on top of me, burying me alive. I couldn't think straight, and I destroyed what we had, and I'm *so sorry*."

Something bursts deep inside me—a wave of emotions breaks over me, emotions I thought I'd gotten over long ago.

Slowly, I open my eyes again.

"You hurt me so badly," I whisper.

James looks at me in despair. "I so regret that; I hate having hurt you, Ruby. I wish I could make it unhappen."

I shake my head. "I don't know if I can ever forget it."

"You don't have to. And I won't either. What I did that eve-ning was the biggest mistake of my life." He takes a shuddering breath. "I understand if you can't forgive me. But you have to know that I'm sorry, from the bottom of my heart." He presses his lips together and glances down for a moment. Then he blinks several times. I can see him fighting against tears. My eyes have started stinging too, at his words.

James takes a moment to catch himself. "I know it's not your job to make me happy, Ruby. I didn't mean it like that. I don't see you as some miracle cure for my sorrows. That just came out to-tally the wrong way." He runs his hand over his face. "You don't have to forgive me. And we don't have to get back together. I just want you to know how much you mean to me. I don't want to live any life that you're not part of. Whatever that means."

James's chest rises and falls rapidly; his eyes are glassy. "The person you got to know in Oxford . . . *that's* the real me. And I'd like to have more days with you where I can prove that."

Our night in Oxford was the most beautiful of my life, but I haven't allowed myself to truly think about it since then, because I was afraid that doing so would break me. But now I let myself remember. I remember our conversations. The way he told me about his fears and his dreams. The way we held each other.

Seeing James like this reminds me of Oxford. At this moment, he is back to being the man he showed me for the first time there. The man I fell in love with.

I take a cautious step toward him and put my arms around his waist.

James stiffens as if that was the last thing he'd been expecting. I'm very still as he carefully puts his shaking arms around me, as if he'd forgotten how to hold me right. I shut my eyes as he gently runs his hands over my back and whispers another apology.

After a while, I let my hands drop to his hips and grab his shirt in my fists. The fabric crinkles under my fingers as James moves his lips to my temple. "I'm so sorry," he murmurs again.

"I know," I whisper.

We stand there like that, beneath the chandeliers in the center of Boyd Hall, right next to the sound desk. James is holding me gently so that I could shake off his arms at any moment, if I wanted to. But it doesn't come to that, because it's an eternity since anything felt this right—as though I've finally come home after a long journey.

James's hands are gentle on my back, his breath is tickling my hair, and his ribs rise and fall in unison with mine, while the words he's whispering are giving me the feeling that there might be hope for us after all.

19

Ember

Maxton Hall is just insane.

Obviously when Ruby applied for the scholarship here, I looked at photos of the school on the internet, but seeing the buildings for myself, with their towers, imposing façades, and arched windows, is something else.

I'm halfway across the parking lot before Ruby's even got out of the car. It's hard to keep the hem of my long dress out of the mud. It rained last night and there are puddles everywhere. We took the pictures for my blog post last night, but I still don't want to arrive at my first Maxton Hall party in a mucky dress.

"Hang on, Ember," I hear Ruby shout as I approach the huge, intricate wrought iron gates, topped with the school's initials, that lead into the front courtyard.

It's a breathtaking sight.

I pull out my phone, switch it to the front camera, and hold it up. I try to get as much of myself, the gate, and the school in the background into the photo as possible, but it's not as good as I was hoping.

"Can you take another picture of me?" I ask Ruby as she catches up with me. Without waiting for an answer, I slip off my jacket and hold it out to her, along with my phone. "It would be perfect if you could get the school in the background too. It looks dreamy, lit up like that."

"One photo," Ruby says, getting herself into position. "Then we're going in."

I nod. "Yes, ma'am."

Ruby counts to three and I beam into the camera.

After that, she hands me my jacket back, waits till I've put it on again, and then passes me the phone.

"You look so lovely," says my sister.

"And so do you," I reply as a matter of course. Then I lift the phone, switch back to the front camera, and pull Ruby in close to my side. "Say *cheese*!"

The two of us grin into the camera. Once I've pressed the shutter button at least ten times, Ruby pulls away from me and I hurriedly glance through the photos.

The ones of me outside the school make me smile.

Just three years ago, it was absolute hell finding clothes that even fit, let alone looked good. Plus-size things are often weirdly cut—I might be fat, but I have a waist, and most designers seem to think that everyone who's overweight will have the same body shape. Which is obviously not true. And that makes me all the happier about the progress I'm making with my blog. Because it's given me the chance to wear a dress like this, on an evening like this, and feel more glamorous than ever in my life before.

If I had to express my feelings in letters, it might look something like: KDJGDHUSGUAOHBS!

Which makes me realize that I may have been spending a bit too much time on my laptop.

"Ember? Are you coming?"

I hurry over to Ruby as she squints at the clock on her phone. We've got plenty of time, we must be ages early, but my sister is really antsy. She's always like this before the events she organizes for Maxton Hall. I can't help wondering where she gets the energy to plan these parties. I'm busy enough keeping up with schoolwork and my blog, and I don't have A levels this year, with the pressure of getting the grades for Oxford on top of that. Sometimes it feels like she's a machine—a machine with occasional deep, dark circles under her eyes. Mum keeps asking if this isn't all a bit too much, but Ruby insists that she's enjoying all the work. And I believe her.

"It'll be fine," I say, but I don't think my voice is as soothing as I hoped. I'm too distracted and jittery myself for that.

"Thanks." Ruby gives me a worried sideways glance. "You'll stick to our deal, right?"

"I'll stay by your side and not speak to anyone unless you say they're OK," I parrot back to her.

Ruby nods with satisfaction.

I roll my eyes. Ruby's in a panic that I'll make friends with people she doesn't approve of. But that's what I'm looking forward to the most. The kids at this school have politicians, actors, aristocrats, bankers, and all that as parents, and it's the ideal opportunity to make connections. I'm good at small talk and making friends, provided people are prepared to see *me* and not stick me in some stupid pigeonhole because of my weight.

As we walk into Boyd Hall, Ruby links arms with me.

"Whoa!" I breathe, looking around.

The entrance to the hall is one of the fanciest places I've ever been. Hard to believe it's just a school. At my school, events are held in the sports hall, but the floor here is marble rather than puke-green lino. The walls must be fifteen feet high, adorned with white stucco and golden accents. In the center, a wide staircase with curving wooden banisters leads up to a gallery.

I can't take it all in. Everywhere I look, there are expensive suits and haute couture dresses in chiffon, silk, and tulle, and my heart is beating faster with every second. And this is just the lobby.

We hand our jackets in at the cloakroom, then I pull Ruby into the actual hall, which takes my breath away altogether.

Boyd Hall looks like something out of a fairy tale. On the way here, Ruby told me about all their work yesterday, and everything they had to build and decorate, but I never imagined that it would look this dreamy.

There are waiters holding trays with flutes of champagne or orange juice flitting between the tables, and there's a pianist in a tailcoat at the grand piano by the stage, playing something classical that fills the entire room.

"I can't believe you organized all this," I whisper, digging my elbow gently into Ruby's ribs. She narrows her eyes and studies the round tables in the center of the hall, where some of the guests have already taken their seats, then scans the long tables to our left, where the buffet is presumably going to be served later on. I know that look—Ruby is checking whether everything looks the way she had in mind.

"Ruby!" exclaims a voice I definitely don't know.

I turn my head and see a pale boy with chin-length dark hair and attractive onyx eyes framed by thick lashes. He has a striking jaw and high cheekbones that don't really fit the boyish grin and cheerful look in his eyes.

"Kieran, hi," Ruby replies, adopting a smile that I've never seen on her before. It's polite, professional, but kind of reserved. Whatever it is, it isn't my sister's smile.

"The caterers arrived ten minutes ago and they're setting up next door," Kieran says before he sees me. "Hi. I'm Kieran. You must be Ember." He holds out his hand and I take it on autopilot. I glance at Ruby in confusion. I'd assumed that nobody here at this school would know about me or our family, seeing that Ruby's always made such a massive mystery of Maxton Hall at home. I thought she was really strict about keeping her school and home lives apart on both sides. So it's a bit surprising that this boy knows my name.

"Nice to meet you, Kieran," I say.

When Kieran lets go of my hand, he smiles at Ruby and his cheeks flush unmistakably.

Aha.

Clearly Ruby has more than one admirer at this school. I'm not surprised that she hasn't mentioned it to me. Ruby practically never speaks about her feelings. I sometimes wonder how she can exist like that without exploding. I could never bottle up my emotions—either positive or negative—the way she does. If I don't like a thing, I say so. Loudly. When I'm happy, you can tell. Ruby is way more controlled than me, and much less impulsive.

I'm so lost in thought that I don't even notice Ruby and Kieran walking over to the stage. I hurry after them, but all they do is spend ten minutes talking about everything they have to remember this evening. I sneak a glance around, but Ruby keeps darting looks at me like she's afraid I'll take the first opportunity

I get to throw myself into the arms of some random Maxton boy. I wonder how long it'll take for her to relax a bit, or else to be too busy to watch my every step like a hawk.

When the gala finally officially begins, I'm sitting at a half-empty table right at the back, so that I can hardly see what's happening on the stage. These are the events team's seats, Kieran explains a little later, and there are indeed a handful of people who turn up at irregular intervals, sit down for a bit and have a drink, and then leap up three minutes later and vanish again.

Right now, there's a young man talking about depression and how it was only thanks to the Family Center that he got through it. It's a very moving speech and everyone is under his spell. I can see a few people dabbing their eyes with fine handkerchiefs, while others nod, frowning deeply. Beside me, Kieran too seems absorbed.

"Hey," I whisper. "I'm going to get a drink. Want anything?"

"I'll come with you," Kieran says, instantly moving to get up.

"Don't worry." I wave him to sit back down. "I'll be fine. Do you want anything though?"

Kieran hesitates a moment, his eyes darting from me to the speaker and back, then he shakes his head. "No, thanks."

I nod and walk to the bar, where one of the waiters smiles politely and asks me what I'd like to drink.

"Champagne, please," I say, as if it's no big deal, but either he can see that I'm only sixteen—nearly seventeen!—or they've been told not to serve alcohol to anyone school-age. Either way, he slowly shakes his head.

I sigh. Looks like I have no choice but to try the kiddies' punch on the buffet table next to the bar. I pick up one of the pretty crystal glasses, hold it up to the light, and watch the kaleidoscope-like spots of light dancing around the room in soft colors.

As I start to ladle punch from the big bowl into my glass, thunderous applause rings out around the room. Seems like the speech is over.

I take a few steps to one side so as not to block the way for anyone else heading for the table.

"Hey, beautiful," says a voice close beside me.

I freeze. Then I grit my teeth.

This isn't the first time I've been spoken to like that. There are a few boys in my year who laid bets on who could chat me up the fastest—just as a joke, obviously.

I immediately shut down and turn, glass in hand.

There's a young man standing there. He has a handsome, attractive face; full lips, and eyes so dark they almost look black; and such curling lashes that I could be quite jealous. He's a little taller than me, his hair is short and wavy, and there's a hint of stubble on his face. Like most men here, he's wearing a tailor-made suit but looks way less neat and tidy than everyone else. His tie is a bit loose, and his black jacket is unbuttoned. I get the impression that he's gone to a lot of effort to look this messy. Like he's been to too many of these things and is bored of them now.

He's probably only speaking to me because he's bored.

I look around as discreetly as possible. Usually in these situations, there's a group of lads standing a few feet away, enjoying a laugh at my expense. But nobody seems to be watching, which makes me even more suspicious.

"Hello," I reply, my voice hard and dismissive, the mirror image of my emotions.

The guy looks me over from head to toe, his eyes resting a little too long on the low neckline of my dress.

"I've never seen you here before," he continues, looking me in the eyes again. And as his mouth slowly curls into a smile, something clicks into place.

I know this boy.

OK, I don't *know*-him-know-him, but I follow him on Instagram. His handle is @kingfitz, but I know that his real name is Wren Fitzgerald. His feed is full of luxury, parties, and girls, and his stories are full of selfies and videos where he's half naked and apparently half asleep. But I don't buy it. Nobody could look that good if they'd only just woken up.

"Probably because I don't go to Maxton Hall," I reply, sipping from the glass. My mouth feels dry and my heart is beating kind of fast. Why the hell do I care that this lad is flirting with me?

"I thought as much," Wren murmurs, a hint of a smile at the corners of his mouth. It's relaxed, almost like he's too lazy to go to the effort of a proper smile. Like he'd rather not waste the energy he's saving for something else, something dirtier. The idea makes me flush hotly.

"I'm Wren," he says after a while, holding out his hand.

I hesitate a moment and look around again—his mates have to be here somewhere. I don't believe this isn't some joke. I mean, OK, I'm not lacking in self-esteem. It doesn't seem totally impossible that a guy would talk to me at a party. But not a guy like him.

"Where are they?" I ask.

He blinks in confusion, lowering his hand. "Where are who?"

"The friends who dared you to hit on me."

"Why do you think anyone would have to dare me to talk to you?"

I raise an ironic eyebrow. "Oh, come on."

We look at each other and both frown. The pianist is playing again, but I can't really hear the tune. I'm too busy finding out what Wren is up to here.

"Believe me, I'm perfectly capable of speaking to a pretty girl of my own free will," he says in the end.

I open my mouth and shut it again. Then I take a closer look at Wren. His lips aren't twitching like the boys who've come on to me at my school, and there's no funny glimmer in his eyes.

Maybe he genuinely wants to flirt. Not for some dare, or some stupid joke, but just because he finds me as attractive as I do him.

I'm pretty sure he's the last person I ought to be speaking to this evening. I don't know what to make of this, and I can't get a handle on him—but that's exactly why I'm curious.

"I'm Ember," I say belatedly.

"Nice to meet you, Ember."

I like the way he says my name. Kind of uncertainly, like he needs to practice it a bit.

"Likewise, Wren."

I am actually good at small talk. But at this moment, I have absolutely no idea what to say. I know Wren's online image, just as I know the way *I* appear to my followers—always cheerful, optimistic, and up for fun. But there are so many evenings where I'm feeling down and cry in secret in my room. Nobody knows about that, not even my sister. So I'm hesitant to judge people by the way they present themselves on socials. And I'm curious about what Wren is really like—whether there's anything more behind the façade.

Maybe I should pull myself together and push my prejudices down a bit. At any rate, there's no harm in having a conversation with him.

"What school are you at, then?" Wren asks, nabbing a glass of orange juice from a tray as a waiter pushes past us. "Eastview?"

I shake my head. "Gormsey High."

For an instant, Wren seems to freeze. He stops in mid-sip and looks wide-eyed at me, then he blinks and the moment is over. "Sounds exotic."

I wonder if I was only imagining his weird reaction. "It's in the middle of nowhere," I say slowly. "Not surprising if you've never heard of it."

"So are you somebody's plus-one?" he asks, looking at me with interest.

"I'm here with my sister. She switched to Maxton Hall a couple of years ago."

"Well, that's lucky for me, isn't it?" says Wren.

At first I'm not sure what he means. "Why's that?"

Now he's smiling properly—showing his teeth and the little lines around his mouth. "Well, if your sister wasn't at this school, we'd never have met. And that really would be a shame. Don't you think?"

He whispers those last words, sounding so intimate that it gives me goose bumps. I can only nod, as if he'd hypnotized me, even though every single alarm bell is going off in my head, warning me to be careful.

"Why are you looking at me like that, Ember?" he asks quietly, the smile slowly ebbing away and making way for something else. He takes a step toward me until we're almost touching. I'd only have to stretch my hand out a little way to take hold of his. I'm wondering how that would feel. Whether his skin is warm.

I clear my throat. "I . . ."

Wren comes closer still. So close that I can feel his breath on my temple. Again, I feel the urge to look around, but I ignore it.

"Maybe we should find somewhere a little quieter so we can get to kn—"

"Wren." A deep voice interrupts him, and I'm snapped out of my trance. I instantly take a step back and turn my head.

It's James Beaufort.

The James who broke my big sister's heart.

The James who kissed another girl, as a result of which, Ruby spent Christmas acting like a lovesick zombie.

A wave of fury washes over me as he speaks again.

"I see you've met Ruby's sister," he says, his voice free of any intonation.

A funny look crosses Wren's eyes. "Ruby's sister, huh?"

I nod slowly and look in confusion from one to the other.

"Evidently I have good taste," he continues, his voice almost mocking and totally different from his tender tone just now. "If you still want to—"

"I don't think Ember does want to. Whatever it was. Fuck off, Wren," James says, cutting him off again. There's an authority in his voice that won't be contradicted. I ask myself if he always speaks to his friends like that, and if so, why the hell he still has so many of them.

The smile is wiped off Wren's face and he's looking pretty pissed off. He shakes his head and mutters something extremely rude. Then he looks at me again. "I wish we'd been able to continue our conversation, Ember."

The next moment, he bends down and presses his lips to my cheek. As he pulls away, he's looking at James, not me.

Before I can say a word, he turns and disappears into the crowd. I lift my hand to where he kissed my cheek while James glares after Wren. Why do I get the feeling that Wren only kissed me to annoy James?

"Sorry about that, Ember," James murmurs.

Then he runs after Wren and I'm left on my own at the bar.

James

I find Wren out in the lobby with the lads. As I join their little circle, Cyril lifts his hand.

"Beaufort! To what do we owe this honor?"

I ignore him and give Wren a dirty look.

"What were you playing at?" I snap at him.

He doesn't answer, just takes a long swig from a flask.

"Wren."

He rolls his eyes. "We were just talking. Stop making such a big deal of it."

"She's Ruby's sister, for God's sake. Keep your hands off her."

Wren snorts. "I've had it up to here with constantly making allowances for you."

I raise a mocking eyebrow. "Allowances? What the fuck are you talking about?"

"You know what, Beaufort? Fuck you," he retorts, draining the flask in one and wiping his mouth with the back of his hand.

"Wren," says Kesh warningly.

"No, Kesh. I've had enough of sparing James's feelings." Wren turns back to me. "All the stuff you said back in the summer was just talk. You're skipping training because you're on the fucking events committee, you walk out of parties to go and see your girl-friend, and now you're coming over all prissy because I want to chat someone up. I get the feeling you don't give a shit about us anymore. You don't even listen when anyone tries to tell you any-thing."

"That's *bullshit*," I reply.

He shakes his head. "You know what? You deal with your own shit. That's all you're fit for at the moment anyway."

I look at him in confusion. "I have no idea what you're on about."

Wren walks away, takes two steps, then turns on his heel and jabs his finger at me. "That's exactly what I mean," he hisses. "I've been trying for ages to have a normal conversation with you, but you're just not interested."

"Leave it out, Wren."

Deep down, I know he's right. The last time we were out to-gether, he hinted at something that I just blanked on because I was too busy thinking about Ruby. Now I'm starting to get a guilty conscience.

"Leave what out? I'm right and you know it. There's no room in your head for anything but Ruby. She's all there is left in your life," he shouts.

"I . . ." My voice trails away. But anger flares in my chest. "There's a lot going on right now, but that's nothing to do with her." I wish there was any other way of getting that through to him.

"You've only been like this since you met Ruby, so don't go trying to protect her. It makes me sick. I don't even know you anymore."

"Hey, Wren, cool it," says Kesh, but Wren pushes him out of the way and takes a furious step toward me.

"You act like Ruby can fix everything in your oh-so-shitty life. Like she's some kind of a saint. But she's not," he hisses.

I stare at him with a frown. "I get that you're angry. I've been a shit friend and I'm sorry—but leave Ruby out of it. You don't know her."

Wren shakes his head scornfully. "I know Ruby very well indeed. If you'd listened to me for more than two seconds any time in the last few weeks, I could have told you *how* well I know her."

I open my mouth, but the words stick in my throat.

I know that tone of voice. And I know what it means.

Wren seems to clock that he's said too much too. He grits his teeth so hard that his jawbone juts out.

"What are you saying?"

"This might not be the right place for this conversation," suggests Alistair, but I shake my head.

"What did you mean just now?" I insist.

Wren hesitates, but my glare isn't letting him off the hook. After a second or two, he clears his throat. "Ruby and I had a little something going on at a Back-to-School party once upon a time."

My heart starts to pound; my throat is constricted.

"Well, there's a surprise," says Cyril, sounding almost pleased. "Ruby's spent all this time keeping the fact that she got off with your best friend a secret."

"Shut it, Cy," I growl.

"Looks like she's not the sweet girl next door after all," he continues, unfazed. "So maybe now you'll finally stop putting her on such a fucking pedestal."

"Say another word, Cy, and I swear to God . . ."

"He's right," Wren interrupts. "If you mattered to her as much as she does to you, she'd have told you about it months ago."

I spin around and grab him by his collar. He doesn't struggle or fight back, just looks at me with his dark eyes.

"You know it's true. Or else you wouldn't be losing your shit like this."

His words echo in my head; my breathing is ragged. Wren's suit jacket is about to tear, I'm gripping it so hard.

I really have been thinking about nothing but Ruby. I've spent the whole time trying to win her back and neglecting everything else around me. Not just Lydia, but all my friends. And what for?

And what the fuck for?

"What are you lot doing out here?" I hear a voice whisper fiercely behind us.

Ruby.

I turn toward her and feel a painful stab in the chest. I'm out of my depth here. I'm only dimly aware that there are a few guests behind Ruby, looking on in concern.

She comes right over to us. "What are you doing here?" she whispers again, looking from me to Wren and back again.

"James just learned about our little secret, Ruby."

All the color drains from Ruby's face.

For a moment, I long to punch Wren's lights out. But then I remember my dad's clenched fist. I snatch my hands away from Wren. I can't stay in this hall a second longer.

"James . . ." Ruby whispers.

I just shake my head and leave.

Ember

I'm kind of disappointed.

Ruby always made such a mystery out of these parties that God knows what I was expecting—but it was definitely not that I'd spend most of the evening standing around on my own, bored to tears. While Ruby dashes around the room, from one corner to the other, to discuss whatever with whoever, I've managed to get into a conversation with exactly two people. One was the daughter of someone who owns a chain of cafés. I loved her dress so much that I had to ask her who the designer was, and if I could take a photo of her. The other was the head girl of Maxton Hall, who made such a great opening speech that I wanted to congratulate her on it. Not that she seemed remotely interested in my opinion, seeing as she spent the whole time glancing at the people standing around us, like she was looking for someone more important to talk to.

Kieran hardly leaves my side all evening. Ruby must have ordered him to take care of me, I'm one hundred percent certain of that. He's kind, but after a while we've run out of things to say to each other and just sit staring in silence at the stage or into our glasses. I feel a bit sorry for him. He must have better things to do than to babysit his team leader's little sister.

While the last speaker gives a passionate call for more love and understanding in the world, I sneakily glance around for Wren, yet again. He's the only person out of everyone here who's genuinely caught my interest this evening. Something about him fascinated me, and I'd love the chance to spend longer chatting with him and learning more about him.

The round of applause snaps me out of my thoughts. The speaker thanks her audience and finally leaves the stage. Ruby is waiting for her at the foot of the few steps. I catch my breath at the sight of her face—something has changed. The smile doesn't reach her eyes and looks fake to me. Now that I think about it, this is the first time I've seen her in hours. Has something happened? It can't have anything to do with the gala, because everything is running like clockwork. I'm wondering whether to go over to her when she and the speaker vanish off into a side room together.

I sigh.

And at that moment, I see Wren.

He's leaning against the wall by the main doors. And he's smiling over at me. For a moment I'm tempted to look around, to make sure that he really is looking at me, but . . . no, he is staring straight at me. Like he was before.

I think about it for all of two seconds. Then I mumble "excuse me" to Kieran and, taking no notice of his protestations, walk over to Wren—who doesn't take his eyes off me the whole time that I'm slowly approaching him, and it suddenly seems a much longer walk than it really is.

"You're back," I say, once I've come to a standstill a little way away from him.

He nods and smiles. "We hadn't finished what we started, had we?"

I don't know if that's intended to sound like a double entendre. Did I do the wrong thing in coming over to him? Because while he is undoubtedly flirting, all I want to do is talk—nothing more.

"No, we hadn't," I answer all the same. The attentiveness and interest in Wren's eyes make a welcome change from the indifferent expression on every other face here. Maybe this evening won't be a total waste of time after all.

Be careful, though, a voice whispers in the back of my mind.

The next moment, Wren reaches for my hand. I look in surprise at our interlaced fingers and then up at his face. He raises an eyebrow while giving my hand a squeeze, like this is the most natural thing in the world. I'm finding it really hard to know what to make of him.

Wren nods toward the exit.

I think for a moment, and glance over my shoulder. Ruby still hasn't reappeared, and Kieran's vanished too now.

Wren squeezes my hand gently again. I don't think I've ever seen such an interesting boy. His Insta account doesn't do him justice, in my opinion. His photos look deliberate—deliberately cheerful, deliberately cool—but in real life, his personality is much more likable. And kind of mysterious. I really want to know what was going on earlier. Why he's faking a relaxed smile while his eyes are troubled.

In the end, I nod, and we walk out into the lobby of Boyd Hall. A woman in a drop-dead gorgeous burgundy dress walks past us, and I turn to watch her. The sight of the low-cut back with its delicate lace trim makes me sigh.

Wren gives me a sideways glance.

"I'm into fashion. And all the dresses people are wearing here . . . I wish I could find patterns for all of them, to sew them myself."

I look at Wren, trying to decide if he thinks that's weird, but his eyes are sparkling. He points to the curved staircase that leads upstairs. "I've got an idea."

I follow him, careful not to tread on the hem of my dress as we walk up the wide steps. When we get to the top, Wren heads off to the left and leads me down a long dark corridor.

Corridors in my school are grubby, and the white paint on the walls is yellowish with age. The dark green paint on the lockers peels more with every year, and people have graffitied pictures on the walls. This landing couldn't be more different. There are expensive-looking paintings in heavy frames alongside photos of famous old Maxtonians. There are glass display cases featuring artworks on loan to the school, and sculptures made by pupils here.

I'm so busy staring that I almost bump into Wren when he comes to a sudden stop. He looks around for a moment and then sits down on a wooden bench. He pats the empty space beside him and I take a seat too.

"Look," he says, nodding toward the banister right in front of us.

Curiously, I peek between the wooden posts.

A smile spreads over my face. From up here, we have the best view of the Boyd Hall lobby and can watch people without them seeing us. I doubt that anyone would even notice us if they looked up. This part of the gallery is too dark.

"You're a genius," I say with a grin.

Wren grins back. "I've never been called that before."

"Well, in that case, I hereby bestow the title upon you." I tap his shoulders as if I'm knighting him with a sword. At that moment, Wren catches my hand and holds it tight. His facial expression changes. Suddenly, his eyes are serious and there's a meaning in them. It starts a tingling feeling that spreads from my stomach.

Nobody has ever looked at me like that before. Absolutely never.

There are no boys like Wren around where I grew up. To most people at school, I'm just Ember. I've known most of them since nursery school, and none of them think I'm anything special, or desirable. I'm actually struggling to breathe here.

Wren's eyes wander from my lips to my eyes and back down again. He's still holding my hand. With his other hand, he strokes a strand of hair from my face. His thumb brushes against my temple and a shudder runs through my body.

There's chemistry between us, getting stronger by the second. I've never experienced anything like this. Every second—every breath—feels good and exciting and like we're doing something wrong all at once.

"Sorry for vanishing on you like that earlier," he says quietly. "Some people seem to think you need to be protected from me."

"Why do they think that?" I whisper back.

He doesn't take his eyes off my face. "Because they know me."

That's the only thing he says, then he comes closer and presses his lips onto mine. I squeak with surprise and Wren puts an arm around my back to pull me closer. His lips soften and open slightly. And then I taste it.

Alcohol.

I immediately push him away with both hands and budge a little over to one side. Then I shake my head.

"Wren."

He looks confused. "What?"

My heart is pounding like crazy. That might have been the shortest kiss in human history, but I can still feel his mouth against mine.

"This isn't how I imagined my first kiss," I admit quietly. My hands are shaking. I fold them in my lap and turn my face away so as not to have to see Wren's reaction to my words. I just keep looking down, through the banisters. There's a young woman walking through the doors, her dark blue dress almost like the night sky. There are little shimmering specks in the train, catching the light with her every step.

"Your first kiss, hmm?" Wren's voice is suddenly very gentle.

The man at the woman's side puts his hand on her lower back and I watch them step into the hall together. "Yes."

For a moment, he doesn't speak. Then . . . "Sorry."

The couple vanish into the crowd and I look back at Wren.

"I've had a pretty crap week. I thought we could cheer each other up a little bit."

"I'm happy to talk about it, if you like," I say. "But I'm not up for more than that. Especially not if you're drunk."

"I'm not drunk. Just a bit tipsy, maybe. So I know exactly what

I was just doing. And I'd want to do it again, without a drop of booze inside me," he says, eyebrows furrowed. "Just so you know."

"OK."

Wren nods again and sinks back into the bench. He crosses his arms over his chest and looks up at the chandelier over the lobby.

"So why was it a bad week?" I ask after a while.

He holds his breath. I can tell by the way his body tenses that he wasn't expecting the question, and that he's making his mind up whether he wants to answer it or not.

We can just about hear the school choir singing, but I only dimly take in their gentle harmonies.

After a while, Wren takes a deep breath and shuts his eyes. "My parents went bankrupt a while back."

"What happened?"

Wren gives a barely perceptible shrug. "Dad lost almost his entire fortune playing the markets."

Oh, wow. I can imagine what it must be like for someone at Maxton Hall to lose practically everything from one day to the next.

"I'm sorry."

Wren presses his lips together and stares at the railing.

"What does that mean for you?" I ask cautiously.

"We're moving. After that, I don't know. I got into Oxford, but God knows how I'll pay for it now."

"Well, you can get a student loan, and there are scholarships and stuff. My sister is applying for one. Maybe you could get a job too."

He nods absently. "Yeah, I guess."

For a moment, we listen to the choir down below, who've

switched to a cover version of a pop song. It feels almost peaceful up here—not like Wren just told me something so sad.

Suddenly, his upper body turns toward me and he looks at me again. I don't know how much effort it costs him, but from one moment to the next, his expression is no longer lost, but as curious as it was at the start of the evening.

"Your turn," he says. "Tell me something about you. So far, all I know is that you're Ruby's sister and that you're into fashion."

I smile at him, unsure what I'm prepared to tell him. "I've been running a plus-size fashion blog for about eighteen months. It's called *Bellbird*," I say, deciding to start with the most important yet most innocuous thing. As far as I'm concerned, the entire world can know about my blog. I'm proud of what I'm doing, especially since the rebrand.

The smile is back on Wren's face. "That sounds cool. How did you get into it?"

I'm surprised by his question, but in a good way. I lick my lips. "I've been fat all my life." I pause for a moment, keen to see how Wren will react to this statement, but he surprises me a second time by just looking attentively at me, waiting for me to go on. "And it's not because I eat too much, like people always think. That's just the way it is. And it's really hard to find attractive and fashionable clothes for my body shape. So eventually, I started to sew my own. And I've been sharing them on my blog ever since. And I write stuff, encouraging people to accept themselves the way they are."

Wren's smile doesn't budge an inch. If anything, it's broader now. "You sound like a superhero, Ember."

I feel the heat creep into my cheeks. But false modesty is not exactly my thing, so I say: "I *am* a superhero."

Now he laughs. It sounds raw and lovely, and I think I'm going to remember it all night long. For a moment, I regret breaking off the kiss. But deep down, I know that it was the right thing to do. I'd regret it a lot more if I hadn't, I'm sure of that.

"Well, now I know what I'm going to be doing tonight," Wren says after a while.

"What's that?"

His dark eyes start to sparkle. "I'm going to read your blog. Every single post."

Now I have to smile too. "That's quite an undertaking. I've written at least twice a week, for a year and a half."

"Ooooooh-kaaay," he drawls, stretching the syllables out. "It might take me a little bit longer, then."

Just then, the choir stops singing, and I break into a mini round of applause. A man down below seems startled, stops, and looks up. I hastily duck my head down, hoping he didn't spot us. I have no idea if we're even allowed up here.

Wren laughs softly. "Anyone would think you didn't want to be caught with me."

"If my sister finds out I've been spending time with a boy, alone in a dark corner, she'll freak out."

Every bit of amusement drains from Wren's eyes. He opens his mouth and shuts it again. Whatever he wants to say, he can't psych himself up to it. In the end, he sighs.

"Then I should probably take you back downstairs. I hope Ruby didn't notice that you snuck out."

For a moment, I'm disappointed, but I guess he's right.

Wren stands up and holds out his hand. Automatically, I put my hand in his and walk along the corridor with him and down the stairs, until we're outside the doors to the hall.

"Thank you for rescuing my evening," Wren says, and he sounds like he means it.

As he gives me one last smile, I feel a sudden urge to stop him leaving. But he's already turned away.

Something in my belly clenches with longing. I sincerely hope that that wasn't my last encounter with Wren Fitzgerald.

21

Ruby

I didn't sleep a wink.

I spent the whole night thinking about what happened at the party. About a setback like that happening right when James and I had been cautiously getting closer to each other again. I'm most frustrated by the fact that I can't tell James in my own words what happened between Wren and me that time. Before the party finished, I messaged him to say I wanted to explain, but he hasn't replied. I get that he's disappointed in me. But on the other hand, him going silent is really winding me up.

Lying in bed, I stare, lost in thought, at my acceptance from Oxford, which I printed out and pinned up on the board over my desk. As always, my stomach does a little leap for joy at the sight of it, but I'm thinking about what James told me two days ago.

The person you got to know in Oxford . . . that's the real me. And I'd like to have more days with you where I can prove that.

The thought that it might already be too late makes my throat clench. I groan with annoyance and get up and dress. I absolutely have to leave this room and take my mind off things or I'll go mad.

I creep over to Ember's room and breathe a sigh of relief as I see light under her door.

"Ember?" I whisper.

"Come in," she calls out, and I open the door.

My sister is lying on her front on her bed, smiling at her phone. As she sees me glance over curiously, she blushes and shoves it hastily under the duvet.

"What are you doing?" I ask.

"Reading the comments on my new post." Her reply is instant. If her cheeks weren't so pink, I'd believe every word of it.

"You look like I've caught you in the middle of something naughty," I say, sitting on the edge of her bed.

"I'm in my PJs, so it can't be that disreputable," she retorts, waggling her eyebrows.

I grin back at her. Then I nod toward the landing.

"Are you coming down to breakfast? I don't want to face Mum and Dad's curiosity on my own. They're going to be full of questions."

Ember sighs but slides out of bed and into her slippers. She doesn't bother to get dressed, just heads downstairs in her pajamas, with their cute print of squirrels and nuts. She's holding tight to her phone, and I see the screen light up again and again. I wonder if it's Kieran texting her. The two of them seemed to be getting on last night.

"Good morning," says Dad as he sees us come through the kitchen door and slides his reading glasses up his nose. He's reading something on the Kindle that we all share, which therefore has a really wide range of books on it. Everything from contemporary romances to thrillers, fantasy, and the classics.

"Morning," Ember and I reply, sitting down at the kitchen table with him.

"Hey," Mum calls, coming into the kitchen too. "You're up early." Her eyes narrow as she looks at me. "Did you get any sleep at all, Ruby?"

Dad and Ember turn their eyes on me curiously.

I look away and help myself to toast. "Yeah, sure."

"Well, I'm not surprised if you're knackered," Ember says suddenly. "I had no idea how much work goes into those parties, or all the stuff you have to think about. It's crazy!"

I smile thankfully at her. "You're welcome to keep on with the compliments."

Mum pushes the butter over to me, followed by Dad's apple jam. "Tell me about your evening, you two."

"It all went to plan," I say, starting to butter my toast. "Which is a relief."

Mum's used to my concise answers to anything to do with Maxton Hall, so she turns her attention to Ember. But my sister is busy texting someone, her phone under the table, so she doesn't even notice Mum speaking to her.

"What are you grinning at, Ember?" Dad asks, about a second before I got to ask her the same thing.

Caught, she glances up. "I'm not grinning at anything."

Dad raises an eyebrow and Mum repeats her request, more firmly this time. "Come on, tell me about yesterday evening."

I shrug and take a bite of my toast, looking just as expectantly as Mum and Dad at Ember.

"It was lovely," she says in the end, sounding genuinely enthusiastic. "The school is so pretty—it doesn't come across properly online. And the dresses the women were wearing! They were all so beautiful."

She sighs and pours herself a cup of tea.

"Is that it? All I'm getting?" asks Mum.

I can't help wondering why she's being so persistent. Is it because she's finally got a chance to get the details of a Maxton Hall party from someone? Or is she worried about Ember? It took us a bit of work last week to get Mum to agree that she could come with me. Or maybe there's a completely different reason.

Ember doesn't let it faze her. She leisurely butters her slice of toast, then looks up. "I met a boy. Is that what you want to hear, Mum?"

My head whirls around and I stare at her. "Was it Kieran? Please tell me that it was Kieran."

"Who on earth is Kieran?" Dad asks, putting the Kindle down. He looks from Ember to me and back again.

"A nice boy on the events committee."

Mum breathes a sigh of relief. "Thank God for that. There was me thinking I was about to have you curled up on the couch like a lovesick beetle too."

"Hey! I wasn't a lovesick beetle."

Mum and Dad glance at each other, a long look that says more than a thousand words.

"If you say so, love," Mum says after a while, but not with her usual smile. "Anyway, Ember, tell us about this boy."

"Oi!" Ember exclaims, glaring furiously at Mum and then at me. "One, it's none of your business. Two, I don't owe anyone here an explanation of anything. And three, 'met a boy' doesn't mean I've got a boyfriend now. I turned him down, as it happens, and now I'm waiting to see how he reacts. So don't go making it into some massive deal."

I stare at my sister. "Who is it, Ember?"

Ember stares back at me, eyebrows raised. "I'm not telling you."

"Ember, I . . ."

"Forget it, Ruby. Now, can we please have breakfast in peace?" She bites demonstratively into her toast.

The rest of breakfast drags by at a snail's pace. After a minute or two, Dad tries to lighten the mood, but without much success. My thoughts are whirling. I'm running through yesterday evening in my mind, wondering when Ember had the chance to spend longer than five minutes chatting with a boy who wasn't Kieran. It *must* have been him. But then she wouldn't be being this mysterious about it, would she?

After breakfast, Ember and I load the dishwasher in silence, and then go upstairs together. Before she vanishes into her room, she gives me another thin smile, which I return wearily. We never normally snap at each other like that, but I can't shake the feeling that something happened last night, something I should have done better at protecting Ember from.

I sigh and push open my bedroom door, and at that very second, my phone pings. I snatch it up from my desk and tap on the message with shaking fingers.

Can we talk?

I type my reply so fast that my phone can't keep up and all the words come out wrong, and I have to start again at the beginning.

Of course. When and where?

I count the seconds until James answers, holding my breath as my phone gives another quiet ping.

Right now, if I can come over? I can head over in a minute.

I hesitate a moment. I've never invited James into our house before. Introducing him to my parents would be a huge step.

But deep down, I can sense that I'm ready. I can be around him without crumbling now. And the fact that he wants to talk to me proves that, despite everything that happened yesterday, he feels the same way.

So I reply:

OK.

Then I go back downstairs, phone in hand. Mum and Dad are in the living room now. Dad's engrossed in his Kindle book again and Mum's going through the week's post. Cautiously, I walk over to them and clear my throat.

"Is it OK if James comes round in a bit?" I ask.

Mum pauses with the letter opener still in her hand and glances at Dad in surprise. I can still hear her words about a "lovesick beetle" in my head, and it's an effort not to look away from their concerned expressions.

"We only want the best for you, love," Dad starts slowly. "And we couldn't help noticing the bad way you were in for the whole of December."

"That wasn't my Ruby," Mum says quietly. "I really don't want you meeting up with that boy again."

I open my mouth and shut it again.

My parents have never forbidden me to do anything. Probably because there's never been much to forbid. My whole life has always revolved around my family and my academic ambitions. Something fires up inside me. I think it's a mixture of confusion and irritation that they'd say that.

"James is . . ." I can't find the words. I have no idea how to explain to my parents what happened between him and me.

Maybe there's some way I can get through to them how much he means to me. And that my heart will always cling to him. But I need time. After all, I don't know what's about to happen.

"Please just trust me," I say in the end, looking pleadingly at them.

The two of them exchange glances again.

Mum sighs. "Ruby, you're eighteen. We can't exactly ban you from seeing him. But if this boy is coming here, we'd like the chance to get to know him."

I nod. Meanwhile, I'm wondering whether Mum's done her research into James and the Beauforts online. That had never occurred to me before, but it wouldn't surprise me if that is why she's dubious—after all, I know what you can read about him on there.

"He's not a vegetarian, is he?" Dad asks suddenly, looking inquiringly up at me.

I have to think about that. "I don't think so."

"Good. I was planning to do spaghetti Bolognese later. James is invited." That's all Dad says. Then he turns back to his book.

"That's a great idea," Mum agrees, smiling broadly at me. She's really trying not to look so anxious, but there's still a skeptical glint in her eye. She gives Dad a fleeting pat on the arm, then grabs the next letter and opens it.

It seems like the conversation is over, so I creep backward out of the living room. Then I head into the kitchen, where you can watch the cars turning onto our street. When Ember and I were little, we always used to sit on the dresser when we were expecting family and watch out for them to arrive.

In less than ten minutes, the Rolls comes round the corner. I start running. No way can I let Dad get to the door first and glare at James with eagle eyes.

I open the door before he's even gotten out of the car. The air is still fresh and I shift my weight from one foot to the other to keep warm, but it's no use. I stop as James comes closer. He opens the little wooden gate with a practiced hand and then looks up at me. For a tiny moment, his steps slow, but then he comes through the front garden and up the steps, until he's standing in front of me, at our front door.

"Hey," he says, his voice scratchy.

I long to give him a hug, just for that pathetic little word. There was a time when him greeting everyone like that really wound me up, but these days it just sounds natural from his lips. And pretty much normal.

"Good morning," I reply, holding the door for him. I nod to him to come in.

The moment in which he clears his throat quietly and steps through the doorway into our house seems immensely significant to me. I wonder if he knows that he's the first boy I've brought home. The first to mean so much to me, and who I—even now—trust enough to introduce to my parents.

The sight of James in our little hallway is weird, but at the same time, I'm asking myself how I was ever so scared of this moment. Everything about it feels right.

James is wearing a gray coat with subtle checks over black

trousers in some soft fabric and a simple black wool jumper. His leather shoes are black too. His red-blond hair is disheveled as ever and curling slightly, like he's just had a shower. I long to touch it.

"Can I take your coat?" I ask instead.

James nods, lost in thought, as he looks around. Of course he catches sight of the cringeworthy photos of Ember and me when we were kids. There's one where we're dancing in the garden, another where we're picking apples, and another where we're in a paddling pool at my aunt's house, beaming with gap-toothed smiles. James takes them all in while slipping his coat from his shoulders in one fluid movement and then handing it to me.

I have to really force myself not to stare at him—after all the time I've spent lately forbidding myself from doing so, the temptation is even greater.

I focus on hanging his coat neatly on the hook, then I walk to the living room. James follows, but before I open the door, I whirl around and look up at him.

"Are you a vegetarian?"

James blinks several times. One corner of his mouth twitches as he slowly shakes his head. "No, I'm not."

I exhale. "Good."

As I press the handle down and walk into the room, James on my heels, my stomach is fluttering nervously.

"Mum, Dad, this is James," I say, gesturing toward him.

James takes an audible breath, then walks over to my mum, holding out his hand. "Pleased to meet you, Mrs. Bell."

"Hello, James," Mum says, smiling warmly at him. "Do call me Helen."

There's no sign of her earlier skepticism, and I wonder if she's really this good an actor, or if she's cutting him a little slack because she knows how devastated he was after his mum died and she feels sorry for him.

"No problem, Helen," says James.

Dad isn't as good at hiding his suspicion. His eyes are cool and appraising, and it looks like he's crushing James's hand as he shakes it. James doesn't flinch.

Fortunately, Mum breaks the awkward moment. "We'd like to invite you to dinner, James," she says, "so that we can all get to know each other a bit."

I shut my eyes and fight down the urge to press my fingers to the bridge of my nose. I hope James isn't already overwhelmed by my family.

"That would be lovely," he replies, without a moment's hesitation. "I don't have anything on for the rest of the day."

"Great," Dad says, with no emotion of any kind in his voice.

There's a moment of awkward silence and I grab James by the sleeve to pull him upstairs and set him free. We're on the stairs before I realize what I just did—I touched James, just like that, like it was no big deal. Like it's something we always do, because we're friends.

I hastily let go of him.

"I haven't tidied up or anything," I say as we stop outside my room.

James shakes his head. "That's OK. I turned up out of the blue, didn't I?"

I nod and open the door. I let James step in ahead of me. It's so weird to be in this room with him, this space that's so familiar and safe. I automatically feel good, but there's also this tingling uncertainty inside me—what is this conversation, this day, going to bring?

A quiet sound cuts into my thoughts.

Or rather, a hoarse laugh.

I turn to James. His laugh sounds kind of rusty, like he hasn't found anything funny for ages. As he sees my confused expression, he waves around the room, taking everything in. "What does your room look like tidy, if this is in a mess, Ruby Bell?"

A warm feeling spreads through my belly and then my whole body, making me smile.

I really like seeing James here.

Seeing him laugh makes me *happy*.

A wave of yearning washes over me. It's trying to drive me over to him, but I stay where I am and close the door quietly behind me. As it clicks gently, James's smile fades.

For a moment, we just stand there, face-to-face, looking at each other.

"I'm sorry about yesterday," I say eventually, breaking the ice.

James shakes his head slowly.

"I should have told you sooner. It—"

"Ruby," he interrupts me softly. "You don't owe me an explanation."

He's right. I know that. Even so, I wish I could turn back time and stop a situation like last night ever happening.

"Why did you run away like that?" I ask cautiously.

He gulps hard. "I was just out of my depth with the whole thing. Wren and I haven't fought like that for ages."

"I know your friendship with Wren means a lot to you," I say quietly. "I'm sorry."

James walks over to my desk and runs his finger over the spines of the books that have been stacked there all week. "You don't have to apologize. And I didn't come here to talk about Wren."

"You didn't? What, then?" I whisper. God knows where my voice has disappeared to.

He glances at me briefly, then turns his full attention back to the chaos on my desk. "Do you know why Wren got so angry?" he asks.

I shake my head and take the two steps that bring me to stand beside him. "No."

"He was angry because he feels like you're more important to me than anything else now."

James pauses for a moment before he continues. "And he's right."

He's still standing by my desk. And he's not looking at me while he's saying these important words.

"James," I whisper, to make him turn toward me.

He does as I wish, and the look in his eyes overwhelms me. I can see all the same emotions that are flooding through my body.

At this moment, such a powerful wave of affection for him washes over me that I almost have to look away. Cautiously, I raise my hand and stroke the messy strands of hair off his forehead. Then I lay my hand on his cheek. His face feels warm to my touch, and as I run my fingers softly over his skin, James wraps his hand around them.

It hasn't been that long since we were last standing like this. That time, I touched his cheek, plucked up all my courage, and confessed to James that I didn't want to lose him. Then he took my hand from his face and turned away from me.

But now the opposite happens.

James holds my hand tight and shuts his eyes. As I stroke my thumb over his skin, a tremble runs through his whole body. He opens his eyes again and I hold my breath.

"I don't want anything to come between us again, Ruby," he whispers.

I can hardly breathe with James this close to me. The weight of his words hangs in the air, and at this second, I realize that I feel exactly the same.

I don't want to be apart from him anymore.

I can't be angry or sad any longer.

I want to feel that rush again, at long last, that James and I give each other. I want to talk to him again, message him again, share my worries and fears with him.

I want to *love* him.

Even after two months, the all-encompassing longing for him hasn't faded. On the contrary, it's grown stronger, day after day. And there's nothing I can do about that.

"I feel the same," I whisper.

He makes a quiet, despairing sound, and the next moment, he pulls me to him. He wraps his arms around me tight as my eyes start to sting and tears run down my cheeks. James mumbles something into my hair. And although I don't catch the words, I know deep inside me what they mean.

James

I don't know how long we stand there like that. At some point, I find myself semi-sitting on the desk surface with Ruby leaning against me. My heart is hammering so hard in my chest that I feel sure she must be able to hear it. Her arms are tight around my waist and her face is buried in my shoulder. Her tears slowly dried up, but I can still feel the damp patches they left.

I breathe in deeply, and the familiar, sweet scent of Ruby fills my nose. I can't believe this is really happening. At this second, my life is no longer a shambles. Everything feels right. I could stand like this forever.

"I've missed you so much," I murmur after a while, my lips brushing her hairline. I would love to let them roam somewhere else—but I won't let that happen. I'm not going to kiss her. Not now, not today. That isn't why I came here.

"I missed you too," she answers, equally quietly, and my heart leaps.

I stroke Ruby's back, one big circle, and then a smaller one. The thin blouse feels so soft to the touch. And so like *her*.

"I'm sorry for what I said when I came before. I didn't mean to put anything on you." I get the feeling that I need to say that again, one more time.

"I'm sorry too. I shouldn't have been so mean."

I shake my head right away. "You weren't mean. What you said was right. I don't want to be a burden on you. That's not how a relationship works," I reply.

At the word "relationship," Ruby raises her head and pulls away from me slightly. Her watchful eyes are on me, and my next words just flood out by themselves.

"It's just that . . . When I see you, I feel like everything in my life is going right. It feels like I'm at home—really at home, I mean. I've never felt like that before, Ruby. With anyone. You gave me the feeling that I'm not alone. And that's what I missed most of all. This feeling of . . . being whole."

Ruby's breath catches.

"I don't know if that even makes sense," I add.

"It makes sense," Ruby says. "Of course it makes sense."

"I don't want you to feel that I'm pressuring you."

Ruby's gaze strokes over my face. I'm sure that my cheeks are as flush as hers. I feel warm, and I've been fighting the tears too. But Ruby isn't looking at me like she finds that cringe, or thinks I'm an idiot.

There's a warmth in her green eyes that pierces right through me. She is looking right inside me and I know that she understands everything.

That's what Ruby's like. She finds solutions to the hardest tasks. She finds meaning where there isn't any. And now she's finding something in me that moves her to fling her arms around me.

"I don't," she whispers. "Not anymore."

The next moment, she stands on tiptoe. She looks me in the eyes for a heartbeat. And then she kisses me.

I give a muffled exclamation of surprise. For a moment, I don't even know what's going on, and I grab hold of the desk with one hand as my fingers tighten their clutch on her back of their own accord.

Ruby comes closer still until there's no space left between us.

This wasn't my goal when I came here. But now she's kissing me and her hands are on my body and she's so close that I'm losing my mind . . .

"James?" Ruby leans back a little and looks uncertainly at me. It's only now that I realize I'd been too overwhelmed by the situation to kiss her back.

"I . . ."

Suddenly, Ruby's eyes widen and she puts a little distance between us. She swallows hard and shakes her head. "I'm sorry. I thought . . . I shouldn't have . . ."

"*Ruby*," I manage. Freed from the shock, I pull her back to me with both hands. Then I lean over her, shut all thoughts out of my head, and kiss the girl I love for the first time in two months.

I press a hand to the back of her neck and wrap the other around her waist to pull her close to me. Ruby sighs in my mouth.

Oh, wow.

I've missed this so much.

The way Ruby moves. Her beautiful lips. The quiet sounds she makes when our tongues touch.

I stroke the back of her neck, from her hairline down to her throat. Her skin is so warm and soft. I'd love to cover her whole body with kisses. Ruby gasps as if she's just had the same idea.

The sound awakens me from my trance. Breathing hard, I pull away from her.

Although we're closer than we've been for ages, we're not ready for more. There's still a boundary between us that neither of us can yet cross, and as Ruby buries her face in my neck and just holds me, I know that she's thinking the same thing.

I stroke her back and hold her tight—seconds, minutes, hours. It's as though, in this moment, she and I are all there are. Only the two of us in the whole world.

———

I don't know how long we've been standing here, but when we finally let each other go, it feels like it's been half a lifetime.

We look at each other and smile. Ruby smooths down her fringe and I straighten my jumper. It's clear that neither of us knows what to do next.

I clear my throat. "I should . . ."

At the same moment, Ruby says, "How's . . ." and we both start to laugh.

"You first," I say.

Ruby smiles. "I just wanted to ask how Lydia's doing. I didn't see her yesterday evening."

"She's fine. She still feels sick from time to time, so she didn't come to the gala."

Ruby frowns with concern. "But everything else is OK, isn't it?"

I nod. "Yeah, it's normal, apparently."

It's good to know that I don't have to watch my words with Ruby. She knows all our secrets; there's nothing I couldn't talk about with her. I don't know if I'll ever be able to show her how much that means to me.

Suddenly, Ruby takes my hand and pulls me to her bed. My stomach does a nervous somersault because for a moment I have no idea what this means, but then she drops cross-legged onto the bed and pats the space beside her. I feel a strange mixture of relief and disappointment as I sit down next to her.

"How are you feeling about Oxford?" she asks in the end.

The warmth inside me gives way to icy cold. I stare at Ruby in shock.

"OK, I guess that answers that," she says, smiling understandingly at me.

"You know what I feel about Oxford."

"That sounds like you're in a relationship with the university."

I raise an eyebrow. "Look who's talking. Don't think I haven't spotted the love hearts you've drawn on that email you've printed out," I say, pointing to the pinboard over her desk.

Ruby looks sheepish. Then she smiles. "Yeah, OK. Got me. But you didn't answer my question."

I think a moment. "I'm happy that you're happy. You can be pleased for both of us," I say, as diplomatically as possible.

Ruby rolls her eyes. Before I can respond, she's grabbed one of her pillows and whacked me with it. For a moment, I'm just blinking in confusion, but then I turn to Ruby. "Lydia always does that too. And now I can't defend myself against her, in case I damage anything. But you . . ." Fast as lightning, I snatch another pillow and throw it at Ruby. "It's completely different with you."

She reacts quicker than I'd have thought possible. She grabs the pillow I threw at her and pummels me with it twice. When she tries to repeat the trick a third time, I catch her wrist and hold it tight.

Ruby's cheeks are flushed, she's breathing fast, and her hair is messed up. Everything within me is crying out to lean down and kiss her again.

At once, I let her go. I clear my throat and move away a little.

"Are you accepting the offer?" Ruby asks after a while.

I nod. "Yes. I don't even need to ask, do I?"

I dare to glance at her once the heat that flooded my throat has ebbed away a little. Ruby is looking warmly at me, and while she's clearly holding back too, the glint in her eyes shows me how happy she is.

"Of course I am." She hesitates. "But I'm worried about money. I've looked into all the loans and scholarships, and I'm sure I'll get a bursary, but I can't afford it without a loan, and it's such a lot of debt to take on." It's almost painful to see the joy gradually fading from her eyes to be replaced by fear. "And I don't know if I'll have time to get a job."

"I'm sure you'll work it out," I say confidently.

"Well, I'm doing my best," she says firmly, and at that moment, I have no doubt that Ruby can do *anything* she puts her mind to.

"Mum always made sure Beaufort's supported various social projects every year. I bet there are grants in there somewhere. I can ask, if you like," I suggest cautiously. I'm not sure if this is crossing a line. I hope not.

Ruby hesitates a moment, but to my relief, she's looking thoughtful, rather than mortally offended by my idea.

"That's kind," she says in the end. "How are things at home?"

Her eyes went soft as I spoke about Mum, so I'm not surprised by her sudden change of subject.

I think for a bit. "Lydia's doing well, and Dad . . . is my dad. I don't see much of him and we've barely spoken since December. Lydia and I will never be able to forgive him for not telling us what happened to Mum."

"I never get into fights, but I think I'd have hit him too."

The idea almost makes me grin. Sadly, that impulse soon fades. "I hate the way he treats Lydia," I say seriously. "Especially now, when she's got so much to deal with all at once."

"How do you mean?" she asks, furrowing her brow.

"He always makes her feel stupid, which seriously winds me up. He hasn't really acknowledged that she got into Balliol."

The corners of Ruby's lips twitch disapprovingly. "Everything you tell me about him makes me so cross. No wonder you're glad when he's not at home."

I normally hate this kind of conversation and usually change the subject or avoid answering, but it feels perfectly ordinary to be sitting here with Ruby, on her bed, talking about my family problems.

I feel like I could get used to this.

"What are you thinking?" Ruby asks out of the blue.

I can only shake my head. There's a lump in my throat that won't disappear, no matter how often I cough.

"James?" Ruby says uncertainly.

"I'm just happy that you let me be here," I croak.

The next moment, Ruby scoots over to me a bit. She puts her hand on mine and I link fingers with her.

"I'm happy you're here too," she whispers, and warmth fills my whole body.

"I'm not going anywhere anytime soon," I declare, my eyes fixed on our hands. "So get used to it."

Ruby

James and I have about another ten minutes undisturbed before Ember knocks on the door exaggeratedly loudly, bringing in a plate of cookies Mum had sent her up with. James jumps up from the bed like he's been bitten by a tarantula. As she walks away, my sister leaves the door wide-open with a pointed look that just makes me roll my eyes. James and I were only talking, not ripping each other's clothes off.

If Mum seriously thinks that . . . well, I don't know how to take that idea.

After Ember leaves, James stands uncertainly around in the middle of the room, then points to the books on my desk. "When do you need to be done with those?" he asks.

I sigh. "I should have read most of them already. I'm way be-hind thanks to the gala."

"OK," he murmurs, holding up John Stuart Mill's *Utilitarianism*. "This one is only a hundred or so pages and I've already read bits of it. We can go through it together if you like."

I blink. "You want to do homework with me?"

"Sure," he says, pointing to the desk. "Got another chair?"

I'm so confused that for a moment I'm lost for words.

Then I nod and slide off the bed. "I'll be right back. Don't move."

I dash into Ember's room. She's sitting on the floor by her bed, back against the frame, laptop in her lap. At the sight of me, a significant grin spreads over her lips, and she pulls her headphones off her ears.

"Sooo?" she asks. Apparently, our conversation this morning is already forgotten—or else she's just too nosy to ignore me right now.

"Can I borrow your chair?" I ask.

Ember's grin widens. "Of course you can borrow my chair."

I ignore her suggestive tone and push the office chair into my room. Meanwhile, James has sat down at my desk, *Utilitarianism* open in front of him.

"Are you sure you want to go through my reading with me?" I ask as I sit down beside him.

He looks up and a slight smile lightens his face. "I want to do anything with you that you'll let me, Ruby." The moment the words leave his mouth, he grimaces. "That came out kind of wrong . . ."

James's cheeks flush pink and mine blush hot too. I look away and turn to the first page, then clear my throat. "D'you need some paper?"

Beside me, James nods twice. "Yes, please."

For the next two hours, we do indeed study *Utilitarianism* together. I find it hard to focus at first—partly because James is sitting next to me, and partly because my thoughts are all over the place—but after a while, I get to grips with the theory and start to shape my own opinion on the topic. James and I discuss each other's ideas and again I realize how bloody intelligent he is. He might not love the idea of Oxford, but when he gets there, he'll be ahead of the field.

When we're finished and I've highlighted a last keyword in my little notebook, I lean back with a sigh.

"What now?" asks James.

I frown. "What do you mean?"

"Well. Whenever I've crammed my head full like that, I have to clear it somehow before I can do anything else."

"What do you like to do?" I ask curiously. How weird that I know James's darkest secrets but almost nothing about his daily life.

"Go to the gym mostly." He shrugs. "Or watch travel videos."

When I don't reply, he looks at me, eyebrows raised. "I'm sure you have your own way of clearing your head."

I hesitate a moment. "Yeah, 'course. But it's a bit weird. You're not allowed to think I'm silly."

James's lips twitch. "I can't wait to hear it now."

"You have to promise me, James."

James nods and raises his hand in a three-finger salute. "Scout's honor."

I reach for my laptop and go into my favorites. I find my relaxation folder and click on the first video I've got saved in there.

A blond girl appears on the screen and whispers hello. The video starts with her opening a parcel and slowly stroking the paper in which various items are wrapped. I dare to dart a sideways glance at James because I know this one by heart anyway. He looks at the screen and then at me. "What the hell is this? Why's she so quiet?" His eyes flick back again. The girl in the video is scratching her long nails over a sponge. "Why's she doing that?"

"This is an ASMR video."

James's whole face is a question mark.

"It's a thing," I explain. "I really don't know how to describe it. They're videos where people speak quietly and make crinkling or rustling noises, for example."

"But why?" It's kind of sweet how confused he is. I've never seen him like this before.

"It's soothing," I explain. "My brain totally responds to it."

"So, you watch this to relax?" he asks dubiously.

I nod. "It gives me kind of goose bumps on my head. Sometimes I watch them to fall asleep too."

James grins. "I think you must have to really get into it for it to work. Right now, I'm finding it too weird to get goose bumps. It's . . . It really is kind of odd."

"There are hundreds of videos," I say, clicking on the next favorite on my list. Now there's a doctor, quietly telling a patient to raise their arm and shut their eyes.

It doesn't take long for my scalp to start tingling.

James shakes his head. "That's fascinating. In a totally messed-up way."

"Watch one tonight before you go to bed. And then tell me if it worked," I say with a knowing grin.

"It would be cool if it did. I've been sleeping so badly for weeks."

The grin falls from my face. I don't want to kill the mood, but when he says a thing like that, I can't just ignore it. I have to ask the question, however sad it is.

"Is that because of your mum?" I ask carefully.

James takes a breath. For a moment, he doesn't move a muscle, then he exhales audibly and nods. "Yes. I . . . sometimes dream about her."

"Do you want to talk about it?"

The doctor on the video is still going through his consultation, and I press the space bar to pause it.

James is quiet for a while, like he's trying to find the right words. Again, I cautiously take his hand, like earlier, before Ember interrupted us. James turns his palm up so that we can link our fingers.

"I never thought it would feel like this," he begins.

"What do you mean?" I whisper.

He gulps hard. "Without my mum."

I press his hand to encourage him to go on. And he does.

James starts to tell me about the last two months. Faltering at first, then a bit more smoothly as the words flood out. He tells me about the guilty feelings toward his mother, because he feels like he's not grieving properly. About being afraid for Lydia, the fear that's with him when he wakes up and when he goes to sleep. About the Beaufort meetings where it feels like his soul isn't part of his body and he's watching everything like an outsider. He tells me that his father won't let him or Lydia visit their aunt Ophelia. That Lydia really wants to find a private midwife, but she's scared of revealing her secret. And that he feels bad about letting his friends down recently.

We sit in my room all day, talking. Not just about James's family. About all kinds of things. School, Ember's blog, my chat with Alice Campbell last night, which I still haven't processed properly.

Just before five, Dad calls my phone. He prefers that to yelling across the house like Mum does, or sending Ember up to my room.

"Dinner's ready," I say.

Hand in hand, we walk to the door. I'm about to open it when James pulls me back again. He hugs me and holds me tight for a moment.

"Thanks," he whispers, right into my ear.

I don't have to ask for what.

James

Mr. Bell's Bolognese is amazing.

The spaghetti is al dente and the sauce is so perfectly balanced with herbs, tomatoes, garlic, and a dash of red wine that I absolutely can't help the little appreciative sound I make as it crosses my lips.

Once I've tasted my first mouthful, there are four pairs of eyes fixed on me. Ruby's whole family is staring at me. Mr. Bell's expression is making me particularly nervous. Since I got the cutlery the wrong way round when laying the table, he's had his eye on me, like he's just waiting for me to make my next mistake and prove that I'm not good enough for his daughter. And of course, I know which way round to put the knives and forks! At business dinners at home there can be a whole array of the things, a set for each course. I'm not stupid, just a bag of nerves.

I clear my throat, sit up straight, and say with utter conviction, "This is the best Bolognese I've ever tasted."

Ruby's mother smiles at me. Ember mumbles something under her breath that sounds like "creep." But at least Mr. Bell's smile is a little friendlier now. I realize that both Ruby and Ember have his eyes—not just the color, but the intensity of their gaze.

"James," says Mrs. Bell—Helen, I correct myself mentally—just as I've put another forkful of pasta in my mouth. "What are your plans for when you leave school?"

At once, I stiffen. But I see Ruby look expectantly at me, which reminds me that these people are her family and I don't have to fake it with them.

"I've got an offer from Oxford," I reply hesitantly, without the usual steel in my voice. "And I'm already on the board of Beaufort's."

"Have you always wanted to do that?" Helen persists.

OK. I might not have to fake it with them, but at the same time, I can't lay my entire inner life bare to these virtual strangers. I just can't. So I chew my spaghetti slowly and pretend that I'm thinking my answer over.

"Ruby knew that she wanted to go to Oxford so young. Sometimes I wonder if everyone at Maxton Hall is as ambitious as her," she adds, smiling at her daughter, who is sitting to my right, squirming uneasily in her chair.

I swallow and take a sip of water. "No, not everyone is like Ruby, I can assure you of that."

"What's that meant to mean?" Ruby inquires, outraged.

"I don't know anyone else who's as desperate to go to Oxford as you. My friends and I have put the work in, but I'm sure nobody else is as dedicated as you." I wonder for a moment if that sounds like I'm trying to suck up to her family by praising Ruby in front of everyone. "But maybe I'm biased."

That makes them all laugh. Like they found that genuinely

funny. I frown. I meant every word I said. I didn't expect them to be amused by it. I feel an unfamiliar emotion in my chest, and take another forkful of pasta to suppress it.

After dinner, I help to clear the table. I'd never do that at home—that's why we have staff—but here, everyone gets to work so automatically that I don't hesitate a second.

Besides, I really do want Ruby's parents to like me.

I totally understand them being dubious about me. I would too in their shoes.

"Will you two join us in the living room for a bit?" Helen asks once it's done. "Or do you have to get home, James?"

I shake my head. "No, I don't have to get home."

"If they ask you questions you don't want to answer, you don't have to say anything," Ruby whispers in my ear as we follow her mother out of the kitchen at a little distance. "I'm sorry it got so awkward earlier."

"That's OK," I reply, equally quietly. "Don't worry about it. I like your parents. And Ember too."

A smile spreads over Ruby's lips. I'd like to take her hand, or touch some other part of her, but we're walking into the sitting room, where the rest of her family have already settled down comfortably.

I notice how spacious this room feels and how minimalistic the furniture is. Unlike Ruby's room, which is full to bursting, there's a lot of free space here. As Mr. Bell maneuvers his wheelchair to stand next to the sofa, I figure out why. Then he picks up a remote control and suddenly the sofa rises up, until it's level with the seat of his chair. Mr. Bell slips from one to the other. When he first catches me watching him, I want to look hastily away, but I resist the impulse. I don't want him to think I have a problem with something that's so everyday to him. So I hold his gaze and point to the sofa, which is now sinking back down again.

"I've never seen anything like that," I say honestly. "Is the mechanism built into the sofa, or . . . ?"

Mr. Bell nods. If he's surprised by my question, he doesn't show it. "Yes, or more precisely, underneath it."

Ember drops down next to her dad. She leans against his shoulder for a moment, and the look of love that spreads over his face softens all his features. So that's what it looks like when a father doesn't just see his child as a business partner he can manipulate for his own ends.

"Sit down," says Helen. I turn uncertainly to Ruby, who takes the decision out of my hands by pointing to the armchair opposite the sofa. She herself sits next to Ember.

"Shall we play Jenga? You know how to play, right, James?" Ember asks suddenly, and her mum puts a game made up of wooden blocks in the middle of the coffee table. I shake my head, looking embarrassed. "No, actually, I've never played it."

Ember's mouth drops open. "OK. Wow, that's . . ." She coughs. "I don't know how to feel about that."

I shrug my shoulders. "Sorry."

"It doesn't matter," Ruby jumps in, glaring at Ember in a way that clearly tells her she'd better shut up now.

"No problem," Helen agrees. "It's easy-peasy."

Mr. Bell snorts. "You say that because you always win."

"Don't be silly." She smiles at me and points to the tower she's built with the bricks. "Everyone takes turns to pull a brick out of the tower and add it to the top. You're only allowed to use one hand, and there has to be at least one brick left in every row."

I nod. "OK."

"And the fun part is," she continues, with a look at her husband, "there are always lots of winners and only one loser."

"That's not true," Ruby says. "If you add up the last eighteen years, we're all losers because Mum never knocks the tower down."

Helen's only response is to smile to herself, and at this moment I realize that I shouldn't be deceived by her cheerful manner—she's a force to be reckoned with.

The game starts. I'm next after Helen and pull one of the little blocks out by the side. Then it's Mr. Bell's turn, followed by Ember, and then Ruby. On just my second turn, the tower collapses. I jump in shock as the wooden blocks clatter down all over the place. "Shit," I mutter.

"No offense, James, but you're terrible at this," says Ember.

"You just need a bit of practice," says Ruby, sounding more confident than I feel.

Next time around, I do better, but even so, it's me who brings the tower down. And the time after that. But as Ember and Mr. Bell seem happy, I'm fine with it. Round four goes better. I've been trying to copy Helen's technique, and using just your fingertips definitely seems to make the difference. After that, I take my time, even though I can feel everyone's eyes on me. I'm really trying to pull the brick out as slowly as possible, and this time it works.

In the end, the tower is so wobbly that Ruby shakes her head in despair as her turn comes around. Her cheeks are slightly flushed as she leans in with an air of great concentration to pull out a brick. The stack rocks from side to side as she leans back and we all wait with bated breath. As the wobbling subsides and it seems still to be standing, I breathe a sigh of relief. Ruby hears and looks at me over the tower. I'll never forget the smile on her face. Seriously, never. It fills my whole body, and for a moment, I'm so caught up in her eyes that I don't even notice Helen stretch out her hand and . . .

The tower crashes down. Ember shrieks triumphantly and jumps up, pointing her finger at her mother. "Ha!"

"James made Mum lose," cries Ruby, clapping her hands.

Even Mr. Bell is laughing quietly, looking at his wife with amusement.

"I think we're going to have to put that to the test again," Helen says, looking at me. Then she nods toward the scattered blocks. "Help me build it up again, James."

This family fascinates me. Their enthusiasm is infectious, and I'm feeling more lighthearted than I've done for ages.

"You're on, Helen," I reply, far too late, and get up to rebuild the tower. Little by little, brick by brick. Just like Ruby and me. And everything else.

23

Ruby

I've never been this nervous on a Monday morning before. The bus to school seems to take twice as long as usual, and I'm far too antsy to enjoy it like I normally do. As we finally cover the last few yards and the bus comes to a stop, I tell myself sternly to get it together.

This is a perfectly ordinary school day.

Nothing has changed.

So, heartbeat, you can calm down a little, if you please.

I'm the last person off the bus. And as I step down, I see him.

James is leaning against the fence by the field, opposite the bus stop. His smile looks almost shy, even if nothing else about his body language does. I remember that one morning over three months ago when he surprised me like this. That time, we'd been at Cyril's party, and he'd wanted to protect me from prying eyes at school and stop people asking silly questions.

This time, he doesn't wait for me to reach him, but comes over. His smile doesn't slip—far from it. Yesterday evening, I couldn't help noticing how often he smiled, for real, when we were playing games with my family. I can hardly believe that this is the same boy who cried in my arms back in December. It's good to see him like this.

"Hi," I say, smoothing down my fringe. It's windy and I'm afraid my hair must be all over the place. But James is still looking at me like I'm the best thing that's ever happened to him.

"Good morning." He lifts a hand and tucks one of the stray strands behind my ear. He's so close to me that I can smell him. His familiar scent. Warm. Kind of like honey. One day, I'll have to ask him what cologne he uses.

"Shall we?" he asks, nodding toward the main doors.

My heart skips a beat. This all feels exciting and new—even though he's met me off the bus and walked me to my classroom before.

"Yes," I say, wondering if I can take his hand. Are we at that point yet? Am I allowed? What will everyone think? James makes up my mind for me by wrapping his hand around mine. The tingle spreads from my fingertips through my whole body.

"Is this OK?" he asks.

"More than OK," I reply, squeezing his hand.

Then we walk together toward Boyd Hall. We don't pass many people I know, but everyone knows James. And everyone seems fascinated by the fact that he's holding my hand. I hear some of them whispering; a few heads turn in our direction. For a moment, I'm uneasy and feel a bit queasy. I glance sideways at James—and the feeling fades slightly.

Because James looks as though walking across the courtyard, hand in hand with me, is the most normal thing in the world.

"By the way, I'd like to take you out on a date," he whispers to me, just before we reach the hall.

I fight the smile that's trying to spread over my face. I raise an unimpressed eyebrow. "Oh, really?"

James nods. "Uh-huh. Next Saturday. If you're free."

I act like I have to think, and James starts to grin. "You're killing me, Ruby Bell."

Now I do smile.

"I'd love to go out with you, James Beaufort," I say, looking him in the eyes so that he knows how seriously I mean what I'm saying.

As we walk into Boyd Hall, he whispers: "I was hoping you'd say that."

After assembly, James walks me to my class. We reach the door just as Alistair, Cyril, and Wren come around the corner behind us. Wren glances at our linked hands, turns on his heel, and heads through a doorway. I notice James stiffen, and at once I want to pull away, but he's holding my hand tight.

"Morning, you two," says Alistair, giving me the hint of a smile.

Cyril just nods almost imperceptibly, which I return. I haven't forgotten what he said to me in December, or how hurtful those words were. It's up to James who he's friends with. But that doesn't mean I have to like him.

"Morning," James replies, his voice calm and unemotional.

"Does this mean you're going to be a bit less unbearable now?" Alistair asks, looking at our hands again.

James lifts his free hand to stick his middle finger up at his friend. Then he turns to me. "See you later."

It sounds more like a question than a statement, so I nod.

"Later," he whispers, stroking the back of my hand with his thumb. The tiny motion sends shivers through my whole body.

"See you later."

He lets go of my hand and walks toward the classroom he and his mates are in next. Cyril and Alistair follow, and I watch them until James glances back and smiles at me over his shoulder. I need to get to my own lesson, but I'm rooted to the spot.

When I think how things started between us, I can't believe we're now holding hands at school, in full view of anyone and everyone.

But it feels good.

More than that: It feels right.

———

"Everywhere I turned today," Lin says in the afternoon, as she drops onto a chair in the little circle we've been arranging for the last fifteen minutes, "you and James were all anyone could talk about."

I glance hastily at the door, but it's still shut. We've got the group room to ourselves. "Seriously?"

Lin nods. "When I went to the dining hall for a coffee at break time, pretty much everyone was talking about you."

Her words make me feel kind of uneasy, but I decide not to let them faze me. It was obvious that I'd lose my cloak of invisibility if I walked around Maxton Hall hand in hand with James Beaufort. Anyway, so much has changed since the start of the year that I don't really care whether people are talking about me or not anymore. Or not much, at least.

"I'm dying of curiosity here, by the way," Lin adds.

"I'm sorry I didn't tell you," I say. "But even I don't really know what happened. He turned up at my house yesterday, and . . ." I allow myself a tiny smile. "It was nice."

"Did you talk? About everything?"

I nod. "Yes. It was so hard. And I don't think we can act like nothing happened. But . . ." I take a long breath in and out again. "Even so, I have some kind of hope that we can get through it."

It's definitely not true that everything between James and me is fine again now. Too much has happened, and I'm too scared of him hurting me again. But yesterday, I just felt happy—and I want to hold on to that feeling for as long as possible.

Lin sighs. "That sounds good. I'm really happy for you, Ruby."

Her wistful tone takes me by surprise. But then I remember that Lin went to the pub with the others on Friday so that she could talk to Cyril. All at once, I feel guilty. There was so much going on that I totally forgot to ask her about it on Saturday.

"Do you have any news?" I ask cautiously.

Lin presses her lips together. For a moment, it looks like she's going to change the subject, but she suddenly exhales with a sigh. "Yeah. The news is that, as of now, I can officially focus one hundred percent on my exams."

I look sympathetically at her. "What happened?"

She shrugs. "Cyril dumped me."

I breathe in sharply. "Shit."

"It's what I thought. He's in love with Lydia," she goes on. "And he hopes the two of them might have a chance."

"Did he say that?" I ask in disbelief.

She nods, slowly. "Pretty much, yeah."

"I'm so sorry, Lin. If I can do anything to help . . ."

"No, but thank you. I think it's good that he's finally told me. Otherwise, I'd probably still have been chasing after him when we got to Oxford, messing up my fresh start there. I just read too much into stuff."

Hesitantly, I put a hand on her back.

"It's all good. *Honestly*. If anything, I'm just relieved that I finally know where I stand."

After watching her uncertainly for a moment, I give her back a quick pat, then pull my hand away. "Are you up for a girls' night on Friday?"

Lin looks unsure but forces herself to smile. "I'll let you know, OK?"

We sit in silence for a moment, side by side, staring at the tables we've pushed to the side to make room for our circle of chairs.

"Do you think everyone will be pleased?" Lin asks, her voice deliberately cheerful.

"Definitely," I say. "We all need a breather after Friday, I think."

Lin's about to reply when the door opens and Jessalyn and Kieran walk in.

"What's going on?" Jessalyn asks in confusion, looking around.

Kieran just mumbles "hi" and sits hastily down. Am I seeing things, or is he even paler than normal today? He won't look at me, just digs furiously around in his bag.

I see Lin look at me, and then at him, and then back at me, but I don't know what I can do to make this moment any less weird.

Fortunately, Camille and Doug now join us, and there's more surprise about the rearranged seating. The last person to stroll into the room is James. He lifts an eyebrow and looks around, then walks right through the ring of chairs to drop into the one opposite mine with a wry smile.

Next to me, Lin clears her throat. "Ruby and I have planned a little surprise for today," she says. "I don't know if you're the same as me, but there's always a rough patch at some point in the school year, when everything seems really hard." There are murmurs of agreement around our little circle. "I get the feeling we might be in for one of those after all the mayhem of the last few weeks. But we don't really have time for a break, because there's the Spring Ball coming up soon too."

"So," I add, "we thought that we'd do things a bit differently for today's meeting. You all worked so hard and the charity gala was a total success. So, I think we all deserve to take things a bit easy today."

Lin bends down and pulls a large bag out from under her chair. She opens it and pulls out two large thermos flasks and a handful of mugs. "We thought we'd liven the meeting up with tea, coffee, and cake."

"Ohhh," says Camille, and Jessalyn cheers beside her. "How cool are you?"

Lin hands out drinks and I stand up to get the paper boxes I hid under our coats on the other side of the room. "I brought muffins from my mum's bakery," I announce.

I put the boxes down in the center of our circle and lift the lids; Jessa leans in right away.

"Mmm. They smell delicious."

"Help yourselves."

As the others dig in, James leans over to me. "You didn't have these this morning."

"Mum dropped them off at lunchtime," I explain with a smile. "They're really fresh."

"They're the best muffins I've had in ages," says Camille, and

Doug nods his head. "Where's this bakery?" she asks then. "Mum's spent weeks trying to find someone to make her a birthday cake. Maybe she should try there."

"In Gormsey," I reply. "It's small, but everything they do is delicious and made with love. I can give you a card."

"That would be amazing," says Camille, and I'm surprised by the sincerity of her words. I've noticed something different about her lately. She's been putting more effort in, and for the last few meetings, she's stopped looking like she loathes everyone and everything in this room. I wonder what's up.

"This is such a nice idea," says Jessa. "Last week was so stressful. I had an English essay to do on top of all the work for the gala."

"How did it go?" Lin asks.

"I screwed up. I totally lost the thread and it made no sense at all."

"Sounds familiar," says Kieran. "I had a test last week too and my mind was totally blank. I couldn't remember a thing."

"What was it on?"

"The Cold War." Kieran pulls a face. "How about yours?"

"*A Midsummer Night's Dream.*"

"Poor you," says Camille. "I hate Shakespeare."

Jessa shrugs. "The play itself is fine. We watched a film of it too, and it made me think that it would be an amazing theme for the ball."

I pause with my muffin halfway to my lips. "Yeah, that could really work," I say slowly, turning my head to Lin.

"Yep . . ." She's looking thoughtful. "When we got all those quotes for the Halloween party, one of the firms had a kind of magic forest set you could rent. With fake trees, fairy lights, a fog machine, the whole works."

"Were they the ones who had the wooden swing you could use for photographs?"

"Yes, that's them."

"Yeah, I can really see it," says Jessa, and Camille sighs.

"It sounds lovely. What would the dress code be?"

"Everyone could dress up as elves," Doug suggests at once.

For a moment, we stop and stare at him. Who'd have thought Doug's quiet demeanor would hide a love for fairy folk?

"Yes," I say, but add hastily: "Or just floral for women and black tie with pastel shirts for the men?"

Jessa nods. "Perfect."

Lin and I exchange glances. Have we just accidentally stumbled on the perfect theme for our next event?

"What's the budget?" Kieran asks, frowning slightly. For the first time today, he's looking directly at me. "Sounds kind of expensive."

"True. But we didn't have to pay the décor firm for the charity gala."

Opposite me, James snorts. Clearly that's still a touchy subject for him. I don't know why, but I find that kind of sweet.

"So with that plus the money Lexie's promised us for this event, we can really go to town. There should be plenty."

"Well, I'm in," says Camille. "Guys?"

"Should we vote on it, just to be certain?" suggests Lin. "All in favor of *A Midsummer Night's Dream*, raise your mugs."

There are no mugs left behind.

As I look at the relaxed faces of my team, I get a warm and

fuzzy feeling. I don't know why, but it feels like the last half hour has really brought us closer together.

James

The week flies by, and they're the best five days I've ever spent at Maxton Hall. Ruby and I spend as much time as we can together, which isn't easy as we're in different groups for all our subjects, but it still works out better than we'd have believed.

I meet her off the bus every morning and walk her to her classroom. Saying that, on Wednesday, Ruby insists on walking me to *my* classroom, and as that's in the east wing, she has to practically sprint across the school to get to her own lesson on time. We have a couple of free periods at the same time, which we spend together in the library, where I try to focus on my revision, despite Ruby's presence. On Thursday, we manage to eat lunch together, although I get the feeling that Lin is anything but thrilled by my being there. There are times when I'm scared she'll jam her spoon into my eye, but she seems to be holding back.

For the first time since Mum died, I don't feel like everything's hopeless. It's as if a huge weight has been lifted from my shoulders, although I could do without all the gossip and unashamed nosiness of everyone at this school.

But the lads are more suspicious of Ruby than ever, and things are still tense since that bust-up with Wren. On Friday evening, Alistair invites us all over, in a blatant attempt to clear the air. I'm longing to spend the time with Ruby, but I know that I really need to speak to Wren. We haven't said a word to each other since last Saturday, and I want to patch things up, on top of which, I want to know what's wrong for him at home. And how I can help.

Annoyingly, Alistair's brother, Fred, has crashed our little party, and he's been droning on at me nonstop for over half an hour. He's twenty-two and the Ellington poster boy: He's at Oxford, he's got a fiancée, and—unlike Elaine and Alistair—he's keen to uphold the family traditions. None of us can stand him, mainly because their parents dote on Fred while acting like Alistair doesn't even exist.

"Is it true that you're on the Beaufort's board already?" he asks, swirling a finger of whisky around the glass he's holding.

"Yep," I reply, not looking at him. I pull out my phone and see that I've had a message from Ruby:

> **JAMES! Alice Campbell invited me to see her in**
> **her London office!**

I feel Fred's curious eyes on me, so, much as I'd like to grin from ear to ear, I fight it down.

> **How did that happen?**

"What's it like?" Fred asks, totally oblivious to my blatant hint that I'm not putting up with his interrogation.

"Thrilling." I growl my standard answer while waiting for Ruby to reply. "A real honor."

I hear Cyril snort, despite his efforts to muffle the sound behind his hand. Unlike Fred, who just keeps on asking questions, he knows that what I really mean is *Would you kindly shut the fuck up?*

"Come on, Beaufort, spill the beans!"

At that moment, my iPhone lights up. Ruby's sent me a screenshot of Alice's email, above which she's commented **Eeek!**

Dear Ruby,

I was very inspired by our conversation last Saturday at the gala. Any time you happen to be in London, you are very welcome to pop into my office for a chat.

Best wishes,
Alice

My fingers type my reply almost by themselves:

So when shall we go?

Suddenly, Fred nudges my shoulder. I turn to look at him, raising an eyebrow. He clocks that he's made a mistake and moves back slightly. Then he clears his throat.

"After all, we're the only people in this room who've already achieved anything, got anywhere in life. So we should stick together."

He laughs like he's said something hilarious.

Nobody agrees.

"You're full of bullshit, Frederick," says Kesh quietly.

Fred gasps with outrage.

"Leave it, Kesh." Alistair's voice is flat. He's always like this when his brother's around. Cold and distant—the total opposite of the Alistair we generally hang around with. If he'd known Fred was going to be here this weekend, he'd have invited himself round to someone else's, instead of having us all here.

"So, what exactly have you achieved?" Kesh insists, his voice so deep and calm that it sends an icy shiver down my spine. "You got into Oxford. Congratulations. And you're getting married. Congratulations again. That doesn't make you some big shot, though—you're still a spineless little weasel." Kesh takes a slow sip from his highball glass, not taking his dark brown eyes off Fred for a second.

"If you had an ounce of class, you wouldn't talk like that," Fred says. He's trying to sound cutting and to look bored, but I can see one of his eyelids fluttering nervously.

"Don't talk to me about class. Unlike you, I know better than to treat my family like shit. The fact that you don't stick up for your brother tells me everything I need to know about you, you absolute—"

"For God's sake, Keshav, shut up!" Alistair jumps up, his fists clenched and his face flushed bright red.

"Fine friends you have, Alistair. Mum and Dad have every right to be proud of you," says Fred, pulling his phone from his pocket. He gets up. "Sorry, I have to take this. My fiancée."

We hear him answer the call, addressing his girlfriend by a soppy nickname, then he flounces out of the sitting room, leaving us in peace.

"What the fuck, bro?" Alistair snarls, having not moved a muscle.

"He was being a dick," Kesh retorts.

"So? If any of your family acts like a dick to you, do I get involved? No!"

"That's because my family would never treat me the way yours act to you. Just be glad I've got your back."

Alistair snorts. "You're such a hypocrite. You only have my back when it suits you. I can do without support like that, thank you."

Kesh flinches like Alistair's hit him. His eyes flit to Wren, Cyril, and me, and then back to Alistair. I frown and look from one of them to the other, but before I can make sense of what's going on, Alistair turns and runs out through the same door as Fred.

"What the . . . ?" Wren starts, but Kesh instantly begins moving and chases after Alistair. The door slams behind him.

". . . fuck was all that about?"

Wren, Cyril, and I all seem equally confused.

Then Cyril groans and leans his head against the back of his armchair. "This isn't how I was expecting this evening to go." He fiddles with his phone and turns up the volume on the music.

"I hope they don't kill each other," I say after a while.

Cyril grins and shakes his head. "Doubt it. But my money's on Alistair."

I'm not really listening, still looking at the door they just vanished through. I've never seen Alistair and Kesh fight like that.

When Alistair came out as gay and his family practically disowned him, he spent a lot of time at each of our houses because he couldn't stand it at home. It brought us all closer together, but especially him and Kesh. Kesh's parents are friendly and accepting, and they became like a second family to Alistair.

"Something's not right with those two," Wren says.

"Yeah, I noticed that."

Wren raises an eyebrow and for a moment I get the feeling

that he wants to say something, but instead he just takes a huge swig from his whisky and Coke.

I sigh. "Wren," I begin.

He looks cautiously at me.

"I've been a crap friend lately," I say. "I'm sorry for being too caught up in my own shit to be there for you."

"It's not like you didn't have a good reason," Wren replies quietly. He exhales audibly. "Your mum died. I acted like a dickhead. Sorry, bro."

"I should have noticed that you've got stuff going on too, though."

Wren shrugs his shoulders.

"Now would be a good time to tell me," I say. "That's the main reason I came tonight."

Wren looks uncertain. He glances at me over his glass. Then he shuts his eyes like he's psyching himself up.

"We're . . . moving."

I scoot a little closer to him. Did I mishear that? "What?"

"My parents lost all their money. We found a buyer for the house last week. We're moving in March. To a semidetached."

I stare at Wren. The words echo around my head, but I can't make sense of them.

"Why the fuck didn't you say anything?" Cyril asks. He stands up, comes over, and drops onto the sofa beside Wren. "We could've helped."

That frees me from my state of shock. "Cy's right," I say. "There must have been some way you could have kept the house."

Cyril nods. "My parents would have bought it and let you keep living there."

Wren raises his hands in an appeasing way. "You know how

proud my folks are. They'd never accept charity. Anyway, having your parents as landlords would be super weird, Cy," he replies. But Cyril just shrugs.

"What happened?" I ask.

Wren sighs and rubs his chin with his free hand. "Dad was playing the markets. He put all our eggs in one basket—and lost."

All I can say is, "Fuck." I don't know exactly how rich the Fitzgeralds were, but I know their house and their various holiday homes. I know the companies they had shares in. It's hard to imagine that they could have lost it all—and in such a short space of time.

"Is there anything we can do?" I ask after a while.

Wren twitches one shoulder. "It's all a bit chaotic at the moment. And Dad . . . He's kind of down."

"Just let us know—anything at all," I say, and Cyril murmurs in agreement.

"It's a lot. I can't keep up at school at the moment. And now I have to think about loans and scholarships for Oxford too. I . . . I really don't know if I can deal with it all."

Wren buries his face in his hands while Cyril and I exchange glances. I'm sure we're thinking the same thing. In the worst case, we'd all chip in to lend Wren some money. Hell, we'd give it to him no questions asked, but we know him well enough to know he'd never accept that.

"You've got this. And we'll help," I declare, bumping shoulders with Wren. He slowly lowers his hands from his face.

"James, the thing with Ruby—"

"Is in the past," I interrupt him.

At this moment, this isn't about me, or Ruby, but about the

fact that Wren's been carrying all this around for ages, without his best friend having a clue. That's not how things should be. Not with us.

I don't care about our fight now. All that matters to me is that I want to help Wren. Even though I have no idea how.

24

Ruby

My heart is hammering in my throat as I open the door. Percy is standing there, and he nods slightly, a smile on his lips.

"How nice to see you again, Ms. Bell."

"It's nice to see you too, Percy," I reply, following him to the car, gripping my silver clutch bag tightly. James refused to tell me anything about our date all week, so I've just had to guess at what to wear. But Ember's helped me put together an outfit for all occasions: a simple black dress, shoes with tiny heels, and the little silver bag. My hair is half up and I've glued my fringe down with a ton of hairspray in case we're spending any time outdoors in the wind.

"We're meeting Mr. Beaufort there," Percy explains as he holds the door for me and gives me a hand into the Rolls. I smile up at him to thank him. To my shock, I see that there are dark rings under Percy's eyes and his skin is pale and dull. And he looks miles away, like his thoughts aren't really present.

"How are things, Percy?" I ask.

"I'm fine, miss, thank you for asking," he replies mechanically.

Smiling politely, Percy shuts the door behind me and walks around the car. The screen isn't up and I watch with a frown as he sits down behind the wheel. Is it my imagination, or is there considerably more white in his hair since Cordelia Beaufort's death?

"How long have you been working for the family?" I ask, edging forward slightly on my seat.

"Over twenty-five years now, miss."

I nod sympathetically. "Wow, that's a long time."

"I started driving Mrs. Beaufort when she was in her early twenties."

"What was she like?"

For a moment, Percy seems to be hunting for the words to describe her. "Fearless and intrepid. She turned the firm upside down, even before she finished university, which didn't please her parents. But it paid off." I can see in the mirror as his eyes narrow as if he's smiling. "She always had a good eye for the trends. She continued working all through her pregnancy, and set so many things in motion. Nothing went out under the company logo without her personal approval. She—" Percy breaks off. "She was an amazing woman," he concludes, his voice hoarse.

I feel a wave of compassion. It seems like Mrs. Beaufort meant a lot to Percy. Maybe more than that, if I'm reading the look in his eyes correctly.

"Are you really OK, Percy?" I whisper.

The chauffeur clears his throat. "I'll get there, miss. I just need a little time."

"Of course. If I can ever do anything to help . . ." I have no idea how I could ever help Percy, but just now, offering seems like the right thing to do.

"There is actually one thing you can do for me." Our eyes meet in the rearview mirror. "Please take good care of James."

My breath catches and I have to gulp.

"I will," I say after a short while. "I promise."

═══

Twenty minutes later, we've arrived. As Percy parks the car, I look through the tinted windows to the outside of the restaurant. I know that we were headed in the direction of Pemwick. But I don't know this area.

Percy opens the door and helps me out. The sun is just setting and bathing the building in front of me in an orangey-red light. The sign is already lit up, and I read *The Golden Cuisine* in fancy lettering. As Percy holds the restaurant door for me, my heart is suddenly racing.

"Mr. Beaufort is waiting inside. Have a nice evening, Ms. Bell."

I thank him, then walk inside nervously. The minute I step through the door, I see James waiting for me. A smile spreads over my face. I'm so relieved that I can feel like this with him again.

He's wearing a black shirt and a blue Beaufort's suit with broad checks, which fits him like a glove. I can see his tiny monogram on the breast pocket.

James smiles hesitantly back, looking me over the way I just did to him. My throat dries out as his eyes glide down my body.

"You look beautiful," he whispers.

I get goose bumps. "Thanks. You look stunning too."

He offers me his arm and leads me further into the restaurant. It's full, and as I can only see one table free, I assume that that's ours, but James walks through a side door and leads me up the stairs beyond it.

As we emerge into some kind of upstairs conservatory, I catch my breath. There's a tree in the middle of the room with colorful lanterns in its branches. The ceiling and windows are decked with chains of fairy lights that give a warm glow. The whole place is magical. And only one of the round tables is set.

James leads me to our table. He's the perfect gentleman, pulling out my chair for me, and then pushing it in behind my knees as I sit.

As he takes his seat opposite me, I glance out of the windows. The view is breathtaking. Now, you can still see the countryside around Pemwick, but I'm sure that the rolling green hills will be swathed in darkness within half an hour.

A waiter appears from nowhere and sets a jug of water on the table, then hands us our menus. I flick through, constantly glancing up at James. Am I this nervous because this is my first official date with any boy—or because it's *James* sitting opposite me, smiling at me over his glass?

I smile back at him. "It's beautiful here."

"It really is. Mum sometimes brought Lydia and me to eat here. I have nice memories of this place," he replies.

James's words make me flush warm with affection for him. I love the fact that he wants to share somewhere so special with me, especially as I know how difficult his family relationships are for him.

"Thank you for inviting me here."

I reach over the table for his hand and stroke it gently. James's expression darkens.

"I wanted to show you that spending time with me isn't just misery. It can be more."

"James . . ." I begin, but the waiter comes back to our table just then, to take our orders. I choose gnocchi with goat cheese, and James opts for a stuffed chicken leg. After that, we're alone again and I'm longing to pick up our conversation from earlier. Sometimes I wish I was a genius at small talk, like Ember. No matter how difficult the situation, she finds a way to break the ice.

"I've set up a Goodreads account, by the way," James says, out of the blue.

I prick up my ears. "Really?"

He nods. "I want to tackle the list. The . . . one we made in Oxford." He coughs, and I can virtually see the memory of that night flickering in his eyes. "The books thing seemed like a good starting place."

"I love that!" I blurt. "So, what's on your reading list, then?"

The corners of James's lips twitch suspiciously. Then he pulls out his phone and opens the app. He taps on it a few times, then looks up again.

"OK, so, I read *Death Note*," he says.

"I saw that," I say. "And what did you think?"

"It was great. But there was only one thing that really bothered me," he adds seriously.

"I think I can guess," I reply.

"It was just . . . I couldn't believe it. I almost didn't read the rest of the series." James shrugs. "But you were right about what you said."

I look inquiringly at him.

"About it being an important part of a rounded education to read it."

I gasp. "You remember that?"

He tilts his head. "Of course I remember it. I remember everything, Ruby."

I gulp hard. "Me too," I say quietly.

There's something in James's turquoise eyes that I haven't seen for such a long time, and I'm suddenly seized by a longing that's so sudden and so strong that I have to clear my throat and reach for my glass of water.

"Show me your list," I croak.

James blinks a few times, like he needs a minute to get himself together. Then he pushes his phone over the table toward me. I scan through the list of what he's read, and I'm surprised by how much there is already—a few mangas, and a whole bunch of classic children's and YA books, like the Percy Jackson series, and books by John Green and Stephen Chbosky.

"Wow, you've read all these already?" I ask in surprise.

He hunches one shoulder awkwardly. "Mostly at night, when I couldn't sleep. Or at break time at school. I've been looking for things to take my mind off it all, and books are pretty good at that. And now I've kind of gotten used to reading before bed."

"It's a great new habit." I keep scrolling through his account. "Can I put a couple of things on your *Want to Read*?"

"Knock yourself out. I'm following some book bloggers now too, and I sometimes check out the stuff they recommend."

I laugh and shake my head. James and his blogs. He really ought to have a chat with Ember sometime, I think, gradually adding to his list.

"You're unstoppable," James says after a while, amused.

"You said to knock myself out."

James laughs. When the meal arrives, I realize to my surprise that we've been here more than an hour already, chatting, and there hasn't been a single awkward moment, and we've never been desperately trying to think about what to say next. It's been ages since we've been able to talk this freely. Maybe we never have.

═══

Our time in the conservatory is lovely, and over way too soon. James says he wants to make a good impression on my parents by dropping me back before midnight, which I reluctantly accept. If it had been up to me, we would have sat there under the lanterns, chatting away forever.

Before I put my jacket on, I walk over to the wall of windows. It's dark now, but the view is still amazing. There are no clouds and I can see so many stars in the sky.

I've never had such a magical evening, and I want to remember it forever. So I pull out my phone and take a photo. But I have to admit that you can't really see anything in it.

James steps up behind me, so close that the hairs on my arms stand on end. But it's still not enough. I lean back and into him. Hesitantly, he raises an arm and wraps it around me. He presses me to him while I let my head sink back. The moment is so lovely, so intimate, that I have to shut my eyes for a moment. I listen to his breathing, and the quiet music filling the conservatory. Suddenly, I have an idea.

"Can I take a photo?" I ask quietly.

I feel him nod as his hair tickles my cheek. I hold up my phone and switch to the selfie camera.

"Smile," I order James.

The two of us smile into the camera, him with his arms

around my body, behind us, the tree bedecked with lanterns in this magical place.

This photo is going to replace the one I nicked off Instagram and secretly saved on my laptop, I decide. But the thought fades as James nuzzles his face into me. He takes a deep breath and presses his lips into the crook of my neck. My breath catches, while a hefty tingle runs through my body. I put my hand on his and hold it tight while the desperate longing to be even closer to him floods over me. I lean back, almost grind into him, until I hear him inhale sharply.

Suddenly, James isn't moving a muscle. My own breath is way too fast. As I squeeze his hand a moment, we no longer need words. James swings me round, and the next second, our lips automatically find each other.

James wraps both arms around me and holds me tight. My hands are on his chest and I let them stray down until they're touching his stomach, which makes him groan. It sounds as desperate as I feel. At this moment, it's as though there's no boundary between us any longer. We are just us. Just like before, and yet changed. Everything feels more meaningful. Feeling James's lips on mine is just as exciting as during our first kiss, yet I know him now. I know the movement he makes with his tongue, the feeling of his teeth on my bottom lip. When his hand reaches for my bum and he pulls me closer, I can feel his erection against my hip.

My knees are weak. I press against him until he almost stumbles back, kiss him harder, let myself be guided entirely by my feelings and the hot burning deep inside me.

But suddenly, he snatches his lips away from me. I was so carried away that now I'm dizzy. James breathes hard as he presses his brow against mine. His hand moves from my bum, up to the back of my head, which he strokes gently.

"We have to stop."

It takes me a moment to work out what he just said. "Why?" I whisper.

He just shakes his head.

"Mr. Beaufort?" I suddenly hear the waiter's voice.

James grunts, not letting me go.

"I just came to tell you that your driver is here," the waiter continues, clearly embarrassed.

James lets go of me, and our hands find each other without any conscious decision of mine. We leave the restaurant hand in hand, like it's the most ordinary thing in the world, both red-cheeked, mumbling goodbye to the poor waiter, who can't meet our eyes.

Outside, I'm hit by a wall of cold air. Percy is standing by the car, holding the door for us. I thank him and get in, James close behind me. I sit in the same place as on the way here. James drops into the seat beside me.

His eyes are dark and his lips are as red and swollen as mine. I can still feel the slight throb in my bottom lip—and elsewhere too. I'm electric, my whole body charged. I can hardly sit still for the urge to pick up where we just left off.

The streetlights of Pemwick pass us by and Percy heads out into the country lanes. The screen is up, and I glance to see if the little red light on the intercom is flashing.

It's not.

I turn to face James, who followed my gaze. His lips are slightly parted and his chest is rising and falling rapidly. There's no mistaking that he was as caught up in that kiss as I was.

"James," I whisper.

He holds his breath.

I move like I'm on autopilot. The attraction emanating from James is so all-encompassing that it's impossible to sit here for twenty minutes without doing something.

Surprise flickers in his eyes as I scoot closer.

"Kiss me, James," I whisper.

He just shakes his head, but in the same breath, he takes my face in his hands and presses his lips firmly to mine. We sigh simultaneously, and the sounds mingle and buzz in my body. The world around me fades. There's only James and me—no past, no future. Just us and the nighttime lights flickering past.

"I missed you," I whisper.

He makes an almost despairing sound and kisses me more deeply.

I'm not prepared for what he does to me. I didn't think it could feel like this. However often James and I are together—it just gets stronger. The yearning inside me grows with every kiss, an unquenchable longing for him and to be close to him, and I don't think that will ever disappear.

I dig my fingers into his hair and pull him closer to me. This is all going too fast, and I can't help myself. James's firm body is pressed against mine and I need him. In this second, I need him like I've never needed anybody.

I'm about to say those words when James pulls away slightly. He looks mistily at me and strokes my cheek with one hand, then lets his mouth move down my throat.

"I missed you too," he whispers to my neck. He sucks on the skin and my breath catches. "Any time I saw you at school, I wanted to do this."

I sigh and shut my eyes. "Next time, please do. I give you permission," I gasp.

He barks out a raw laugh. "Good to know."

Slowly, James works his way down, but I want to feel his mouth on mine again, so I pull him up and hold him there. His tongue plays around mine, and my other hand is exploring his body. All these clothes are in the way, regardless of how amazing he looks in that suit. I undo his top shirt button.

"Ruby," he interrupts quietly.

I keep on. At the third button, James grabs my wrist and holds it tight. I look up and into his dark eyes. James stares at me, breathing hard.

I can see him gulp. "Normally, I'd let you undress me anytime. Seriously. Anywhere, for all I care. But . . ." He breaks off and looks around the car. Then he looks back at me. "I really wanted our next time to be something special. And if we don't stop now, I . . . I don't know if . . ."

I feel the heat shoot into my cheeks. He's right. "I wasn't thinking."

My face is still burning as I slowly start to rebutton his shirt. But even once I've done them all up, I can't look him in the face.

"Ruby," James whispers suddenly.

I pretend to straighten his collar, which is perfectly neat already. "Mm?"

"Ruby," he repeats. "Please look at me."

I breathe in and look up again. The first thing I see is that James's face is as flushed as mine feels. The second is the look in his eyes. It's so tender. "I'm not ready . . . I mean, we should take things slow."

"Because we have time," I croak.

"All the time in the world," James confirms.

I nod, my breathing ragged. Then I lean back with a sigh and shut my eyes. For a few seconds, we're silent.

After a while, James takes my hand. "Thank you for saying yes. To the date, I mean," he whispers.

I squeeze his hand. "It was a lovely date."

"I thought so."

There's something in his tone that makes me look up at him again. His eyes are glimmering dangerously and his smile is so hot that for a moment, I feel disarmed.

Just two weeks ago, I'd never have thought it possible that he'd look at me like that again, let alone that I'd have another moment like this with him. There's so much more I still want to say to him—but I can't. It's too soon. The wounds are too recently healed. James seems serious, but I'm still afraid that he'll reject me again.

I try to imagine him in a few years. Grown up, more mature. More confident in his decisions, without the unpredictability I've gotten to know in the last six months. What kind of a person would it make me if I only let him have a place in my life again at that point? Am I even certain that we'll still be there for each other by then?

But—who am I kidding here? There'll only ever be James for me. I could never love anyone else the way I love him—in this all-powerful, devouring, passionate way.

"What are you thinking?" he whispers suddenly, stroking my skin with his fingers.

That I'm in love with you.

That you're the only man for me.

That that scares me.

"I was thinking that in future, we need to talk more. About our problems. So that nothing else . . . bad happens," I answer hesitantly.

James looks hard at me. There's a determination in his eyes that I've never seen before. "We can do this, Ruby."

I gulp hard. "Are you sure?"

He nods curtly. Just the once. "Yes, I am."

Relief washes over me. Hearing James with the certainty to say that quiets my doubts.

For a while, we sit side by side, studying our linked fingers. Then James leans back and grins at me.

"Best date in the world," he murmurs, lifting our hands so that he can kiss my fingers.

I nod. "I thought so."

Suddenly, his eyes light up. "Come round tomorrow evening," he says. "To see Lydia and me. I know she'd love to see you too."

I hesitate.

"Your dad . . ."

"Dad's in London all weekend. We can order sushi."

At this moment, James seems so excited yet so jittery that I instantly absorb all his nerves. I've only been to his house twice, and I only have sad memories of those occasions. I'm ready to replace them with new—nicer—ones.

"OK, great. Tomorrow evening. I'll bring Ben and Jerry's."

"Perfect. Percy will pick you up." Suddenly, James frowns. "Speaking of Percy . . ." He leans forward. "Shouldn't we have gotten to Gormsey by now, Percy?"

For a moment, there's just the quiet crackle. Then . . .

"I thought you might need a little . . . privacy, sir."

Eyes wide, I look at James. He seems as surprised as me. Then I burst out laughing.

James joins in, burying his face back in my throat.

25

Ruby

I see Lydia's messages the moment Percy turns onto the Beauforts' driveway.

> **Change of plans!**
>
> **Dad just came home**
>
> **Better tell Percy to turn around**
>
> **Ruby?**

She sent the first a good fifteen minutes back, and the last three minutes ago; there are three missed calls from James too. The panic starts to rise within me as I stare at my phone and wonder what to do. But before I even manage to get my thoughts together, Percy is pulling up outside their house.

I watch with growing unease as he gets out, walks around the car, and opens the door. I gulp hard as I pick up the little bag with its three tubs of Ben & Jerry's, take the hand Percy is holding out to me, and let him help me. Once out of the car, I take a deep breath of the cool evening air and look cautiously around me.

I can see James and Lydia standing, waiting for me at the top of the steps outside the enormous front door. James has his arms crossed over his chest, but Lydia gives me a quick wave. I turn back to Percy. "I don't know how long I'll be able to stay. Will you be here for a while?"

A thin smile spreads over the chauffeur's lips. "I'm always here, Ms. Bell. Mr. Beaufort just has to drop me a line and I'll be ready to take you home." He tips his hat slightly, then gets back into the car, presumably to park up in the huge garage at the side of the house.

I hurry up the front steps.

"Hey," I whisper, as soon as they're in earshot. "I only saw your texts a minute ago. Your dad is here?"

James and Lydia nod. The pair of them look anything but happy, but James pulls me into a quick hug. "Hey," he murmurs into the crook of my neck, which gives me full-body goose bumps.

Once we've pulled apart, Lydia sighs. "Dad came home early especially to have dinner with us."

"I'd better go, then, hadn't I?" I ask uncertainly. I don't want them to feel like I'm running away the minute things get complicated. After all, James put up with a whole evening in the company of my family. But they look so miserable about the idea of spending time with their father that I don't want my presence to make things even worse.

James gives me a crooked smile. "I just don't want to subject you to this ordeal."

At that precise moment, Mortimer Beaufort appears in the hallway.

At the sight of me, his eyes widen for a split second.

I stiffen.

"Kindly invite your guest inside and shut the damn door. Do we live in a barn?" he thunders. Lydia and James look startled as they whirl around.

For a second, we stare at each other. Lydia is the first to react, pulling me gently into the house by the arm. She shuts the door behind me, and suddenly I'm just feet away from Mortimer Beaufort, who scans me over from head to foot.

I do likewise. He's wearing a tailor-made navy suit and his sandy hair is gelled into place with a neat side parting. He's paler than he was the last time we met, but the look in his eyes hasn't changed—cold as ice, without even a hint of emotion. I gulp hard. My throat feels like I've swallowed a mouthful of sand.

The next moment, I find myself wondering why I let this man intimidate me so much. I don't care what he thinks of me; after all, the only things I feel for him are rage, scorn, and revulsion—certainly no respect.

So I straighten my back and meet his eyes. "Good evening, Mr. Beaufort," I say.

"Dad, I'm sure you remember Ruby," James adds.

Mr. Beaufort just gives me a nod. Then he turns to James. "Dinner is ready. Your . . . girlfriend is welcome to join us."

He turns on his heel without a second glance at either me or Lydia and disappears into a room at the other end of the hall.

I hear Lydia beside me as she suddenly lets out her breath. "Oh God, Ruby," she says with a grimace. "I'm so sorry. We wanted to have a nice evening, and now we have to face Dad. There's probably coq au vin, not sushi."

James's eyes are piercing as he looks at me. "You still have time to escape."

"Your dad knows I'm here."

"Doesn't matter."

"Would you prefer it if I left?"

James doesn't miss a beat. "No, of course not. The sooner Dad gets used to the idea that you're one of us now, the better."

Warmth fills my body at his words. I take James's arm and give it a quick squeeze. "I won't leave. And I like coq au vin." I pick up my bag. "Plus, I've brought ice cream."

"I'll just take that down to the kitchen," Lydia says. "You two go ahead."

James's hand is on my lower back as we walk into the dining room. It's huge, with a high ceiling and wide windows that look out over the Beauforts' extensive gardens. The walls are painted a dark green that's echoed in the seat covers; over the long dining table hangs an impressive chandelier that's easily a match for the ones at Maxton Hall. The table is set with rows and rows of cutlery, dainty porcelain, and gilt wineglasses.

But it isn't only the furniture and décor that makes this dining room—if that's even the word for it—so different from home. It's mainly about the atmosphere. Everyone is tense and the mood is chilly, nothing like the warm, relaxed house I grew up in.

Just the same as that time at their London workshop, Mortimer Beaufort's presence is dominating the room. His brusque manner and cold eyes make it utterly impossible to feel at ease. It's incredible.

We all take our seats, Mr. Beaufort at the head of the table, James to his left with me at his side, and Lydia opposite us. Two of the kitchen staff come into the room and set a deep bowl of soup in front of each of us; it smells delicious. I follow James and Lydia and spread the folded damask napkin over my lap.

"To a pleasant evening," says Mr. Beaufort, raising his glass.

James and Lydia mumble some kind of agreement, and I lift my glass too.

This is already the most *un*pleasant evening I've had in ages.

The first ten minutes pass in silence. The room is so quiet that it feels unnaturally loud every time I swallow or set my glass down on the table. I'm desperately trying to think of something to say—or wondering if I should even speak at all. I have absolutely no idea.

I dare to glance at James and he flashes me a quick, thin smile.

In the end, Lydia speaks up. "The charity gala went well, didn't it, Ruby? Or at least, I've only heard good things about it."

I'm relieved that she's picked a subject I know about, where I have something to say. "Yes, it was brilliant. We raised over two hundred grand, which was way more than we even hoped."

"Wow," says Lydia. "Was Lexington happy?"

I nod. "Yes, luckily. But he's usually pleased with us."

"With a few exceptions," murmurs James.

As I turn toward him, he's grinning into his glass.

I know what he's thinking. I remember the day we sat side by side at Lexie's desk, when James was ordered to join the events committee as a punishment, as vividly as if it were yesterday. I smile back at him.

"Well, one exception, maybe. But that was hardly my fault, or anything to do with my team."

Mr. Beaufort interrupts our conversation, and I feel the grin immediately wiped off my face. "I hear you're very involved in school life, Ruby."

"Yes, I've been on the events committee for the last two years."

He just nods. Blink and you'd miss it. "Uh-huh."

"Ruby is the head of the events committee," says James, not looking up from his soup.

His father pays him no attention. "And will you be going to university too?"

"I hope to be starting at Oxford next year."

Now Mr. Beaufort looks up, and, for the first time this evening, I get the impression that he's actually taken notice of me.

I hold my breath. Everything within me is rebelling against talking about Oxford with this man. It's sacred to me, and I don't want anyone who doesn't get what studying there really means to me to trample on my dreams.

"Oh, really? What will you be reading?"

"PPE," I reply.

"A solid degree. And which college has taken your fancy?"

"St. Hilda's."

He nods. "Just like James. How convenient."

I ignore his insinuation. "It's a lovely college. At the interviews . . ." I fall silent. It was during the interview period that Mrs. Beaufort died. I glance at Lydia, who has frozen, her spoon halfway to her lips, and is now staring blankly into her soup. "I really liked everything there, and I'm looking forward to it a lot," I conclude hastily. I can hardly imagine how painful it must be for James and Lydia to think back on that time. I venture a glance at James, but he's not letting anything show, just spooning up his soup.

Just the starter takes more than an hour. During the main course, Lydia and I try to make the best of the situation and chat about all kinds of things—from films and music to books and blogs. When Lydia mentions that she used to do ballet, Mr. Beaufort even manages a fleeting smile. It only lasts a split second, after which I start to wonder if I'd imagined it.

"I once had the tiniest part in *The Nutcracker*, but I was so proud," Lydia reminisces. She cuts into her chicken, which is beautifully garnished with griddled vegetables. The cook has put so much work into the presentation that I can hardly bear to destroy his mini work of art.

"I'd love to see photos."

"No, you wouldn't," James mumbles beside me. "She was a little rat. The pictures are terrible."

"Why don't you tell Ruby about the times you did ballet too?" Lydia mocks from across the table. As James glares at her, she pops a huge forkful into her mouth and shrugs.

"Did you really?" I ask in surprise.

A muscle in James's jaw stands out. "Lydia made out that it was really hard. She used to kick up a major fuss every time. So I said it couldn't be that difficult and that anyone could do a bit of jumping up and down."

"And then he came along to three lessons. You should have seen him. He was so awful!" She bursts out laughing.

"Why did you stop?" I ask, grinning.

"Because I made Lydia promise to stop moaning about ballet at home."

"Such a nice brother," I remark.

"One does one's best," James replies.

"It's just as well it was only those three lessons. Otherwise, I probably would have stopped as well and not kept it up another two years," Lydia says.

"Why did you stop?" I ask.

"Lack of discipline," Mr. Beaufort replies, as if I'd asked him the question and not Lydia. "My daughter generally only persists with things she finds easy. The moment she faces a challenge, she gives up."

An unpleasant, heavy silence spreads over us, like a dark thundercloud that will start rumbling any moment.

Lydia's lips are set into a pale line. Beside me, James grips his knife and fork so hard that his knuckles are white. The only person to keep eating at his leisure is Mr. Beaufort. He doesn't even seem to notice that his unkind remark has killed the mood around the table.

How is it possible to be that insensitive to everything going on around you? To be so ignorant when it comes to your own children?

My friend Lydia faces up to every challenge. Speaking about her like that shows how little he knows his daughter.

"Well, I'd still love to see the photos," I say in the end, keeping my tone cheerful to break the oppressive silence. "I'm sure you looked really cute, even as a little rat." I've never had to be the bridge between this many people before, or not in an atmosphere like this, and I don't know if I'm helping or just making things even worse. I only know that I want to ease a bit of the pressure on James and Lydia.

"I'll show you after dinner," Lydia replies with a forced smile. She raises her head, and for a moment it looks as though she's looking at their father. But then I see that she's looking past him, to the enormous family portrait hanging on the wall over the antique fireplace. It's an oil painting of the whole Beaufort family, including their mother with her fox-colored hair. James and Lydia can't have been more than six or seven when it was painted.

"So," Mr. Beaufort says suddenly, dabbing his mouth with the napkin and standing up. "I have another video conference. Good evening." He nods to us and leaves the room.

I look in disbelief from James to Lydia, but neither seems particularly surprised by their dad's abrupt departure.

"He just walked out," I whisper, glancing over my shoulder to the door through which Mr. Beaufort just left.

"He does that. Don't worry about it," Lydia declares, leaning back in her chair. She smiles and rubs her belly. The fact that she does that around us, without a second thought, fills me with a warmth that's very welcome after Mr. Beaufort's icy glares.

"He always finds some excuse to get out of an awkward situation," James remarks, taking a large sip from his glass of water. "Even when it was him who forced us into it in the first place. I can barely ever remember seeing him for longer than two hours at a time." He snorts. "Which is fine by me."

"I bet he doesn't even have a call. Mum would never have allowed it," Lydia mumbles.

James holds his breath. After a moment, he lets it out again audibly. "If you want to get away, I hereby set you free," he says, glancing sidelong at me.

I furrow my brow. "What do you mean?"

"We can knock this depressing evening on the head now and try again next week."

Lydia nods. "Nobody would mind if you'd rather go home."

I stare at them both in outrage. "I'm not wasting this delicious meal." I point my fork first at my half-eaten chicken, and then at Lydia. "Besides which, I'm not going anywhere until I've seen your ballet photos."

Lydia laughs and James shakes his head with a smile.

I turn my attention back to my food, trying not to let anyone see how much the encounter with Mortimer Beaufort has unsettled me.

===

The rest of the meal is much more relaxed, but I'm still glad when we can go up to Lydia's room after pudding and shut the door behind us. Now we're sitting on her large, comfy sofa, looking through old photo albums.

"You were so sweet," I sigh, pointing to a photo of James and Lydia hugging each other, their chubby little cheeks pressed close together.

"That's from when we were three. Look at the curls I used to have," Lydia says, pointing to her hair in the picture.

"You don't anymore?" I ask.

She shakes her head and runs her hand over her ponytail. "No, thank goodness. I'd probably go mad if I still had to tame those every morning."

"Oh, but they were so cute. James never had curls."

I look at him as he sits in one of the armchairs opposite the sofa, flicking through a travel magazine.

"His hair always looked pretty much like it does now," Lydia says, tearing me away from my thoughts.

I lean closer, to get a better look at the picture. "He's always had that serious expression too," I remark.

Lydia snorts and turns the page. On the next page, there's a glowering mini-James, holding an empty ice-cream cone.

"He dropped the ice cream out of the cone," Lydia explains with a grin.

"Poor baby James," I murmur, grinning too. When I glance over at him, his only response is to raise an eyebrow.

"Lydia, don't act like you were sorry for me. I still remember the way you laughed," he says dryly.

"That's not true!"

"Isn't it? You didn't laugh at me?" he retorts.

"OK, I did. But then I let you share my ice cream."

"Yours was banana. What kind of a person likes banana ice cream?"

"Not me," I say.

James points at me. "There, you see."

"You're both nuts." Lydia shakes her head and flicks on. In the next few pages, the twins are six or seven, and now Alistair, Wren, Cyril, or Keshav turn up more and more often.

"It's mad that you've all known each other so long," I say in amazement.

"Yeah, isn't it? Sometimes I feel like we're brothers."

I nod and look at a picture of a chubby-cheeked Alistair, his golden curls sticking up all over the place. Then my eyes are caught by a younger version of James with mini-Wren in a headlock.

"Did you and Wren ever talk?" I ask James quietly.

"We discussed one or two things." He hesitates. "He's got a lot on his mind."

"Bad stuff?" Lydia asks at once.

James shrugs his shoulders. "I promised not to tell anyone."

Lydia frowns with concern. I can see that she still has a lot of questions, but after an internal struggle, she just nods. "OK. But do you think it's going to work out in the end?"

James nods. "Wren's going to be fine. After all, he's got us."

Lydia and I exchange skeptical glances.

All the same, I'm relieved that James and Wren seem to have

made up. During that long phone call on my birthday night, James told me how important it is to him to enjoy this last year of school together with his friends. He wanted to make the most of it and not worry about what will come next. His mum dying changed things, but that makes it all the more important to have friends he can count on. And vice versa.

A little later, I say goodbye to Lydia, and James drives me home. Or rather, Percy drives me home, but James comes along for the ride in the Rolls-Royce. We're quiet as we leave their property and head for Gormsey.

However little I like it, it feels as though the run-in with Mortimer Beaufort is a shadow hanging over us. I've met the man on three occasions in my life, and he's tried to come between James and me every time. I so hope that James won't let him do that again. That the thing we have now is stronger than his father's influence.

"What are you thinking?" he asks suddenly, his voice deep and warm.

I look up and meet his turquoise eyes. My stomach starts to tingle.

I take a deep breath. "That I'd like to spend more weekends like that with you."

James looks up into my eyes and then down again, as if he doesn't know how to defend himself against me.

"And at the same time, I'm wondering . . ." I pause.

James waits, still looking at me. "What are you wondering?" he asks after a while.

"I'm wondering how things are going to work out. For you," I whisper. "For you and your dad, I mean. With him telling you how to live your life, and you letting him drive you into a corner where you don't want to be."

James lowers his eyes and stares at the car footwells, as if there's something fascinating to see there. He takes a deep breath. And another. After a while, he slowly shakes his head.

"It's not just about him," he begins after a while, his voice rough. "Everything comes down to Beaufort's, Ruby. It's not just Dad's life's work that I'm going to inherit." I gulp hard as he glances up again and looks straight at me. "I . . . I don't want to disappoint my mum."

I inhale sharply.

I'd never thought of that. Of course his mum's death has changed things. I spent the whole time thinking that everything would work out fine so long as James could follow his own dreams, rather than his father's. But now I realize that that isn't what matters anymore. James isn't only tied to Beaufort's by his dad. The main person keeping him there now is his mum.

"You won't disappoint your mum," I whisper.

"But what if I do? What if I can't do this?" The expression in his eyes is one I've never seen on him before: fear. It flickers on his face and seems suddenly to fill the massive car.

"I'm there for you," I say. Only four words, but at this moment, I'm putting everything I can into those few syllables.

James gives me a long look. He seems to understand everything else I'm trying to say. Gradually, the sheer panic fades from his face, to be replaced by tenderness and the warmth that's been in his eyes for me all evening.

The next moment, James takes my hand. He links his fingers into mine and squeezes gently.

"And I'm there for you. Whatever happens."

I let myself sink back and lean my head against his shoulder.
It's a little easier to breathe now.

We can do this.

James

It's after half past one when a loud crash startles me awake. I jerk upright so fast that the e-reader falls off the bed and lands on the floor, but that's the least of my worries. I run at top speed over the landing to Lydia's room. But when I fling her door open, she's just sitting up in bed, rubbing her tired eyes.

"Are you OK?" I ask.

She nods. "What was that?"

"Must have been Dad," I reply, feeling my pulse quicken.

I don't want to go downstairs.

I don't want to know what else he's smashed.

I don't want to fucking worry about him.

Everything in me is yelling at me to go back to bed, but I head down the stairs. Another crash. Whatever Dad's up to, he's in the dining room.

I creep quietly down the hall. The closer I get, the more clearly I can hear him. He's mumbling something; he sounds like he's angry with somebody. Could it be Mary or Percy?

Just before I get to the dining room, I press myself against the wall with the door on my left.

"You bitch," my father slurs. "You shouldn't have done it."

I frown and creep closer. Who the hell is he talking to?

"I'll never forgive you. Now I'm on my own with the two of them and I can't do anything right and it's all *your* fucking fault!"

He roars those last words. I lean out from my hiding place just in time to see him hurl a full decanter of whisky at the family portrait over the dining table. I gasp as the decanter shatters, the sound ringing in my ears. The brown liquid runs down from Mum over Lydia and me. It looks as if the paint is running. Mum's face smears like a melting waxwork, gradually transforming into a monster. A grotesque mask, looking down on my father from above, mocking him.

At this moment, the anger at him that's always slumbering inside me awakes into new life, and the heat that flows through my veins is one that only he can trigger. I clench my fists, and I'm about to walk into the room to confront him when he suddenly makes a new sound.

From behind, I see his shoulders shaking. He gasps for breath, again and again, then suddenly his knees give way and he sinks to the floor. Among all the broken glass. He claps his hands to his face, and then I hear it again.

My father is sobbing.

I can't move; I'm rooted to the spot as I watch him weep. I think about all the times he made me cry. I think about his fists, his shouts, his insults, and the cold way he always looks at me. I think about the day of the funeral when he instructed us on how to act. The way he didn't tell us about Mum's death.

And I realize that I'm not feeling the satisfaction I want to feel. Anything but. My dad is suffering. What kind of a person would it make me if I turned around now and went back up to my room?

It's not easy to take the first step, but I do it. I walk into the dining room, being careful not to step in the wreckage of his fury, and stand behind him. Purely on instinct, I lay a hand on Dad's shoulder and press it for a moment. The sobbing stops at once and he holds his breath.

Just as I'm about to take my hand away, he reaches for it. He clings to it, almost desperately, and I let him. A weird feeling floods over me. Something I haven't felt for my father for ages.

I look up at the portrait of us. Dad has both hands on Lydia's shoulders, and I'm standing in front of Mum, who has her arms wrapped around me. The colors might have blurred, but I remember what it was like that day. I remember what it felt like to be part of a family.

The feeling burgeoning in me now is only a shadow of that, but I hold fast to it.

26

Lydia

For the first time in my life, I have to order a dress online. Instead of strolling down Bond Street and wandering into each of the shops at least once, I'm sitting on Ruby's bed, clicking from one website to another. It's fun, especially because I don't have to do this on my own, but I'm still looking forward to when I'll be able to go back to my favorite shops in person, to touch the dresses for real and see them up close.

That's not going to be an option for the next few months though. Most of the shop owners know me, and it's way too likely that they'd take one glance at my stomach and put two and two together. After that, it would be only a matter of time before Dad found out.

And that thought sends an ice-cold shiver through my body.

No, online shopping will have to do for the time being.

"What d'you think of that one?" Ruby asks, turning her laptop toward me.

I screw up my nose. "It looks like someone slipped with the scissors," I say, running my index finger over the image—the hemline is a good bit higher at the front than the back. "My mum would have been so angry at a cut like that. The color isn't great either. And nor is the lazy bit of lace at the neckline."

"OK, OK." Ruby laughs, closing the window. "Well, let's try here. We're only on page twelve of twenty-seven."

She starts scrolling down, and together we watch an array of dresses in all kinds of cuts and colors pop up on the screen.

"Maybe I should just skip the Spring Ball," I suggest after a while.

Ruby instantly shakes her head. "It's your last Spring Ball, Lydia. You *have* to come."

"I'm starting to think it's going to be impossible to find a dress that will hide this belly. What if someone catches on?" I ask, pointing at the little bump beneath my oversize sweatshirt.

"We'll find a dress. Don't you worry." Ruby sounds a lot more confident than I feel.

Dr. Hearst has told me that I'm a lot smaller than most women expecting twins, but I feel enormous. Over the last few weeks, I've got used to carrying my school bag in front of me, and my blouses are two sizes bigger now. James snuck them home from the sewing room last time he was up at Beaufort's for a meeting. This is the first time that I've been glad our school uniform was designed by Mum and is made in our workshops.

I wish it was that easy to get hold of a ball dress. I'm already wishing I hadn't let James and Ruby talk me into going. And the dress isn't even my biggest problem. My main concern is avoiding Graham outside class at all costs.

But I can't tell Ruby that—and I certainly can't tell James. I couldn't bear it if he gave me even one more sympathetic glance. Not after last Wednesday, when I got a trapped nerve in my back and was lying helpless in bed like a beetle. The pain was so bad that I couldn't move and had to wait for James to hear me calling for help. And then he had to help me *dress*.

It was humiliating, and I wish I could just wipe the whole morning from my head. Forever. So now, if I tell him that I can't face meeting Graham at a party, he's bound to think I'm losing it. And I'd hate that.

"What about this one?" asks Ruby.

I don't like that dress either. It's too young for me, not glamorous enough—it reminds me of a uniform. "What I really want is a dress where I won't totally stand out."

"I'd never have thought it would be this hard to find a suitable dress for *A Midsummer Night's Dream*. I wish we hadn't chosen it as the theme now."

"It's a gorgeous theme. And an Elie Saab dress would work perfectly for it," I sigh.

Ruby types the name into her browser search bar and then squeals enthusiastically. "Yes, they really would be perfect. The appliqué flowers are stunning and . . . oh God, they cost a fortune!"

"Oh, ah, yes. But that isn't the problem. The thing is, you have to try a dress like that on in person, and I can't do that right now."

Quite apart from the fact that it would be totally OTT to go to a school ball like that. I'm saving the dream of Elie Saab for my wedding day. Or someone else's—all my friends will probably be married before me. My love life now consists entirely of reading old messages from Graham and bursting into tears, as inconspicuously as possible.

It's a fiasco.

"We could ask Ember to help," Ruby suggests hesitantly.

"She's great at finding stuff online." She glances cautiously at me. "We don't need to tell her any more than she needs to know."

"Don't you think she'll work it out for herself?" I ask.

"She might. Ember has a nose for secrets," Ruby muses. "But even if she does, I hope you know that she'd never tell a soul."

I take a deep breath. Over the last few weeks and months, Ruby has proved what a good friend she is. She might be the best friend I've ever had. I can't imagine her going behind my back. And if she trusts her sister, then I can too.

"If you think Ember can solve my dress problem, then I'm very happy to ask her."

Ruby beams. Then stands up. "When is Percy bringing James to pick you up? Do we have time?" ·

"Training won't be over for another half hour," I say after a quick glance at the clock. "So there's no way he'll be here before quarter past seven."

"Perfect." Ruby opens the door and beckons to me. I follow her onto the landing. Ember's door is directly opposite Ruby's and slightly ajar. Ruby knocks twice.

"Ember, do you have a minute? We've got a dress emergency."

"Sure, come in," she calls.

The two of us walk into Ember's room. It's the same size as Ruby's and pretty cluttered. A bed, a desk, another narrower table with a sewing machine on it, a tailor's dummy with a dress hanging from it . . . My eyes widen.

"Is that your dress?" I ask Ruby in disbelief.

I'm longing to take a closer look at it, but I remember my manners in time. "Hi, Ember," I say with a wave.

Ruby's sister is sitting on the floor beside her bed with rolls of fabric and assorted swatches laid out in front of her. Her hair is up in a huge messy bun and a few strands have come loose. There's a pen between her teeth.

"Hi," she mumbles, putting more swatches down so that she can take the pen from her mouth. "What kind of emergency?"

"Lydia needs a dress for the Spring Ball. Ideally one by Elie Saab, but that's not an option at the moment. Do you have any ideas where we could get something to fit the theme? We've already tried all the websites you suggested."

"Elie Saab would be perfect. His clothes are so gorgeous." Ember sighs. "I've got loads of them on my dresses board on Pinterest."

"Aren't they?" I say, stepping closer to the dummy. I glance over my shoulder at Ember. "May I?"

She nods. "Sure."

I study the dress in detail. It's in pale rose with a tulle skirt and an embroidered floral bodice. On closer inspection, I notice that it's in two pieces. I presume that Ember is planning to use the wide silk ribbon to join them where it's currently pinned together.

"Did you sew this yourself?"

Ember nods.

"It's stunning," I say straight up.

Ember's cheeks color a little. "We were in luck—I only really bought the tulle for fun. It's not great quality, but nobody will be able to tell once it's finished, unless they really know their stuff."

Suddenly, I hear Mum's voice in my ear.

Talent. Pure talent.

I keep thinking about her lately. In the strangest situations and the weirdest places, I suddenly see her face or hear her voice, and although it still really hurts to think about her, those moments are beautiful and reassuring too. It's like part of Mum will always be with me.

"You're really talented, Ember. I wish I could sew this well."

"Don't you learn that, growing up in a family like yours?" she asks carefully.

I shrug.

I still remember begging my parents at the age of thirteen for lessons from one of the dressmakers. I wanted to be able to make the dresses I was designing for real, but I didn't know how. Dad wanted to see my sketches and designs so that he could decide whether it was worth paying someone to teach me. But the minute he realized that I was drawing dresses for young women, he put them down with a snort.

After that, I more or less taught myself to sew. But not even the skirts and blouses I made were enough to convince my parents that it would be worthwhile for Beaufort's to branch out into a women's collection. And after a while, I found it too depressing to sit for hours at the machine, pouring blood, sweat, and tears into pieces of clothing that nobody would ever wear.

"I used to be able to sew. Now I'm . . . out of practice," I answer after a while.

"How come?"

It's kind of nice that Ember just asks straight-out. Most people are too shy, like they don't know what's OK to ask me. Which means we just talk about superficial stuff. Ember is a rare exception. She gives me the impression of being genuinely interested in the answers.

"I always wanted to have my own line at Beaufort's, but my parents flat refused to consider women's fashion. So eventually, I gave up sewing."

Ember looks thoughtfully at me. "So you aren't designing anymore?"

"No, I am, but . . ." My shoulders twitch. "Only for me, not for Beaufort's."

"That's sad," Ruby says beside me, and Ember nods. "I could say something stupid like 'Never give up!' but I get how down it must get you to be constantly rejected. I'd lose the will after a while of that too."

"Yeah." I feel the dark clouds looming inside me, ready to whirl me into a cyclone of negative thoughts that it takes me hours to escape. Hastily, I try to take my mind off it, to think about other things. "Never mind. Back to business! Where do you think I could get a lovely dress for the Spring Ball? Ruby says that as a blogger, you've got all kinds of insider tips," I twitter. I can hear how fake my cheerfulness sounds.

Ember studies the dummy, then turns to me. "I've still got loads of fabric. If you want, I could sew you a dress too."

For a moment, I can't speak.

Then I realize that I can't possibly ask that much of her. I shake my head slowly. "That's way too much work. Besides, the party's next Saturday."

Ember waves dismissively. "Rubbish. I wouldn't have offered if I didn't have time. You must have a slip from one of your old dresses, right?" she asks. "We'll come up with something lovely. It'll be great."

"Take her up on it, Lydia," Ruby insists, putting an arm around my shoulder.

I'm so overwhelmed by their generosity, friendliness, and helpfulness that my throat constricts and my eyes start to sting. I blink frantically and take deep breaths in and out. It might just be hormones, but right now, I'm finding it really hard not to let go.

"Thanks," I mumble in the end.

"Oh, don't thank me yet. My work comes at a price. Although it's only a little thing . . ." Ember says, looking from me to Ruby with an almost fiendish smile.

I look in confusion at Ruby, who seems anything but happy.

"Ember . . ." she says, her voice serious.

"Oh, Ruby." She turns to me and says, "All I want is to come to the party with you."

"That's a great idea! Isn't it?" I ask Ruby, but she is just staring hard at her sister.

"Lydia would love me to come."

"You still haven't told me about the mysterious boy you met last time," says Ruby.

"What's that got to do with anything? I just want a nice girls' night out with you two," Ember retorts.

Ruby just raises an eyebrow.

"I saw what you ordered from that design company. I'd love to go to the fairy ball. When else will I get the chance?" Ember continues.

Ruby takes a deep breath, holds it a few seconds, then slowly exhales. "We had an agreement last time and you didn't stick to it. I'm just worried."

"I didn't get drunk and I didn't dance naked on the tables. So there's absolutely nothing for you to be worried about."

Ruby sighs. She says nothing at all for ages. She just looks as though she's listing all the pros and cons in her mind.

"The same rules apply as last time," she says in the end. "And this time you'll stick to them, OK?"

Ember's smile broadens.

"Deal?" Ruby insists.

"I would be delighted to accompany you to the Spring Ball, Ruby. Many thanks for your kind invitation!" declares Ember. When Ruby doesn't respond, she exhales audibly. "All right, fine, I'll stick to your rules, Ruby."

"OK." Ruby nods. "Then the three of us have a date."

Ember cheers and digs her elbow in my ribs. "This is going to be amazing."

I hope she's right.

27

Lydia

The dress that Ember has conjured up is dreamy. It's short-sleeved, with a bodice in a floaty, champagne-colored fabric. She's attached a tulle skirt dotted with little flowers—similar to Ruby's—that falls from right under the bust. It has a gentle drape and it's cut to hide my stomach as much as possible. I'm fairly certain Ember knows but, weirdly, I don't feel bad about that.

"I think we need to get going," Ruby says, glancing at the clock on my desk. It's dark wood with gilt patterns on the shimmering dial. Dad gave it to me for my tenth birthday. God knows why I still have it standing there. It's not like it's even particularly attractive, but I can't part with it.

"Lydia?" Ember's voice from right beside me snaps me out of my thoughts.

"Yes?"

"Are you OK?" she asks cautiously. Ember has the exact same

eyes as Ruby: green and penetrating. Sometimes I get the feeling that both sisters can see right into a person's heart.

"Yes, fine." I beam at her. "James and Percy must've been waiting twenty minutes by now. We really should go down."

Ember nods, but her expression is still thoughtful.

"Thanks again for the pamper session, Lydia," Ruby says. "It was just what we needed after all the stress of getting ready." She walks over to give me a quick hug.

"It's thanks to you two that I have something decent to wear, so that was the least I could do," I reply.

I booked hair and makeup stylists to get Ruby, Ember, and me red-carpet ready. A red carpet for fairies, of course. Or for Shakespeare in person.

We walk down to the hallway together, where James and Percy are waiting. They're chatting, and I hear Percy laugh. The sound moves me. It's the first time in ages that I've seen the two of them this lighthearted.

James turns and his eyes instantly rest on Ruby. They light up, as they do practically anytime he sees her or speaks to her.

"You all look beautiful," he says as Percy holds my coat for me to slip into.

"You say that every time," I tell James.

He just shrugs, his eyes still fixed on Ruby. She does a twirl and smiles widely at him. "I feel like a princess."

"You look like one," James replies, caressing her cheek, then bending to give her a gentle kiss.

"I still don't know if I should find that sweet or disgusting," Ember murmurs beside me.

"It's sweet," I say, almost without thinking about it. "It's so much better than seeing the pair of them being miserable."

Ruby

When we were watching the fifteen artificial trees being set up in Boyd Hall yesterday afternoon, I thought we'd made a huge mistake. By daylight, it looked weird, too big, anything but atmospheric. But as I look around now, I breathe a sigh of relief.

The soft light of the lanterns and candles, the scattered petals in blues and lilacs, and the gentle classical music being played by the school orchestra are creating a fairy-tale atmosphere, and the guests in their florals and pastels clearly feel at ease.

"Ruby, this looks amazing." Lydia sighs beside me.

"It's really beautiful," Ember agrees.

She points to the wooden swing hanging from one of the trees. The photographer is standing beside it, ready to take a photo of the couple who are getting themselves into position. The girl holds on to the flower-entwined ropes, and her boyfriend stands behind her with his hands on top of hers. It's dreamily romantic.

"We all have to get a photo taken together later on," Lydia says.

"Didn't I say it would be worth coming?" I ask before I start automatically looking around for Lin. I need to ask her if she's spoken to the caterer and checked the buffet. But before I can go to look for her, James lays his hand gently on my back.

I look inquiringly up at him.

"I know exactly what you want to do right now. But your shift doesn't start for"—he glances at his watch—"another hour."

"Did you check?" I ask in amusement.

He nods. "So now you belong to me and not to the canapés, Ruby Bell."

The next moment, he pulls me away from Lydia and Ember. I just about manage to glance back at them before I have to face the way I'm going to avoid stepping on my dress. At first I think James is leading me to the bar, but then he does a detour in the direction of the swing. Another couple has just struck a pose, and we wait a few paces behind the photographer.

I grin up at James. "Seriously? I remember the days when you were bored to death by our parties," I remark. "And now you want a couple-y photo as a souvenir?"

"You know why they bored me," I hear James say, right into my ear. I get goose bumps.

"You weren't bored, really," I say. "Admit it. It was all a façade and you were actually seriously impressed by the DJ at the Back-to-School party and just jealous that you hadn't booked him for one of your own house parties."

James snorts. "Exactly."

Suddenly, he leans in and runs his lips down my cheek and jaw. I shiver as he presses a kiss on the spot behind my ear.

"You really do look beautiful," he murmurs, and I feel his warm breath on my skin. The goose bumps spread over my whole body, and I'm about to open my mouth to return the compliment when the photographer's voice makes me jump.

"Next," he calls out, sounding bored. When he sees me in the queue, he raises an eyebrow. "Oh, hello, Ruby."

Mr. Foster and I have known each other as long as I've been doing events stuff at Maxton Hall. He does all the official event photography for the school website and blog, and the newsletter that Lexington sends out once a month. He's a pro, and I'm all the more impressed that he's prepared to spend the evening taking these Polaroid swing photos.

"Evening, Mr. Foster," I say.

"I don't think I've ever had the opportunity to photograph you before," he muses aloud, pointing to the swing. "Have a seat."

"Thanks," I mumble, sitting down as James comes to stand behind me, one hand on the rope and the other on my back. Even through my dress, I can feel his warmth. My body tingles again, and I wonder if this feeling of excitement at being close to him will ever fade. I hope not.

"Smile!" says the photographer, but there's no need—I can't help myself.

We're given the Polaroid snap and James shakes it dry before we look at it.

"That's so cheesy!"

I'm sitting on this flowery swing with James behind me, and I bet every couple here will have the exact same photo taken by the end of the evening.

And I already know that I'll grin every time I see this photo for the rest of my life.

"I like it," says James.

He smiles and slips it into his jacket pocket. Then he lifts his hand to stroke my cheek with his fingertips. I get the impression he's not even really aware that he's doing it. As he pulls his hand away, I'd love to hold it there and snuggle my cheek into his palm.

"Shall we dance?" I ask instead. I have to do something to get the heat that his gentle, matter-of-fact touch has fanned in my body under control.

James's eyebrows shoot up in surprise. "You want to dance of your own free will?"

I nod and take his hand. Before I can change my mind, I pull him onto the dance floor, among the other couples who are already moving slowly to the music.

I lay one hand on James's shoulder and start to move with him. This time I've come prepared, and I watched some videos with Ember, but I soon realize that there's no need to worry about where to put my feet. James and I are just swaying to and fro.

"At the start of the year, I'd never have dreamed I'd be here. With you," James murmurs close to my ear. "I'm so grateful."

His words send warmth flooding through me. "I'm grateful to have you too, James."

We keep moving throughout the slow dance. After a while, I raise my hand to stroke the back of his neck. James pulls me so close to him that you couldn't slip a sheet of paper between us. I can feel his breath on my body. His breathing is as uneven as mine. When I slip my other hand from his and wrap my arms around his neck, James inhales sharply. His hands wander over my waist and stroke my sides. I gulp hard and shut my eyes.

Then I feel James's lips brush my hairline.

"James . . ." I whisper, slowly opening my eyes again.

He's looking at me through half-closed eyes. I hold my breath, drink in the sight of him. His beautiful eyes, the gentle curve of his lips.

"Ruby . . ." he says hoarsely.

And then I can't resist a second longer. I stand on tiptoes and he comes to meet me.

As our lips touch, it's like pure electricity shooting through my body. This is how it always is with James. I can't describe it, but a single kiss from him is enough to turn my world upside down and make me forget everything around me.

James strokes his tongue gently over my bottom lip and I allow him in. I bury my hands in his hair and feel his groan against my lips.

"God, get a room," says a cutting voice beside us.

James pulls away and I blink several times. Then I look over James's shoulder and see Camille dancing with a guy from our year. She rolls her eyes.

"We're awful," I mumble, burying my face in James's shoulder. Suddenly, I notice him stiffen. "What . . . ?"

I look up. James is staring at something behind me, and I turn to follow his gaze.

Mr. Sutton just walked onto the dance floor with a woman.

"Isn't that our tutor from the Oxford study group?" I ask.

"Philippa Winfield," James murmurs. He always remembers names—even of people he's only met once. I think it's the kind of thing that gets drilled into you as the heir to a major business.

"They seem pretty friendly," I say as Mr. Sutton puts his arm around Pippa. She smiles at him—her high heels mean they can look straight into each other's eyes—and then leans in to whisper something in his ear, which makes him laugh. It sounds shy, very different from the way he laughs in lessons.

"Fuck," James breathes at the same moment that Mr. Sutton looks over Pippa's shoulder and his cheerful expression dies away.

It's not long before I see why.

Lydia.

She's standing close to the dance floor and saw the whole thing. Now she turns on her heel and leaves the hall through one of the rear doors.

I want to go to her, but James is holding me back by the hand. Before I can ask him why, he nods in the direction that Lydia just fled.

Mr. Sutton is running after her.

"Do you think that's a good idea?" I ask hesitantly.

James's face is unreadable. "The two of them have to talk eventually. And I think they'd rather be left alone right now."

James knows Lydia better than anyone, so I trust him.

"I don't want her to get hurt," I mumble.

That makes James glance warmly at me. "She's got this. I'm sure of that."

The certainty in his words and the way he's suddenly looking at me give me the impression that it's not just Lydia he's thinking of.

For the first time since I met him, he seems to have faith in his own happiness. And that makes me very happy too.

28

Lydia

I wish I hadn't come. I should have listened to my gut and not let them convince me. I knew it wouldn't be easy for me to see Graham. But I never expected this.

Just now, when he was dancing with Pippa, when he put his arm around her like it was so ordinary, when she smiled at him and he smiled back, when the distance between their faces was shrinking more and more—I just couldn't bear it. It was too much.

And even now, in the empty corridor, with no music and no people around me, my heart won't stop racing. I feel sick and my hands are clammy. Dots are dancing before my eyes. My blood pressure must be way high. At once, I lay a hand on my bump, like that will tell me anything about whether the twins are OK.

"Lydia?"

I lower my hand and turn around.

Graham is standing just a few feet from me, his jacket unbuttoned, his eyebrows narrowing pensively.

"What?" I snap. Oh, how sick I am of pretending to everyone that everything in my life is fine. Nothing is fine. Least of all now, with him facing me. He ran after me when I thought he hadn't even seen me. And he's looking at me like he knows what's going on inside me—the way he always used to.

I can't look away. The pressure that has been building up inside me has got to the point that I can't hold it in anymore.

"Did you have fun?"

His expression darkens and his frown deepens. "It was just one dance, Lydia."

I snort disdainfully. "What I saw in there was a lot more than just 'dancing.'"

We've never argued before and now I know why. It feels shit, and snarling at him like this isn't even liberating.

"She asked me, and turning her down would have looked weird. People are already gossiping about me as it is."

I laugh. "So, you were on the verge of making out with my tutor in the middle of the dance floor to stop people wondering if you're seeing someone?"

The words emerge from my mouth louder than I intended, and Graham glances anxiously over his shoulder.

"I hate this, Graham," I say. My voice is cold yet trembling. I've never heard myself speak like this before. "I hate that you can't even speak three words to me without looking all around you in panic." I clench my fists and put all my strength into fighting the stinging at the backs of my eyes.

"Do you think I'm enjoying it?" he retorts suddenly.

I can only snort again.

Now he clenches his fists too. "I'm trying to do the right thing for both of us!"

"The right thing?" I can't believe he just said that. "You think it's right to dance with other women—while I watch on?"

"Do you think I *like* this? Keeping away from you, acting like we never met?" he asks in disbelief. Then he clutches his hair, shakes his head. "It hurts like hell, Lydia, and it's getting worse every day."

"Well, that's certainly not my fault!" I almost scream the words, and then bite my lip. I take a deep breath and remember the stuff Mum drummed into me about composure all my life. "I don't call you," I continue more quietly. "I don't speak in your lessons. I don't even bloody well look at you. So, if you'd be so good as to let me know what else I should be doing so as not to hurt *your* feelings . . ."

Graham shakes his head again. Then he takes a long stride toward me—and holds my face in his hands.

For a moment, it's like I've been turned to stone. Then I push his arms away. He can't touch me like that—if he does, it feels like the old days, and I can't bear that for even a second.

"We can't go on like this, Lydia," he croaks.

"Like I just told you, I've stuck to my end of the deal."

"Me too. But it's going to break both of us."

I feel my anger gradually ebbing away, leaving only pain. Pain that's tearing me apart from the inside, so that I can't breathe.

I wish I hadn't pushed him away. And I wish I'd done it harder.

"It was just a dance," Graham whispers.

All I do is nod. I long to look away, but I can't. Graham and I—it's been ages since we've been this close. I get the feeling that I have to breathe in every second before the moment is over and I'm left here on my own.

"Nothing has changed on my part, Lydia."

I catch my breath. "What—what do you mean?"

Graham comes another step closer but doesn't touch me. "I mean that you're the first thought on my mind when I wake up. I think about you all day long. If I see something funny, you're the first person I want to tell. I hear your voice in my ear when I fall asleep. For God's sake, Lydia, I love you. I loved you from our first phone call. I will never stop loving you, even though I know there's no chance for us."

My heart is beating as fast as if I'd just run a marathon. I can't believe he just said that.

"I'll change schools."

That tears me out of my stupor. I shake my head. "No. You can't do that. You said yourself that Maxton Hall is the best thing that ever happened to you. That you'll never find a better job."

"I don't care. I want to be able to be there for you again. I want to be able to walk into a café with you, to hold your hand. And I want my best friend back. If I have to take a worse job to get that, then I'll be happy to."

I shake my head again, confused by this sudden switch. "I . . . You can't. Why suddenly now?"

"It's not a spur-of-the-moment thing. Since my very first day here, I've been thinking about leaving. Every morning, I ask myself whether Maxton Hall is really worth us having lost each other."

"But we—" I break off, unable to think straight.

"We decided it together. That's why I didn't say anything. I was afraid of pressuring you. But now . . ."

The tears flow faster and I can't hold them back. I pinch my eyes together and a silent sob shakes me. This time, when Graham touches me, I don't stop him, just let my brow rest wearily against his chest and allow him to gently stroke my cheek.

"I'm so sorry that I can't be there for you, Lydia," he whispers.

The longing for him is almost unbearable at this moment. And so is my guilty conscience, because I still haven't told him about the pregnancy, and my grief—not just for our relationship, but for our friendship. I dig my hand into his shirt and hold him tight. "I miss my mum. And I miss you. All the time."

"I know. I'm so sorry." He strokes me again.

His soft touch reminds me of the first time we met. Then we were nothing more than friends who'd met online, but he held me in this same way when a young woman in the café asked me about the newspaper headlines. I tried not to let anyone see how much her words had affected me, but Graham could tell at once, and he took me in his arms. He whispered into my ear that everything would be OK. Just like he's doing now.

His soothing voice eases my pain, and as he runs his thumb over my wet cheek and assures me that we'll get there, I sink into the dream for the moment, into the illusion he's created.

But then Graham stiffens.

"Lydia," he whispers.

I move away from him a little and follow his gaze.

At the end of the corridor, only fifteen feet away, is Cyril.

His face is paler than I've ever seen it, and he's staring in disbelief from Graham to me and back again. His mouth drops open.

But then his face changes. His eyebrows contract, his eyes narrow to slits, and he grits his teeth so hard that his jawbone juts out.

The next moment, he turns on his heel and vanishes back into Boyd Hall.

"Fuck," I mutter, pulling away from Graham completely.

"Lydia . . ."

I shake my head and wipe my fingers over my damp cheeks again. "I have to speak to him. Could we talk later . . . on the phone?"

Graham looks like his whole body is strained, but at my words, a warmth creeps into his golden-brown eyes that I haven't seen in months. It's familiar, like a faded memory that is slowly regaining color and becoming a reality.

"I'll call you," he says. "After the ball."

"OK," I whisper.

For a moment, I'm tempted to hug him again, but then Cyril's disbelieving face looms up in my inner eye and instead I turn tail to look for him.

═══

I run after Cyril as fast as I can and catch him just by the exit from Boyd Hall.

"Cy . . ." I gasp, reaching for his elbows.

He whirls around and snatches his arm away. "Don't touch me."

I raise my hands, shocked by his cold tone. Cyril has never spoken to me like that before. And the way he's looking at me is entirely new: disdainful, disgusted. He shakes his head.

"I can't believe you did that, Lydia."

I frown up at him. "I can't believe you think you're in any position to judge me, Cy. Or do I have to remind you of some of the people you've been with?"

Cyril flinches. "You think I'm pissed off because you're shagging your teacher?"

Now I'm the one to flinch. There's a little group of people behind Cyril, who've just walked out of the hall.

"Why else?" I ask quietly.

He makes a sound of despair and leans his head back, staring up as if the heavens could tell him what to say next. Then he looks back at me and gulps hard.

"I'm pissed off with you because you've been holding out on me for ages."

My mouth drops open. "What?"

"There's only you for me, Lydia. I've been in love with you for years."

"But," I croak. "But we . . . I . . . It was never anything serious."

Cyril looks like I've slapped his face. He opens his mouth, but not a word emerges.

"I didn't know you felt like this," I whisper. Cautiously, I stretch my hand out toward him a second time and touch his arm. He's my friend; I've known him since we were kids. If I'd had any idea that he was serious about me, I'd never have got involved.

"Are you telling me you never noticed?" he exclaims in disbelief.

I nod in silence.

"You never noticed that I haven't been with anyone since our little fling? You never noticed that after your mum died, I was there for you from morning to night, to comfort you?"

"That's what friends do for one another," I whisper tearfully.

"I wouldn't do that for just anyone," he says, his tone bitter. "I'd only do it for you."

I stare at him, unable to move. Nausea washes over me, and

more tears are rolling down my cheeks. "I'm sorry. I . . . I never meant to hurt you."

Cyril hesitantly lifts a hand and wipes away one of my tears. Then his face hardens. "But you did."

With those words, he turns away and walks toward the parking lot.

James

This evening is definitely not going the way I imagined.

The original plan was to spend as much time with Ruby as possible, seeing that each of us was only on duty for an hour, after which we'd be free to do whatever we liked. I wanted to dance with her, party with her, and kiss her as often as she would let me in front of everyone else.

But then Lydia suddenly burst back into Boyd Hall. At first we thought her conversation with Sutton had gone badly, or that he'd said something to hurt her. When we finally got her to tell us what had actually happened, I immediately went in search of Cyril.

Neither Alistair nor Keshav had any idea where he could be, and it took me ages to find Wren, who could at least tell me that Cyril had driven home in a hurry some time earlier. So then I called a taxi and asked Percy to drive Lydia, Ember, and Ruby home.

Now I'm standing outside Cyril's front door, pressing the bell again and again. I can hear it clanging from out here, the sound echoing through the house. I'm sure Cyril's at home—his car is in the driveway and I saw a light on upstairs in his room as the taxi approached.

I ring again. And again. Just as I'm lifting my finger the third time, the door flies open.

And a waft of booze hits me. It's been no more than an hour since his encounter with Lydia, but Cyril's swaying on his feet. His dark hair is all over the place and the top buttons of his shirt are undone.

"What a surprise. Lydia's sent her watchdog round," he slurs.

"Can I come in?" I ask.

Cyril flings the door wider, turns, and walks up the stairs without looking at me. The whole house is dark. Looks like his folks aren't back yet.

I follow him up to the first floor and straight into his room. The window is open, but the clouds of smoke and alcohol fumes hang heavily in the air.

Cyril sits on the windowsill. I can see a cigarette stub glowing in an ashtray. He picks it up, takes a deep drag, and leans back.

"So," he begins, still not looking at me. "You're here to buy my silence?"

"I'm here because I'm worried about you," I reply, walking over to the window.

Cyril turns and looks at me, eyebrows raised.

"And because Lydia's worried too."

He snorts with laughter and takes another puff. Next to the ashtray is a bottle of whisky that's less than half full. Can he really have drunk all that in the last hour?

I'd never have imagined seeing Cyril in this state.

"I'm sorry, mate."

Cyril stubs out the cigarette. Then he grabs the bottle, lifts it to his lips, and tips back his head.

"I don't get it," he mutters after a while, through clenched teeth. He wipes his mouth with the back of his hand and sets the bottle down with a clatter. "I just don't understand why."

I don't know how to answer that. Cyril's been hoping for years that he and Lydia might get together. Learning that all his waiting was in vain must be really doing him over.

"I'd have done anything for her. Anything," he says, shaking his head. That seems to make him dizzy, because he lurches a little to one side. I grab his arm and pull him down from the windowsill.

"I know," I say.

Suddenly, Cyril grabs me with both hands. "You have no idea how it feels, James. To hope for something for years and to see it break in front of your eyes."

His face is twisted with pain. He's swaying, can't stand up straight. Without another thought, I take his arms and steer him toward the bed. I give him a gentle nudge so that he has to sit down. Once I'm sure he's not going to wobble over again, I let go of him and go to shut the window. Then I pull the heavy gray curtains.

I turn to Cyril. He's leaning forward, his face buried in his hands. The sight of him makes me sad. This whole situation is fucked up, and I'm sorry for Cy, but I have to look out for Lydia first. She's the one with everything to lose if her relationship with Sutton comes out.

I sit next to Cyril on the bed. "You mustn't tell a soul, Cy," I insist.

He just shakes his head. Then he lowers his hands and turns to face me. "Do you think I'd really ever do anything to hurt Lydia?"

I look back at him. "No, I don't think so."

He nods.

Then he stares in silence at his hands for a while. "I always thought that what we had was as important to her as it is to me."

"It's not anything you did. That part is obvious."

He just growls and then falls back onto the bed with a groan.

"I'll get you a glass of water," I say after a moment.

Cyril doesn't reply, so I stand up and walk down to the kitchen. When I get back, he's sitting up in bed again. I've brought a bucket up with me too in case he feels sick overnight, and Cyril eyes it mockingly.

"Here," I say, holding out the glass. He takes it and forces himself to have a couple of sips. After that, he puts it down on the bedside table.

"Is there anything else I can do for you?" I ask.

"No, thanks, bro. I think I need some time alone."

"OK, then I'll be going." I gesture over my shoulder with my thumb.

Cyril gives a curt nod. Then he does something he hasn't done for at least ten years—he gets up and wraps his arms around me. I'm taken by surprise, but then I clap him on the back. He's leaning half his weight against me and I'm doing my best to hold him up.

"You'll get through this," I say quietly.

Cyril pulls away from me and won't meet my eye. It's clear he doesn't believe a word of it.

Ruby

It's half past one when James finally gets home. He knocks quietly on Lydia's door and opens it a crack. When he sees me sitting on the bed, beside his sleeping sister, the smile that crosses his lips makes my stomach tingle. Cautiously, I stand up, trying not to make a sound. James's smile broadens as he sees that I've changed out of the dress into one of his T-shirts and a pair of Lydia's leggings.

It's only once I've shut the door gently behind me that I dare to say anything. Lydia was so distraught when we got here—I really don't want to wake her.

"You're here," he greets me softly.

I nod. "I was going to go home with Ember, but Lydia was so upset that I didn't want to leave her on her own. So I told Mum I'd stay over with you. Did you find Cyril?"

James's smile fades. "He was pretty out of it. I don't know if he'll remember a thing in the morning."

That's not particularly reassuring.

"I trust Cy," James adds. "You can rely on him in this kind of stuff."

I eye him skeptically, but in the end I nod. "OK."

James glances down the landing and then looks back to me. I reach for his hand and tug gently, and we walk together to his room.

When we get there, I sit down on his king-size bed.

"Is Lydia doing better now?" James asks, slipping off his jacket and loosening his tie. Then he drops down beside me.

"Yeah," I reply pensively. "I think so. Mr. Sutton called her and they talked a while."

James doesn't seem to know what to make of that. He exhales audibly and rubs his forehead.

"What's wrong?"

He grunts. "I don't want Lydia to get into trouble. I just don't know how to stop all the secrets collapsing in on themselves like a house of cards."

"They won't," I say softly, leaning forward to touch him. I feel a need to comfort him when he looks like this, and I wish I could do more than just stroke his cheek.

James looks at me, his eyes dark. "I'd do anything for the people I love."

I stroke my fingers further down his throat. Hold the nape of his neck in my hand, rub my thumb along his hairline. "I know."

"That includes you, Ruby."

I pause in mid-gesture and gulp hard. Suddenly, there's a lump in my throat that I can't swallow down.

"I love you," he whispers.

There's so much emotion in his voice, along with so much pain that, for a brief moment, I don't think I can breathe.

But the next instant, my body reacts to his admission as if by itself. I lean forward until I'm kneeling on the bed and level with James. Tenderly, I lower my mouth to his and kiss him, just fleetingly.

"I love you too, James," I whisper back, resting my brow against his.

I hear James breathe in. "Really?"

I nod and kiss him again.

It's only meant to be another brief kiss—but then James puts a hand on the back of my head and what began gently is soon more. I lose my balance and fall sideways, onto the soft down. James doesn't break off the kiss, even for a second. All the words I still want to say vanish from my tongue as James parts my lips with his. I sigh gently.

This time, when he pulls away, we're both breathless.

"Thank you for being here for us both today," he murmurs.

We're lying on our sides, our faces turned to each other. James gently strokes upward from my waist, lays his hand on my rib cage. He's drawing little patterns on my skin.

I still remember exactly what it felt like the first time he touched me—it felt like his fingers were burning through my clothes, right onto my skin. And it's the same now, as his hand travels down again, coming to rest on my thigh.

"Thank you for letting me be there for you," I whisper, stroking a strand of his red-blond hair off his forehead. I could run my hands through his hair forever; I love the way it feels under my fingers.

We lie there in silence. The only thing I can hear is our even breathing. We can't let each other go. I have to touch James the whole time, as if I'm making it clear to myself that this, here and now, is reality. That we really have found our way back to each other, and that this new, ever-growing trust exists between us.

I fight against it, but eventually, my eyelids are so heavy that I can barely hold them open. James is there when I fall asleep, one hand in mine, the other nestled gently in my hair.

30

Ruby

"What do you think?" Lin asks the following Monday, pushing her planner over the table toward me.

I study the entry she's made in purple pen. Among the Chinese characters, I read in her neat handwriting *Move to Oxford*; in the field for the next day, she's added *Celebrate with Ruby*. I grin broadly at Lin. And although the whole thing is still months away, I pick up my gold pen from my pencil case, flick through my planner to find the monthly overview of the year, and write the same things.

"Ta-da," I whisper, just as the bell goes for lunch. Lin and I start to pack up our things, but before I can slip on my backpack, we hear the gong again—but briefer this time.

"Will Ruby Bell come to Mr. Lexington's office immediately?" the head teacher's secretary announces over the loudspeaker. At once, every head in the room turns to stare at me.

I frown up at the clock over the classroom door. We're not due to meet Lexie until just before the end of lunch. If he wants to see me now, something must have happened.

Goose bumps spread over my body as I frantically try to guess what it might be.

"Should I come too?" Lin asks as we walk out of the room.

"No, you go and get something to eat." I grip the straps on my bag.

"OK. Do you know what you want? I can pick it up for you so you don't have to come back and queue."

"That would be lovely. I'll have whatever you're getting, thanks."

Lin squeezes my arm for a moment before we head in opposite directions. The way to the head's office feels much longer than normal. A queasy feeling grows with every step. And when the secretary waves me in with a stern glare, my heart feels like it's about to burst out of my chest.

I take a deep breath, knock on the heavy wooden door, and walk in.

My greeting dies in my throat.

Sitting in front of the head teacher's desk is my mum.

Instantly, I'm imagining horrible things like Dad in hospital after another accident.

"Is Dad OK?" I ask, hurrying toward her.

"Your father is fine, Ruby," Mum answers, not taking her eyes off the solid wooden desk.

I look in confusion from Mum to Mr. Lexington.

"Take a seat, Miss Bell," he says, pointing to the empty chair next to Mum. Hesitantly, I do as I'm told.

Lexington folds his hands on the desk in front of him and looks at me over the top of his glasses.

"Nothing is more important to me than the reputation of our school. We have been known for centuries for excellence and achievement. If anyone acts against the interests of the school, I must take action myself. You must surely be aware of this by now."

I gulp. "I thought the Spring Ball was a complete success, sir. But if anything went wrong, then I'm really sorry, but . . ." Before I can finish my sentence, Lexington pulls open one of the little drawers in his desk and pulls out four photographs, which he fans out in front of us.

"These photographs were sent to me over the weekend by a concerned member of the Parents' Committee," he continues unabated.

I hear Mum inhale sharply and lean in for a closer look. The photos are dark, and at first, I can't make anything out. Then I see myself.

They're photos of *me*.

I pick up one of the printouts and hold it up to my eyes.

It takes me a moment to process what I'm seeing—it must be from the Back-to-School party. That's the only time I wore that green dress.

But I'm not alone in the photo. I'm standing close to a man.

Mr. Sutton.

And it looks as though we're kissing.

I remember talking to him. But we never got that close together. I have no idea who took the pictures, but they're clearly intended to harm me—or Sutton.

"I see what that looks like, but I—"

"Miss Bell, I don't think you understand," Mr. Lexington interrupts. "These photos were sent to me by one of the parents, and a fellow student here has confirmed seeing you and Mr. Sutton together."

"We were only talking!" I exclaim in outrage.

"Ruby, watch your tone," Mum snaps. As I glance sideways at her, a cold shiver runs down my spine.

Mum has never looked at me like that before—with that total disappointment on her face. But before I can defend myself, Lexington goes on and Mum looks away from me.

"I have never known anything like this in my whole twenty years at this school, Miss Bell. I will not permit the reputation of Maxton Hall to be damaged by a fling with a teacher."

"I don't have flings!" I cry.

I can't believe this is happening. It must be a nightmare.

"I have a boyfriend," I continue. "I . . . I would never get involved with a teacher. I'd never do a thing like that, I swear."

I can't say that it was Lydia who was seeing Mr. Sutton. That's out of the question. Not after everything she's been through, and everything she still has to face. I'd never abuse her trust like that.

"I don't think you appreciate the gravity of the situation, Ruby," Lexington continues, picking up one of the photos. "I think it is best for all concerned if you leave the school. You and Mr. Sutton are both suspended from Maxton Hall with immediate effect."

Silence.

It feels as though someone's pulled out the plug on me. All I can hear is a ringing in my ears. The seconds drag on in slow motion. Lexington's mouth is moving, but I take in no sound.

"You can't do this," I gasp. "I need to get my A levels; I need my grades for Oxford."

Mr. Lexington doesn't reply, just shuffles the photos together again and puts them back in an envelope. It's brown and I see a stamp in the top left-hand corner—presumably the return address. I squint at it and make out a curving black "B."

My heart skips a beat.

That's impossible.

They can't have done that.

They'd never betray me like this.

"Who was it that said they saw me?" I ask breathlessly.

Now Lexington is looking almost pityingly at me. "That is confidential, Miss Bell. Would you now kindly leave my office? We will confirm the suspension in writing. Good day to you."

He flicks through the pile of papers on his desk and then turns his attention back to his computer—an unmistakable sign that we're dismissed.

No. Fucking. Way.

"Do you know how much I've worked my arse off for this school?" I blurt suddenly.

Mr. Lexington looks up again slowly. "Don't make me call in security, Miss Bell."

"You can't throw me out just because I'm here on a scholarship and don't have rich enough parents to bribe you to ignore rumors about me!"

"I will not be spoken to like this!" gasps Mr. Lexington.

"You absolute—"

"Ruby!" Mum cuts me off sharply. She grabs me by the arm and pulls me out of the chair.

Without another word, she drags me out of the office and into the waiting area outside it. I'm raging, and stare at Lexington every step of the way until Mum slams the door behind us.

This didn't just happen. It can't have done.

I shake my head and turn to my mum. "Can you believe that? How sick would you have to be to dream up a thing like that?" I ask her.

Mum just shakes her head and won't meet my eyes. Her gaze

is fixed on a point somewhere over my shoulder. "I knew something like this would happen if we sent you to this bloody school."

I flinch and my eyes narrow. "Wh . . . What?"

Mum shakes her head. "How could you, Ruby?"

"I'm telling you, I didn't do anything!" I yell.

If my own mother won't believe me, I don't know what else to do. Despair floods through me, runs through my veins, making it hard to breathe.

"Mum, you have to believe me—I'd never kiss a teacher."

"I'd never have thought that you'd lie to us so you could sleep with your boyfriend either, but apparently things have changed in the last few months."

I gape open-mouthed at her.

Mum takes a deep breath and then sighs. "I don't have anything to say to you right now, Ruby. I'm so disappointed in you."

Tears fill my eyes. I try to find the words, but there are none. My body feels numb. The only thought racing through my head is this: *Who the fuck took those pictures?*

"Mum . . ."

"Get the bus home," she says, gulping hard. "I have to speak to your father."

"I didn't do it, Mum."

She doesn't respond to my words, just adjusts her handbag strap on her shoulder, turns, and walks away down the corridor.

I'm left alone.

Lexington's words are echoing in my head on a loop.

You are suspended from Maxton Hall with immediate effect.

Suspended. Just before the Easter holidays. Before my A levels. With my St. Hilda's offer printed out and pinned to my noticeboard at home.

If I don't get the grades, I can forget Oxford.

Everything I've spent the last eleven years working toward.

The recognition of what just happened hits me full force. I sway, have to grip on to the secretary's desk as the world seems to spin around me. I have to fight to walk out of the room without collapsing.

In the corridor, I meet gaggles of younger kids on their way to lunch, and my feet want to turn toward the dining hall. But I'm not allowed in there.

I'm not allowed to go to events committee meetings.

You are suspended from Maxton Hall with immediate effect.

I'm not even allowed to be in this corridor anymore.

"Ruby?" a familiar voice says behind me.

I look up, eyes blurred with tears. James is there. As he sees how shaken up I am, he takes my upper arm gently.

"I heard them call you. What happened?" he asks urgently.

I can only shake my head. Saying it out loud is just too crazy—and it would turn this nightmare into reality. The only thing I can do is fall into James and cling to him. I bury my face in his blazer and let the tears fall for a moment. Just a moment, just until I've got solid ground under my feet again.

"Mr. Lexington . . . said I'm suspended," I manage after a while. I pull away from James and look up at him. He wipes my eyes with his hand, looking confused. "Apparently someone took photos of me and Mr. Sutton which make it look like we're kissing."

James's hand freezes on my cheek. "What?"

I can only shake my head.

James pulls away from me and stares wide-eyed at me. "What did you say?"

"Someone sent Lexie these photos that make it look like it was me in a relationship with Sutton," I whisper urgently. I wipe my eyes, my hand shaking. A few people stare at me as they pass, and among them, I spot a pair of ice-blue eyes.

"That's impossible," James stammers.

"Why?" asks Cyril. "You were the one who took those pictures, Beaufort."

Stunned, I look from James to Cyril and back again. "What?" I whisper.

James doesn't respond. He's just staring at Cyril, who is standing there, head aslant, hands deep in his pockets.

"Go on. Tell her," he insists.

"What the fuck are you talking about, Cyril?" I ask, digging my fingers into James's arm.

Cyril raises a challenging eyebrow. "Ask him, Ruby. Ask him who took the photos."

I look back at James as he stands there motionless.

"James?" I whisper.

As I say his name, he seems to come out of his stupor. He turns to me and gulps hard.

I look into his eyes.

Panic rises up inside me.

This can't be true.

"Who took those photos?"

James is breathing faster now too. He slowly raises a hand as if to touch me but doesn't dare. "It's not like . . ."

"*Who*, James?"

James opens his mouth, then shuts it. He pinches his eyes together and I see him swallow. Once. Twice.

When he opens his eyes again, it feels like someone has stabbed me in the chest.

"He's right, Ruby."

The ground beneath my feet shatters into millions of tiny shards.

"I took the photos."

And I'm falling.

EPILOGUE

Ember

I feel like a traitor.

My gaze darts to the clock, to the counter and the barista behind it, to my cappuccino, and back to the café door. Then the cycle begins again. And again.

Every minute seems to pass more slowly than the one before.

I've missed a whole period of school now. I've never felt this guilty before, not even when Mum caught me pinching a scone from the counter in the bakery after she'd said I couldn't have one.

But this is a million times worse. This time, I'm doing something really wrong.

The excitement builds and I can hardly keep still. I fidget in my chair, wondering if the cappuccino was a bad idea. I don't drink much coffee, really, but I got so little sleep last night, I thought the caffeine would do me good. Probably would have been better off without.

Ten more minutes.

I ask myself if I can hold out. I think about packing up my stuff, getting up, and walking out, only to reappear in thirteen minutes like I've only just arrived. But even I think that's a bit over-the-top.

It's crazy what nerves are doing to me.

I don't normally get this worked up about anything. But then, I don't normally go behind my parents' back, skip school, and meet up with a boy I don't even really know.

I flick absently through the pile of leaflets and forms for grants and bursaries. There are Post-its in some of them where Ruby's highlighted important information, and I'm sure the color scheme is deeply significant.

The bell over the café door rings. I look up—and suddenly everything around me goes into slow motion.

He actually came.

His eyes sweep over the people in the café. His brows crease into a frown for a moment, then he spots me at the table by the wall. I give a hesitant wave. His forehead smooths for a second and his lips curl into a smile.

He strolls slowly toward me.

He's wearing a black leather jacket with wide lapels over a gray T-shirt with a pocket on the chest, dark jeans, and heavy boots. It's a great look, effortlessly stylish. This is the first time I've seen him not wearing a suit—I was wondering how he dresses in his free time.

The half smile doesn't fade from his face as he takes the chair opposite me.

My heart is racing. There's so much darkness in his eyes that I want to get to the bottom of. So much that I'm *going* to get to the bottom of.

"Morning, Ember," says Wren Fitzgerald.

A smile slowly spreads over my lips.

ACKNOWLEDGMENTS

First of all, I would like to thank my editor, Stephanie Bubley, for her tireless work with me on this novel, and for always making the effort to draw everything possible and more from my stories. Here too, my thanks go to my agent, Christiane Düring, and LYX Verlag for making this series possible and doing everything so that the stories can find their way to readers.

Thank you to my beta reader Laura Janßen for her comments on Ember's chapters, which really helped me rework them. I would also like to thank Kim Nina Ocker, who was always there to listen to me—this book is dedicated to you.

Thanks go to my husband, Christian, who always had my back so that I could steer Ruby and James back on track, and who worked on the plot with me in the car when I was stuck.

At this point I owe many, many thanks to Flavia Viotti and Giuseppe Terrano, through whose efforts *Save You* found its way to the other side of the world, to Berkley, where the Maxton Hall trilogy has found its home in English, and particularly to Cindy Hwang.

And finally, I would like to thank all the readers who have come with me to Maxton Hall. It is a joy to me every time to see how much you root for Ruby, James, and friends. See you again soon!

Keep reading for an excerpt from

SAVE US

The third novel in the Maxton Hall series
by Mona Kasten

Graham

When I was younger, my grandfather always used to ask me, "If one day you lost everything, what would you do?" I would never think seriously about my answer to the question, just say whatever popped into my head first at that moment.

When I was six, and my brother had deliberately broken my toy truck, I said, *I'll fix the digger.*

When I was ten, and we moved from Manchester to the outskirts of London, I said, *I'll just have to find new friends.*

And when I was seventeen, my mum died, and while I was trying to be strong for my dad and my brother, I said, *We can get through this.*

Even then, giving up was not an option.

But now, aged almost twenty-four, sitting here in this office where I suddenly feel like a criminal, I no longer have an answer. At this moment I feel as though there's no way out of this situation, that my future is uncertain. I don't know how I'm meant to go on from here.

The drawer squeaks as I pull it out of the heavy cherrywood

desk. I dig around in the muddle of pens and notepads that have accumulated there over the last year. My movements are slow; my arms feel like lead. But I need to hurry—I have to be out of the building by the end of lunch.

You are suspended with immediate effect. You are expressly forbidden from maintaining any contact with Maxton Hall students. If you breach this ban, I will go to the police.

The pens fall through my fingers and clatter onto the floor.

Bloody fucking hell.

I bend down, pick them up, and dump them into a box with the rest of my belongings. It's a mishmash of notes, textbooks, my grandfather's globe, and handouts I'd photocopied for tomorrow's lessons and now might as well leave behind, although I can't bring myself to do that.

I look around the office. The shelves are bare, and there's nothing but a few bits of paper on the desk and the smudged writing pad to show that I was marking essays here until a few hours ago.

You only have yourself to blame, a spiteful voice nags in my head.

I rub my pounding temples as I check all the drawers and cubbyholes in the desk one last time. I shouldn't drag out my goodbyes any longer than strictly necessary, but I'm surprised by how reluctant I am to tear myself away from this room. I'd decided weeks ago to look for a job in another school so that I could be together with Lydia. But there is a major difference between leaving a job of your own accord and being escorted out by security.

I gulp hard and take my jacket from the wooden coat stand. Mechanically, I pull it on, then grab the box and walk to the door. I leave the office without a backward glance.

The questions are piling up in my head: *Does Lydia know? How is she? When will I be able to see her? What should I do now? Can I ever work as a teacher again? What if I can't?*

But I can't find the answers to them now. All I can do is fight the rising panic and walk down the corridor toward the school office to drop off my keys. Kids run past me, and some of them greet me politely. My stomach is throbbing painfully. It's a struggle to smile back at them. Teaching here was fun.

I turn the corner and suddenly it feels as though someone's tipped a bucket of ice-cold water over my head. I stop so abruptly that someone crashes into me from behind and murmurs an apology. But I barely take it in—my eyes are fixed on the tall, red-blond young man whom I have to thank for this entire situation.

James Beaufort's face doesn't flinch at the sight of me. Far from it—he looks totally unbothered, as if he hasn't just screwed up my entire life.

I knew what he was capable of. And I was aware that it wasn't a good idea to get on the wrong side of him. Lexington warned me as much on my first day at this school. "You never know what he and his friends will do next. Watch out for them." I didn't pay much attention to his words because I knew the other side of the story. Lydia had told me how hard all the family expectations were on her twin, and how he'd closed himself off from everyone, even from her.

In hindsight, I feel like a total idiot for not having been more careful. I should have known that James would do anything for Lydia. Having destroyed my career is probably all in a day's work for him.

Standing next to James is Cyril Vega. It's a good thing he doesn't take history, seeing that I can't set eyes on him without picturing him and Lydia together. Walking out of school together and getting into a Rolls. Laughing together. Cyril with his arms around her, comforting her after her mother's death in the way I never could.

After the tiniest hesitation, I grit my teeth and walk on, the box jammed under my arm. I grip the keys in my pocket more tightly as I come closer toward them. They've broken off their conversation and are watching me, each of them with a hard, impenetrable mask of a face.

I stop by the door to the school office and turn to James. "Happy now?"

He doesn't respond, which makes the anger inside me boil over.

"What were you thinking?" I ask, glaring at him. "Didn't you and your friends realize that your childish prank would destroy my career?"

James exchanges glances with Cyril, and his cheeks flush slightly—just like his sister's do when she gets angry. The two of them look so similar and yet, in my eyes, they couldn't be more different.

"You're the one who ought to have been thinking," Cyril spits.

His eyes are more furious even than James's, and it occurs to me that getting me kicked out was probably a joint effort.

The expression on Cyril's face leaves me in no doubt that he has all the power here. He can do what he likes to me, even though I'm older than he is. He's won, and he knows it. There's triumph in his eyes and arrogance in his stance.

I bark out a resigned laugh.

"Beats me why you're laughing," he goes on. "It's over. We know what you are. Don't you get it?"

I clench my fist around the key ring so hard that the little metal teeth cut into my skin. Does this rich brat really think I don't get it? Does he think I'm not entirely aware that nobody gives a shit when and where Lydia and I first met? That nobody will believe us if we insist that we had already fallen in love before I started at Maxton Hall? And that we broke up the moment I found out that I'd be her teacher? Of course I knew it. From now on and for all time, I'm going to be the creep who got involved with a student on his very first teaching job.

The thought makes me sick.

I walk into the office without deigning to look at the two of them again. I pull the keys from my jacket pocket and slam them onto the desk, then turn on my heel. As I walk past the lads again, I glimpse Cyril pushing a phone into James's hand out of the corner of my eye. "Thanks for that, mate," he says. I turn away and hurry toward the door as fast as I can. I dimly register that James is raising his voice.

Every step hurts; every breath feels like a monumental effort. There's a roaring in my ears that drowns out pretty much everything else. The students' laughter, their echoing footsteps, the creaking of the double doors as I walk out of Maxton Hall and into the unknown.

Ruby

I feel numb.

The bus driver shouts out that it's the end of the line, but I can't make sense of her words. Eventually, I grasp that I've got to get off if I don't want to ride all the way back to Pemwick. I've been so sunk in thought that I have no memory of the last forty-five minutes.

My limbs feel heavy yet tingly all at once when I step out into the air. I grip my backpack with both hands as if the straps could hold me up. But it doesn't help to shake off the feeling that I've been caught up in a whirlwind from which there's no escape. Like I no longer know up from down.

This can't have just happened. I can't have been kicked out of school. Mum can't really have thought I'd get involved with a teacher. My dreams of Oxford can't have just gone up in smoke.

I must be losing my mind. My breath is coming ever faster and my fingers are cramped. I feel the sweat running down my spine, but there are goose bumps all over my body. I'm dizzy. I shut my eyes and try to get my breath back under control a bit.

When I reopen them, I no longer feel like I could throw up at any moment. For the first time since I got off the bus, I take in my surroundings. I've come three stops too far and I'm at the far end of Gormsey. Normally, I'd be kicking myself. But right now, I'm almost relieved, because I can't go home yet. Not after Mum looked at me like that.

There's only one person I want to speak to at this moment. One person I trust completely and who knows without doubt that I'd never do a thing like that.

Ember.

I start walking toward her school. They must be nearly finished, because a few primary school kids are coming this way. There are a bunch of boys trying to push one another off the narrow pavement and into the hedge. At the sight of me, they pause for a moment, and walk on with their heads down like they're scared I might tell them off.

The closer I get to Gormsey High, the weirder I feel. It's only two and a half years since I was at this school too. I don't miss it, but being here again is a blast from the past. Except that back then, nobody turned to stare at me for wearing a private school uniform.

I walk up the steps to the main doors. The dingy walls presumably used to be white and the paint on the windowsills is flaking. You can't help noticing the lack of funds flowing into this place.

I squeeze past the stream of people coming out toward me and try to spot anyone I know in the sea of faces. Before long, I see a girl with two neat plaits who is walking out of the school beside a boy.

"Maisie!" I call to her.

Maisie stops and looks around. When she sees me, her eyebrows shoot up. She nudges her boyfriend to wait, then threads her way through the crowd toward me.

"Ruby!" she says. "Hi, what's up?"

"Do you know where Ember is?" I ask. My voice sounds perfectly normal and I wonder how that's even possible when everything inside me is broken.

"I thought Ember was ill," Maisie says with a frown. "She wasn't in school today."

"What?"

That's impossible. Ember and I left at the same time this morning. If she didn't go to school, then where the hell is she?

"She messaged me that she was in bed with a sore throat." Maisie shrugs and glances over her shoulder to her boyfriend. "So she must be at home, right? Sorry, I have to go, do you mind . . . ?"

I nod hastily. "Yeah, sure."

She gives me another wave, then walks down the steps and

links arms with the boy. I watch them go, my mind racing. If Ember had a sore throat this morning, I'd have known. She didn't look ill, and she was acting normal. Everything was fine at breakfast.

I pull my phone out of my pocket. Three missed calls from James. My cheeks flush as I dismiss the notifications.

I took the photos. I can hear his voice in my mind, but I'm trying to ignore the oppressive feeling in my chest. I click on Ember's name in my favorites. It's ringing, so her phone can't be switched off. But she doesn't pick up, even after ten rings. I hang up and text her:

Please call me. I need to speak to you. It's urgent.

I send the message and slip my phone back into my blazer pocket, then I walk down the steps and turn back to look at the school one last time. I feel out of place. I don't belong here anymore. But I don't belong at Maxton Hall anymore either.

The words *I don't belong anywhere* shoot through my head.

With that thought, I leave the school grounds. On autopilot, I turn left and walk down High Street toward our neighborhood, even though home is the last place I want to be right now. I couldn't bear it if Mum looked at me with the disappointment she showed in Lexington's office.

The events of the day are running through my mind on a loop. I replay the head teacher's voice again and again. Those few words that shattered the future I've been working toward for years.

As I pass a row of cafés and little shops, I catch fragments of conversation between people on their way home from school. They're discussing homework, getting angry at teachers, or laughing about things that happened at break. Numbly, I realize that I have nobody to chat like that with anymore. All I can do is walk along with the warm sun mocking me, knowing deep down that there's nothing left in my life. no school, no family, no boyfriend.

Tears fill my eyes and I try in vain to blink them away. I need my sister. I need someone to tell me that everything's going to be OK, even if I don't believe that for a moment.

I'm about to pull out my phone again when a car stops at the curb beside me. I can see that it's a dark green beater, with rusty rims and grubby windows. I don't know anyone who drives a car like that, so I walk on, not paying it any attention.

But the car follows me. I turn to take a closer look and the driver winds down the window.

The face I see then is the last person I'd have expected. I stop in surprise.

"Ruby?" asks Wren. I must look as shitty as I feel, because Wren leans out of the window to squint at me more closely. "Are you OK?"

I press my lips together. There are few people on earth I want to speak to at the moment less than Wren Fitzgerald. The more I think about it, the more I know why he's looking at me like that. I must be the talk of the school by now. A wave of unpleasant heat washes over me and I walk on without replying.

A car door slams behind me and I hear hasty footsteps. "Ruby, wait!"

I stop and shut my eyes. Then I take two, three deep breaths. I turn to Wren, trying not to show how messed up I am or what I'm thinking.

"You look like you're about to pass out," he says with a frown. "Do you need help?"

I snort. "Help?" I croak. "From you?"

At that, Wren grits his teeth. He stares at the ground for a moment, then looks up. "Alistair told me what happened. That's shit."

I stiffen and turn away. Just as I thought. Everyone at Maxton Hall knows about it. Marvelous. I stare at the gym by the road. There are people running on treadmills and others lifting weights. Maybe I should crawl in there to hide. Nobody would find me there.

"Great," I mutter.

I want to turn and walk away, but something makes me pause. Maybe it's the fact that he's not driving around here in a flashy car, but one that looks like it's on its last legs. Maybe it's the expression in his eyes, which seems serious and genuine, not like he's laughing at me. Or maybe it's just the fact that we're here in Gormsey, where I'd never have expected to meet Wren Fitzgerald.

"What are you doing here anyway?"

Wren shrugs. "I was just passing through."

I raise an eyebrow. "Just passing through. In Gormsey?"

"Hey." Wren changes the subject. "Listen, I refuse to believe that James had anything to do with it."

"Did he send you to talk me round?" I ask, my voice trembling.

Wren shakes his head. "No. But I know James. He's my best friend. He'd never do a thing like that."

"The photos make it look like I'm kissing a teacher, Wren. And James admitted taking them."

"Maybe he did. But that doesn't mean it was him who sent them to Lexie."

I press my lips together.

"James would never do a thing like that," Wren insists.

"What makes you so certain?" I ask.

"Because I know how James feels about you. He'd never do anything to hurt you."

He says it with such certainty that my thoughts and feelings are stirred right up again. Would it change things if James didn't send the photos? But why did he even take them?

"I'm on my way to his place now," says Wren. "I want to know what the fuck is going on too. Come with me, Ruby. Then you can find out for certain."

I stare at Wren. I'm about to ask him if he's out of his mind. But I bite the words back.

Today has been the worst possible. It can't get any worse. I have nothing left to lose.

I ignore the alarm bells that start ringing in my head. Without another thought, I walk over to Wren's rusty car and get in.

MONA KASTEN was born in 1992 and studied Library and Information Management before switching to writing full-time. She lives in Hamburg, Germany, with her family, their cats, and an enormous number of books; she loves caffeine in every form, long forest walks, and days when she can do nothing but write. For more information, visit: monakasten.de.

RACHEL WARD completed the MA in Literary Translation at the University of East Anglia in 2002 and has been working as a freelance translator from German and French to English ever since. She lives in Wymondham, near Norwich, UK, and specializes in works for children and young adults, as well as in crime fiction and contemporary literature. She also loves coffee and cats and can be found on social media as @racheltranslates and at forwardtranslations.co.uk.

Ready to find
your next great read?

Let us help.

Visit prh.com/nextread

Penguin
Random
House